DEAD SPY RUNNING

Stock is currently Weekend editor of the *Daily Telegraph* in
..don. He is the author of two novels, *The Riot Act* and *The
..amom Club*, and is also a columnist with *The Week* magazine
..dia. He lives in Wiltshire with his wife and three young children.

Praise for *Dead Spy Running*

'.. smooth thriller aims to inhabit John le Carré territory by
...nding us spies never trust each other. It centres on suspended
.. officer Daniel Marchant, whose father was once head of the
..ce, and who, almost by accident, thwarts a terrorist attack on
.. London Marathon, but whom the CIA suspect of aiding the
..rist. With suspicions of a mole at the heart of operations, this
..ciously John Buchan-like hero could be chasing the 39 Steps.'
The Daily Mail

'..come to the secret services – or their fictional avatars – for the
.. century. Fans of *Spooks*, the slick and stylish television spy
..a, will feel at home in Stock's world: sexy young agents, cunning
..hiefs, lots of clever stuff with mobile-phone and surveillance-
..era technology, an intriguing sexual technique called the narcissus
.. an AQ plot to assassinate Barack Obama. From "Legoland"
..spies' name for MI6's HQ) to Iran to a terrorist lair in a remote
..n village, the pace fizzes and crackles as MI6's Daniel Marchant
.. to stay one step ahead of his many enemies.'
The Sunday Times

'..ck has crammed his thriller with the realpolitik of spookery.
.. authentic paranoia of the trigger-happy CIA about the subtler
..duce-and-subvert British approach to Islamist terrorism brings the
..ophistication of John le Carré or David Ignatius to a narrative
.which never mistakenly thinks that "realism" should be underscored
.either by a tone of dry detachment or thumping urgency. Awash
.vith characters who wouldn't recognise a simple motive if it bit
them on the bum, this is a Jason Bourne sweat-fest with George
Smiley's brain.'
Daily Telegraph

'*Dead Spy Running* is reminiscent of an old Cold War spy thriller,
updated for the 21st Century . . . Stock displays considerable

Also by Jon Stock

The Riot Act
The Cardamom Club

JON STOCK

Dead Spy Running

blue door

Blue Door
An Imprint of HarperCollins*Publishers*
77–85 Fulham Palace Road,
Hammersmith, London W6 8JB

www.harpercollins.co.uk

This paperback edition 2010
2

First published in Great Britain by
Blue Door 2009

A catalogue record for this book is
available from the British Library

ISBN: 978-0-00-735017-9

Set in Sabon by Palimpsest Book Production Limited,
Grangemouth, Stirlingshire

Printed and bound in Great Britain by
Clays Ltd, St Ives plc

Mixed Sources

Product group from well-managed
forests and other controlled sources
www.fsc.org Cert no. SW-COC-1806
© 1996 Forest Stewardship Council

FSC is a non-profit international organization established
to promote the responsible management of the world's forests.
Products carrying the FSC label are independently certified
to assure consumers that they come from forests that are managed
to meet the social, economic and ecological needs
of present and future generations.

Find out more about HarperCollins and the environment at
www.harpercollins.co.uk/green

For Hilary

Therefore I lie with her and she with me,
And in our faults by lies we flatter'd be.

William Shakespeare

1

A bright Blackheath morning and it was already hot, too hot for twenty-six miles. Daniel Marchant scanned the crowd and wondered again why he was about to run a marathon. Thousands of people were stretching in the early sunshine, massaging limbs, sipping at water. It was like the stillness before battle. A woman in a baseball cap strapped an iPod to her arm; the man beside her tied and retied his laces. Another runner poured water over his hair and shook it like a dog, droplets catching the light. Whatever it takes, Marchant thought. In his case, too much Scotch the night before and not enough training.

'One last try,' he said, turning to Leila. She was sitting on the grass, leaning back on her hands, staring straight ahead. Why was she taking it so seriously, he thought, as he strolled over to join a long queue for the Portaloos. If the going got tough, they could walk, enjoy the day out. Wasn't that how she had sold it to him? But he knew that would never happen: they would crawl before they walked. It was a stubbornness they shared, a bloody-mindedness he could sometimes do without.

He inched forward in the queue. The sweet smell of Deep Heat hung heavy in the spring air, reminding Marchant of school changing rooms, the similar imminence of pain. He always felt like this before they went out running in Battersea Park, only for his resentment to subside when the endorphins kicked in; that and the sound of her rhythmic breathing, her easy footfall. He still wondered why he was about to run twenty-six miles, though, and at such short notice. Their longest training run had been the weekend before, eighteen miles down the towpath to Greenwich and back. But how could he have said no when he barely realised she was asking him? That was her job, after all: persuading people to do what they shouldn't, to say what was meant to remain unsaid.

After queuing for five minutes, Marchant changed his mind and returned to Leila, who had stripped down to her running kit. From the day they had first met, he had promised himself not to fall in love with her, but she had never made it easy. Today was no exception. Her limbs were long, but she touched her toes with ease, shorts tightening against toned muscles. He looked away at the hot-air balloons behind her, swaying in the gentle breeze, desperate to rise up into the brilliant blue sky. In front of them lorries were parked up like a military convoy, piled high with runners' plastic bags, ready to be transported across London to the finish line.

Marchant took both their bags and handed them in to a marshal. He tried to imagine how he would feel when they were reunited with them again, three, more like four, hours later. Despite his protests, he knew that it was the right thing to be doing. The training, however inadequate, had kept him sane during the last few weeks, helping him to focus on what must be done.

'Too many people,' Leila said, pushing hair out of her eyes as Marchant rejoined her. He noticed she was holding her mobile phone. He followed her gaze over towards the main start, where an army of 35,000 runners was now massing. Afterwards, he thought, the dead and the wounded would be laid out in St James's, wrapped in shiny foil.

'It'll be fine, a stroll in the park,' Marchant said. 'Just like you promised.' He put a hand on her shoulder as he stretched one calf muscle, searching her large eyes. It was a hint of the exotic that had first attracted him, the dark, lustrous hair, her olive skin. 'You're not nervous, are you?' he asked, trying to sound bullish. There was suddenly something distracted about her, an unsettling distance. She was usually so upfront, eye to eye.

'Not about the running,' she said.

'What, then?'

'Cheltenham picked up some chatter last night,' she said quietly, looking around.

'About the marathon?' Marchant kept his hand on her shoulder, face close to hers, stretching the other calf. Leila nodded. 'Now you tell me.'

'And you know I shouldn't,' she said, pushing him away. 'Paul's just called, heard I was taking part.'

'Paul? What's he monitoring these days? *Runners' World* chatrooms?'

'Come on, Daniel. You know I can't.'

Marchant had been out of MI6 for two months now, suspended on his case officer's full pay. Leila knew how angry he still felt about everything that had happened: his father's death, the rumours that wouldn't go away. She knew the toll it was taking on his health, too, the late, solitary vigils at the pub. Marchant's youthful features were tiring around the eyes, a greyness starting to fleck his dirt-blond hair. He was only twenty-nine, but sometimes, in a certain light, Leila looked at him and thought she saw his father.

'Remember not to go too fast at the beginning,' she said, changing tack as they jogged over to join the crowded start. Leila still worked for MI6, although she often wondered why. The Service was slowly killing them both.

'That shouldn't be a problem.' Marchant surveyed the sea of people around him, more carefully now. 'Remind me why we're doing this?'

'Because you love running and because you love me.' Leila brushed her lips against his cheek as a helicopter arced across the South London sky. 'More than you should.'

She had never kissed him like that before. Earlier she had woken him very differently, pulling him up through the languid hours of dawn with a passion that had almost frightened him.

'Shouldn't we be saving our energy for the marathon?'

he had whispered afterwards, the rising sun filtering through the blinds of her Canary Wharf apartment. His eyes ached at the thought of all that daylight.

'My mother always told me to live each day as if it was the last.'

'My dad used to say something similar, only in Latin.'

She lay with her head on his chest, eyes open, stroking his stomach. A police siren faded somewhere near the Thames.

'I'm so sorry about your father.'

'Me too.'

Later he had found her in the kitchen, stirring a saucepan of porridge for them both as she looked out of the window towards the O$_2$ Dome. There was an empty bottle of whisky on the granite-top island, next to a couple of stacked dishes from the previous night and the remains of a big bowl of pasta. He pedalled the chrome bin and quietly slid the bottle in, his eyes on Leila. She was wearing knickers and an old London Marathon T-shirt with a slogan on the back: 'Never again . . . until the next time'. The whisky had been a mistake, he realised that now. The next time he would realise earlier. The pain behind his eyes was spreading.

'What's this?' he asked, picking up a single sheet of paper from the island.

She turned, and then looked back out of the window. 'You've never really been religious, have you?' she asked.

'Hey, I was a Sufi once, in my year off in India.'

'Who wasn't?'

'Is this a Bahá'í thing?'

'It's not a thing, it's a prayer. My mother used to make me say it every morning, before I went to school.'

Leila wasn't particularly religious either, but she had grown interested in her mother's Bahá'í faith in recent months. Marchant's own knowledge of it was patchy, based on an internal MI5 briefing that had crossed his desk about Dr David Kelly, the weapons inspector and Bahá'í member who had been found dead in a wood in Oxfordshire.

He looked at the sheet again, and read a passage of the prayer out aloud: ' "*Armed with the power of thy name, nothing can ever hurt me, and with thy love in my heart, all the world's afflictions can in no wise alarm me.*" Is it reassuring?'

'She said it would protect us.'

Marchant thought he could do with a little protection now, as he looked up at the blur of helicopter blades above Blackheath. He suddenly felt claustrophobic, pressed down upon from above as well as from all sides. There was no room for personal space any more, normal rules of behaviour no longer applied. A runner next to him fumbled at his shorts with an empty plastic drinking bottle. Another hung his head, clearing one nostril, then the other. Somebody else yelled with joy (or was it fear?). The crowd responded, calling back like restless animals. They were all part of the larger herd now, surging forward as one towards the start line.

Marchant instinctively flexed his elbows as people pushed in, trampling on his old running shoes. For a few seconds he lost Leila, then he spotted her again, five yards ahead, turning back to look for him. Despite himself, he loved her more than ever in that fleeting moment, her beauty framed by a thousand strangers. He moved up alongside, squeezed her hand. She smiled back, but her look was far away. The call from Paul Myers had unsettled her.

Above them two helicopters now circled, the drone of their blades more menacing than ever. There was a new sound, too, top notes cutting through the background noise. Marchant couldn't work out what it was at first, but then he realised. Runners everywhere were synchronising and calibrating, making final adjustments to their bleeping stopwatches and heart monitors. He glanced instinctively at the hands of his own silent watch. In the same instant, the starter's klaxon hooted, oddly hesitant, an uncertain call to arms. The only thing Marchant could do was run.

It was fifty minutes into the marathon that Marchant first noticed him, tucked behind a small knot of runners twenty yards ahead. The man – Asian, mid-thirties, fragile frame, heavy glasses – was moving at a similar pace to them, but looked uncomfortable, stumbling on the cobbles as he rounded the bow of the *Cutty Sark*. He was sweating profusely, too, even for this heat; but it was the belt around his waist that had caught Marchant's well-trained eye.

Leila's talk of Cheltenham had put Marchant on edge, reawakening old skills. The world around him was suddenly full of threats again, of brush passes and dead drops, and the belt troubled him. It consisted of a number of pouches, each one containing an isotonic energy drink. The drinks were in soft, bulging cartons, silver with small orange screwcaps. He'd seen other runners loading up with drinks belts at the start, but none with so many pouches.

It was just a precaution on a hot day, Marchant told himself, lengthening his stride. Running had always come naturally to him, a benefit of being tall. He caught up with the group as they left Greenwich for Deptford, heading down Creek Road. The crowds were thinner here, but still noisy, heckling runners with the names they had written on their vests. 'Where's Grommit?' someone shouted, as a fun-runner dressed as Wallace ran past. 'Go Dan!' two young women screamed. For a moment, Marchant thought they must be supporting someone else, but then he remembered Leila had insisted on writing 'Dan' on the front of his own running vest. He turned his head to take another look but they were already lost in the crowd, cheering on other strangers.

'What are you doing?' Leila called out from behind Marchant. 'We were doing fine.'

'Give me a minute,' he said. The group of runners ahead of the man also bothered him. Two were heavily set, struggling in the heat and bearing all the unsubtle hallmarks – bulging vests, GI One haircuts – of the American Secret Service. The third man was lean and sinewy, a born runner. He looked familiar.

As Marchant drew near, he knew at once that something was not right. He could taste it in his mouth, like corked wine. His father had always taught him to trust his instinct, whether it was a bad feeling on first meeting a potential agent or pulling out of a rendezvous for no other reason than that it felt wrong. It wasn't tradecraft; it was more visceral than that.

Marchant positioned himself as close as he could behind the man, trying to get a better look at the belt, but the running field was still tightly packed. He counted six drinks pouches. They were eight miles into a hot race, but none of the pouches had been opened.

Then he noticed what looked like an oversized watch on the man's wrist. Leila had something similar for long runs. It was a basic GPS receiver, relaying her position, speed and when she should speed up or slow down. (He remembered how she had once said it beeped ruthlessly at her when her pace dropped below a pre-programmed speed.) It wasn't as sophisticated as the military units he and other case officers had been issued with in Africa, but it wasn't a toy either.

'What's happening?' Leila said, appearing on his shoulder. 'We were going so well.'

Marchant nodded at the man in front and slowed up a little, falling away from the group.

'See the guy with the belt,' he said, as they both slowed to their former pace. Marchant was short of breath as he continued. 'I don't think those cartons are for drinking.'

'Why not?' Leila asked.

'And that man up there, the tall one all in white. Isn't he the US Ambassador?'

'Turner Munroe? Dan, what's going on?'

Marchant knew what Leila was thinking. He was deluded, still drunk from the night before, seeing things where there was nothing to see. He'd watched it himself in other case officers who had been called in from the field and tethered to a desk in Legoland (the name employees had given to MI6's headquarters in Vauxhall), drinking themselves to death to alleviate the boredom of captivity. In his case, though, he didn't even have a desk. That was the hardest part: knowing there might never be a way back. And now here he was, hard on the heels of a runner in the London Marathon, convinced that the man was shortly to kill himself and everyone around him, including the US Ambassador to Britain. He'd run agents who were less paranoid.

'What exactly did Cheltenham pick up last night?' Marchant asked, breathlessly.

'Nothing like this.' He guessed Leila was already making her own calculations, weighing up risks. 'How can you be so sure about the belt?'

'By asking him,' Marchant replied.

'Don't be stupid, Dan.'

'For a drink.'

'Dan . . .'

Marchant ignored her and moved towards the runner again, pulling up alongside. The man was clearly in trouble. Sweat was pouring off him as his head bobbed like a donkey's.

'Hot one,' Marchant said. The man glanced at him nervously and looked ahead again, wiping his thick

10

eyebrows with the back of his hand. 'Did you see that last drinks station?' Marchant continued. 'Crazy. Shouldn't have to queue for water, not on a day like this.' Marchant smiled at the man, nodding towards his belt. Inside, his stomach turned. He was right. 'Couldn't have one of yours, could I?'

'Who are you?' the man said aggressively. His accent was thick, from India: another cell from the subcontinent. Marchant knew immediately there would be consequences, for him, for his father, but they would have to wait.

'No problem. Any idea who that is?' Marchant gestured at the US Ambassador. 'Brought his own fan club with him.'

'Please, stay away,' the man said.

The two of them ran on in silence. Marchant's mind was racing. Post 7/7, it was bulky clothing that had attracted attention. Here was a man wearing explosives on the outside, and it was so bloody bold no one had noticed. The pouches must be wired together inside the belt, he thought. But if the man was a running bomb, why hadn't he blown himself up by now? Why was he warning him to stay away? And if his target was the Ambassador, he could easily have bunched in close to him and his babysitters and taken them all out before now.

He remembered the last suicide bomber he had seen, in Mogadishu. They had been talking in the marketplace, making nervous progress. Then a phone rang. Twice. Marchant had run for his life. The man's head was found on the corrugated-iron roof of a nearby café. The bomber hadn't wanted to die, Marchant was sure of that. Afterwards, in the British Embassy bar, as his hand shook the Johnnie Walker out of his glass, he kept telling himself, over and over, that the bomber had not wanted to die. It had made it easier to understand. The handler knew it too, which is why he had detonated the bomb himself.

This time, he had to keep his man talking, establish the method of detonation, hope the mobile networks would be too busy for a phone call from a third party. Like the bomber in Mogadishu, this man was also not a volunteer. He had been forced to wear the belt. It was happening more and more these days: genuine suicide bombers were becoming hard to find. Trust your gut feeling, his father had said.

'That watch you've got there,' Marchant said. 'GPS?'

'Sat-Runner,' the man replied. Better, Marchant thought, much better; a gear and gadgets man.

'Useful piece of kit.'

The man nodded. Then the GPS beeped. Both of them looked at it. 'Please, you must go,' the man said to Marchant. They weren't the words of a suicide bomber hoping to take as many people with him as he could.

'Why's it beeping?' Marchant asked, recalculating the risk to himself, to others. His lungs tightened, making words difficult. 'Does it do that when you slow down, when your pace drops?' he asked, trying to remember how Leila had explained it, cursing himself for not showing more interest at the time.

The man nodded. He had been coerced into this,

Marchant repeated to himself, which meant that he could be talked out of it.

'Then what?' Marchant glanced down at the belt again.

'Can you help me?' They looked at each other for a moment, gauging the fear in each other's eyes.

'I can try. What's your name?'

'Pradeep.'

'Keep it going, Pradeep. You're doing fine. Just fine. Don't go anywhere. I'm coming straight back.'

Pradeep glanced over his shoulder, stumbling again, as Marchant dropped back down the field to search for Leila, but he couldn't see her in the crowd. How much faster than her had he been running? He slowed up some more, looking at everyone who overtook him. He shouldn't have left her, he knew that now. There were too many people, too much noise.

Above him the helicopters circled low again, drowning out the jazz band playing on the roof of a pub. Children by the roadside cheered, holding out bags of sweets. Stout women from St John's Ambulance were offering outstretched hands of Vaseline. And then he spotted her, over on the far side of the road, hidden behind a small group of club runners. He cut across the flow of people to join her, almost tripping on the heels of another runner. His legs were tiring, more than they should have been at this stage of the race. He was desperate for more water, too.

'Leila, we've got a problem,' he said, short of breath. 'A big problem.'

'Where have you been? I couldn't see you anywhere.'

In between swigs from her drinking bottle, he told her about the GPS, and how he thought it was linked in some way to the pouches around Pradeep's waist, which he was now convinced contained explosives – enough to kill dozens of people if he was in a tightly bunched group. He knew how he sounded: a has-been desperate to prove himself in the field.

'My guess is, if he drops below a certain pace, the isotonics will blow,' he added.

'Daniel . . .'

Leila's face told him she was struggling to comprehend the situation, trying to decide whether his reading of it was deluded or credible. She was momentarily tearful.

'You've got to leave this to others,' she pleaded. 'You must. You're no longer . . . I need to make a call,' she said, removing her mobile phone from a pocket at the back of her running shorts.

'You won't get a signal,' Marchant said, glancing at the phone. With its stubby, inch-long aerial, the unit looked very familiar.

She held the phone in front of her, tripping and grabbing at Marchant's arm for support.

'Who are you ringing? MI5? The networks will be congested,' he said. 'Too many people.'

She looked at him again, her face suddenly professional, drained of all emotion, and then she dialled.

'It's a TETRA handset,' she said coldly. The secure encrypted digital network used by the emergency and security services was one of the perks Marchant missed.

'They're not answering. Daniel, please. This is not your responsibility, not mine. If what you say is true, it's one for MI5, Anti-Terrorism Command. We must leave it to them.'

Marchant looked at the road ahead, and reckoned he knew where the runner was, give or take a few hundred people. 'I've got him talking. He doesn't want to go through with it.'

Leila hesitated, weighing up the options. Had she conceded he might have a role to play? She looked at him again, swallowing hard.

'OK. If you take my phone, I'll drop out, find a phonebox and tell Five about the situation. Once the networks have been knocked out, I'll give you a call on TETRA.'

Marchant was thinking fast now, like he used to in the field. The head of station in Nairobi had once predicted that a glittering career stretched ahead of him; he might even follow his father to the top if he quit the whisky and womanising. Next time they met, Marchant was suspended and burying his father.

'Alert MI5. I'll stay with him,' he said, trying not to think about the funeral in the Cotswold frost, how they had treated his father. 'My guess is we can't pull him off the course, even if he keeps running. Deviating from waypoints could trigger the belt too.'

'Daniel, you shouldn't be doing this.'

'I know.' He also knew there weren't many alternatives. If they both stopped, it would be almost impossible to find the bomber again. 'I could tell the Americans.

The Ambassador's got company, and I think they're wired.' Leila glanced at him for a moment. They were both reluctant to involve the Secret Service, who didn't always play by the same rules as everyone else. 'The Ambassador *is* the target here?' he asked.

'He must be.'

Marchant had missed the adrenalin, but it was draining his energy, too. Lactic acid was building in his legs, weighing them down like lead.

'Here,' Leila said, holding out the phone. Their eyes met.

'No blues and twos, nothing to alert him, OK?' he said, taking the handset. He was increasingly short of breath. 'Someone else might have their finger on the button. It's happened to me once before.'

'I know,' she said. 'Keep your distance from him.'

'Who gave you this?' he asked, looking at the handset again. It was a Motorola MTH800. 'Just like my old one.'

'Services. Mine was knackered. If you don't hear from me in fifteen minutes, try calling the office.' She paused. 'Speed-dial 1. They'll find me.'

Marchant glanced back at Leila as she pulled up on the side of the road, feigning a hamstring injury. She looked up at him, and for a moment he wondered if she might never make the call, leaving him to run on in his imaginary world of bombers and belts.

He knew she had tried to walk away from what they had together – God, how they had both tried – but each time one of them had relented. It wasn't like him at all.

For the first time in his life, a woman had got under his skin. Now they might be at the heart of a major security incident, and his involvement wouldn't do her career any favours. Suspicion still hung over the Marchant family like a poisoned fog.

She gave a small wave and disappeared in the sea of runners.

2

It took ten minutes for Marchant to find Pradeep again. His head was bowed, his feet scuffing the road, running like a drunken tramp. The American Ambassador was in the group immediately ahead of him, still with company. He was moving strongly, chest out, no signs of tiredness. Worryingly, the field seemed to be tightly bunched around Pradeep, not as spread out as it was further back. And then Marchant saw the reason why: up ahead, just beyond the Ambassador, was an official pacemaker, running with a sign above him: eight minutes a mile. Stick with him and the marathon was yours for three hours thirty minutes. Marchant looked at Pradeep again, and feared that he didn't have long, maybe ten minutes at most.

'Pradeep? It's me. You're doing great.'

'It's too late.'

'Why?'

'I'm so tired, too weak.'

'Do you want to stop, take a rest?' Marchant said, bluffing. One final check, just to reassure himself about the GPS.

Pradeep's glance at his belt gave him his answer. He was right.

'How about we keep running, but turn off the course, up here, say, right at the pub?'

Pradeep shook his head.

'Is the marathon route programmed into your GPS, your Sat-Runner?' Marchant asked. That was something else his father had told him, shortly after he'd joined the Service: never ask a question you don't know the answer to.

Pradeep didn't respond. He was really struggling now, continually losing his footing. Marchant looked at his frame, lean and sinewy, and thought that in other circumstances he would be a natural marathon runner. No doubt that was why he had been chosen. But the mental pressure on Pradeep was sapping every ounce of his energy. Marchant could feel them slowing moments before the GPS beeped.

'Come on, Pradeep, we're going to get through this,' Marchant said, trying to pick up the pace again. They had to keep running until Leila rang. She would have an answer.

'Two beeps and we're gone,' Pradeep replied, suddenly grinning, almost laughing. Marchant realised Pradeep was losing control. 'You don't understand, my friend,' he continued. 'The American. I can't leave him.'

'The Ambassador?'

Marchant looked up at Turner Munroe, who was five yards in front of him. The Ambassador checked his watch, and for the first time Marchant noticed that its bulky design was identical to Pradeep's.

'Eight minutes a mile. He always runs the same,' said Pradeep, suddenly sounding like a trainer admiring one of his charges.

'Three hours thirty,' Marchant said. 'He's running a 3.30.'

'One hour forty.'

'What?'

'He reaches Tower Bridge after one hour forty minutes.'

'And?'

Pradeep smiled again, tears welling now. They had been running for one hour thirty minutes. Marchant desperately wanted Leila to ring, more than when they had first tried to split up, more than after their first date at the Fort, MI6's training centre in Gosport. He looked at the phone in his hand and saw that the commercial networks had been knocked out. Should he try ringing her? The office would be surprised to hear his voice, but she would have told them and they would patch him through to wherever she was. He lifted his head, looked around, and for a moment he thought he saw his father running ahead of him, trundling along at a surprising speed for his age.

He blinked, wiping the sweat away from his eyes, and looked again at the handset. He had to stay on top of this: Pradeep was wearing a belt of explosives linked in some way to the GPS receiver on his wrist. He seemed to be an unwilling participant, rather than a suicide bomber. If he slowed down, the explosives would detonate: ditto if he took any deviation from the marathon course, the waypoints for which had been entered into his GPS. And for some reason it seemed that Pradeep had to stay close to the Ambassador, possibly because of a similar GPS receiver on *his* wrist.

Suddenly Leila's TETRA phone was vibrating in his hand. A couple of runners ahead of him glanced around at the sound of the loud ringtone.

'Leila?' he said, hearing the panic rise in his own voice. He had to remain calm.

'Did you try ringing me?' she asked.

'No.'

'Don't, OK?' she insisted. 'Please. Just don't. There's some sort of problem with TETRA. Are you still with him?'

'Yes.' Marchant glanced across at Pradeep, managed a smile, then pulled back a few yards, out of earshot.

'Listen very carefully,' Leila was saying. 'I'm on the grid at Thames House. MI5 picked up someone in Greenwich and have been sweating him all morning. You've got to get the GPS off the Ambassador's wrist.'

'Why?'

'It's just like you said. The Asian guy's GPS receiver is linked to his belt using Bluetooth. Only we think the belt can be triggered by Munroe's GPS too.'

'If Munroe drops off the pace as well, you mean,' Marchant said.

'Yes.' Marchant thought of Pradeep's words, how he said he couldn't leave the Ambassador. 'And maybe if the link between the two GPSs is broken, if they're separated,' Leila added. 'Technical's working on the permutations now.'

Marchant could hear other people in the background. He imagined the scene at Thames House, MI5's headquarters, as news of the situation spread and increasingly senior people arrived, duty officer giving way to Harriet Armstrong, MI5's Director General, who had helped to hound his father out of office. Leila would be consulted less and less, particularly once his own involvement had become clear. It was a nightmare for MI5: having to rely on someone from MI6, and a discredited case officer, too. It would confirm their worst suspicions about their rivals south of the river. And then the US Secret Service would try to take over, reigniting old turf wars.

'What about the Americans?' Marchant asked. 'Are they running the show now?'

'Not yet. They wanted to lift Munroe and for us to escort the bomber down a side road, away from the crowds, but the risk of collaterals is too high. We don't know how quickly the belt might be triggered by removing Munroe.'

'So I get to wear the Ambassador's GPS, then what?'

Leila paused. 'You both keep running while Cheltenham tries to intercept the satellite signals.'

'Tries?'

'They're keen to pull you out, Daniel, put someone else in.'

'I bet they are.'

'But it's going to take time, and we haven't got any.'

'Pradeep's knackered.'

'I know. We've got a feed from the BBC helicopter above you now.'

Marchant had forgotten about it, hovering high above him. So Armstrong could see them, he thought. He could never forgive what she and others in MI5 had done to his father. Stephen Marchant was a man who had lived and breathed for the Service, only to be accused, at the pinnacle of his career, of the very thing he had always despised in others. Some people died of a broken heart; his father had died of shame, within weeks of being forced to retire as Chief. There was nothing more important to his father than loyalty. Even the best assets he had recruited, the ones who made his reputation in Delhi, Moscow, Washington, Paris, had filled him with a deep loathing for mankind and its willingness to betray.

'Don't Munroe's babysitters have a radio link?' Marchant asked. Things might become easier for him and Leila after this; the family's reputation might be restored; he might get his old job back.

'They're linked to each other,' Leila replied, 'not to the outside world.'

'That figures. Is there a code for this yet? Something to re-assure the Ambassador I'm not from Albania when I relieve him of his watch.'

'Tell them it's a Defcon Five. Try "Operation Kratos" if that doesn't work. Once you've got the GPS, persuade

Munroe to leave the course as soon as possible. He must be out of there before Tower Bridge.'

'What is it with the bridge?' Marchant asked, remembering Pradeep's words.

'It's where the biggest crowds are, apart from the finish. We're trying to clear the area now. Bomb disposal are on the way. We've got blues assembling in all the back streets, from you to Tower Bridge.'

The line suddenly dropped. There was not much more to say. Marchant moved up to join Pradeep again.

He had some jelly beans on board for the final few miles, but he decided to pull the bag out from his pocket now and offer them to Pradeep, who visibly rallied at the sight of them.

'Beats the gels,' Marchant said, taking a couple himself after Pradeep had grabbed a desperate handful. 'I'm going to talk to the Ambassador, then I'm coming back,' Marchant said. 'It's going to be OK. I promise. *Sab theek ho jayega, Pradeep.* Everything's going to be fine.'

Marchant hoped his rusty Hindi had reassured Pradeep as he moved up towards the Ambassador. He knew a bit about Turner Munroe, who had arrived in London six months ago. He was a hawk, best known for his outspoken views on Iran, where he favoured regime change by military intervention. And he had fought in the first Gulf War, serving with distinction. Marchant now knew that he was also a fitness fanatic, who liked to run with an iPod.

Experience had taught Marchant to stick to protocol when dealing with the Americans (it reduced the chances of being shot), so he approached the Ambassador's outriders first. When he explained that they were in the midst of a critical, Defcon Five incident, they asked him for some ID, as Marchant knew they would. They finally agreed to let him approach the Ambassador when he name-checked one of his old CIA contacts who was still based in London, but only after they had briefed their boss.

'How you doing?' Munroe asked, taking an earpiece out of his right ear. Marchant swore he was listening to Bruce Springsteen. 'Tell me you're kidding about the Defcon Five.'

'No, sir, I'm afraid it's true,' Marchant said, knowing Munroe would appreciate the 'sir'.

'You realise I've never run a 3.30 before? Boston: 3.35.10, Chicago: 3.32.20. Right now I'm heading for 3.29.30, and you're telling me to quit?'

'You might never be able to run again if you hang around here,' Marchant said.

'Is that so?' Munroe said sarcastically. Marchant glanced at one of the sweating Security Service officers, who was nodding towards the side of the road.

'Sir, we need to break off,' the officer said, moving alongside the Ambassador. At the same time, his colleague closed in on the far side.

'But first I need your Sat-Runner,' Marchant said.

'Am I being mugged here?' Munroe said. 'That's what it feels like. Mugged on the London Marathon. Can you believe it?'

'I really need the GPS,' Marchant said, as the

Ambassador's babysitters began to ease him across the road. 'And please don't slow down.'

Munroe looked at him as he undid the strap and handed the receiver over. '3.29.30. A PB was on the cards here, never mind the heat. Somebody's going to pay for this.'

He watched as Munroe was almost lifted to the kerb, where he stopped, reluctantly. Then Marchant strapped the GPS to his own wrist. Pradeep was now ahead of them, glancing anxiously over his shoulder.

'We're in this together now,' Marchant said, coming up on Pradeep's shoulder and showing him his wrist.

3

Paul Myers was unpicking encrypted emails and eating his fourth Snickers of the day when he took Leila's call. He'd always liked her, ever since she had attended his course on *jihadi* chatrooms and had asked the first question, filling the awkward silence that always followed his introductory talks. All MI6's new recruits were invited up to GCHQ in Cheltenham for a week, to give them a break from training at the Fort, and, Myers thought, to show them where the real work was done.

Paul had liked Leila's boyfriend, too, though only begrudgingly at first. On the surface, Daniel Marchant had seemed to be the archetypal obnoxious MI6 man: Oxbridge, well travelled, smooth-talking, handsome and good at games – everything Myers wasn't. But then he read his file and learnt about the dark stuff – the benders, the brawls, the twin brother who was killed when he was eight in a car crash in Delhi, the mother who never recovered, dying a depressive – and began to warm to him. Everyone in life was struggling to keep it together, he thought. According to Leila, Marchant had never got over losing his brother, and had been drinking himself slowly to death until he stumbled out of journalism and into the Service. It must have been like coming home, what with his old man running the show.

They might have been friends sooner if Paul hadn't somehow convinced himself that Leila carried a torch for him, despite the obvious chemistry between her and Marchant. He knew it was insane, an attractive case officer like her falling for a short-sighted, overweight desk analyst, and common sense soon prevailed, but those early feelings for her had stayed with him. Now she was on the phone, breathless and posing one of the most interesting questions he had been asked in months: could he screw up the Americans' GPS network for a few minutes?

Given the history of the navigation system, and in particular the US military's policy of 'selective availability' in the 1990s, when they degraded the signal's accuracy for everyone else, Myers relished the opportunity. Bring on Galileo, he thought, Europe's own network of navigation satellites. The sooner Britain could wean itself off its dependency on GPS, the better.

'Do you think you can do it?' Leila asked, knowing that the challenge would appeal. Myers had been at the heart of a recent exercise in the West Country, when the entire network was jammed to thwart a simulated attack by an Iranian missile flying into British airspace on GPS.

Car Tom-Toms went haywire, and the papers were full of stories the next day of lorries stuck in narrow country lanes.

'Technically it's possible,' Myers said, warming to his theme. 'Each of the thirty GPS satellites has its own atomic clock – well, four clocks actually. 2nd Space Operations Squadron in Colorado Springs sends out a navigational update once a day to make sure they're all telling the same time –'

'Paul, we don't have long.'

'Sure. We'll get on to 2 SOPS now, find out which four satellites this guy is linked in to, and see if they can accelerate those particular clocks.'

'Will that help?'

'It'll trick the receiver into thinking it's travelling faster across the surface of the earth than it really is. The Americans aren't going to like it, but I guess if we tell them their Ambassador is the target . . . How long do you need?'

'The Bomb Squad want ten minutes.'

'Two, maximum.'

'Two?'

'We'd have some serious shipping incidents in the Channel if those clocks are out for too long. I don't even want to think about the main approach to Heathrow. How's Daniel these days, by the way?'

Myers was aware that Marchant was *persona non grata* in the Service, but he had always liked his father, and had been upset by the manner of the Chief's departure and the subsequent news of his death. It had left

Marchant an orphan, which struck a chord with Myers. He was adopted, and had always assumed his own parents were dead.

'Actually, he's running alongside the guy with the belt.' Leila had not intended to tell him, but she needed to focus his mind.

'Daniel?' The line went silent for a moment. 'Christ, what's he doing there? I thought he was suspended.'

'Not now, Paul.'

'Sure.' Paul had changed up a gear. '2 SOPS are on the other line. I'll patch them through.'

Marchant listened carefully as Leila talked him through what he had to do next. Her voice sounded different, faltering, lacking her usual confidence. Tower Bridge had been cleared of all crowds, she said. Half a mile ahead of him, at the twelve-mile point, there was about to be a roadblock, organised by plain-clothed police officers wearing race marshal tops. As he approached they would fan out across the road, using megaphones to order the runners to stop for safety reasons because of the intense heat. It would be the first time the London Marathon had been stopped, but the measure was not unheard of. (The Rotterdam Marathon had been abandoned in 2007 because of soaring temperatures.) In other words, there was an outside chance that the roadblock wouldn't arouse the suspicion of Pradeep's handler, should he be watching.

'Are you all right?' Marchant asked, after another hesitation from Leila.

'Of course I'm bloody not,' she said.

30

Marchant passed on the basic details of the plan, along with some more jelly beans, to Pradeep, who seemed to grow stronger at the news. The police would delay their intervention as long as possible, to avoid a crowd building up in front of them and slowing their pace. However, they should stick to the right of the road, as close as possible to the pavement, where a channel would be formed to let them pass through. To avoid being mistakenly challenged, Marchant was to call out that he was a doctor and must be allowed to pass.

'Have you got all that?' Leila asked.

'What happens when we're through the block?' Marchant replied. His mother had always wanted a doctor in the family.

'As you near Tower Bridge, the Americans are going to tweak the clocks on four GPS satellites orbiting 12,000 miles above you. When I give the word, you and Pradeep should gradually slow down to a walking pace. The Bomb Squad will join you and disable the belt as quickly as they can.'

'How long have they got?'

'Two minutes from the moment you start to slow.'

Marchant didn't say anything for a few seconds. For the first time, he realised that his chances of survival were slim. Somehow he had assumed that everything would work out, but now he sensed that he might never see Leila again. She had already realised that. His life normally felt fairer in these moments of acute danger. Ever since that dark day in Delhi, he had been burdened with guilt: why had his brother been killed, while he walked away from the crash unscathed? When the odds were stacked against him, the weight briefly lifted: intense relief replaced the fear. The greater the danger, the closer he felt to Sebastian, the more able to look him in the eye.

But that wasn't the case now. There was no frisson of higher justice or fateful euphoria. His body just felt more tired than it had ever felt in his entire life, even more than when they had found him drunk in Nairobi, face down in the gutter, his last night as a journalist.

'Are you still there?' Leila said.

'I'm here.' Another pause. He checked on Pradeep, who looked as if he had fallen into some sort of trance, eyes staring straight ahead, unaware of the outside world. But he was still running, that was all that mattered. 'They've let you keep the mike then,' Marchant continued.

'Yes. In the circumstances, it was felt to be the best option.'

Drop the formal tone, he thought, but he knew she couldn't; all the agencies would have live feeds by now: Thames House, Cheltenham, Langley.

Marchant imagined an aerial view of himself, as if taken from one of the satellites far above South London. He could picture the runners, tiny figures moving along toy streets, begin to bunch up in front of the police, who had appeared from nowhere. Zooming in on the scene, he could tell at once that there was no way through. Fifty yards out, he heard himself shouting at the top of his voice that he was a doctor. But no one else heard him. What was wrong with his voice? It sounded so faint, lost in the hubbub of the crowds, who were now jeering, protesting at the race being stopped. He shouted again, but his voice was too weak, barely audible above the sound of his own breathing, the megaphones, the helicopter above them. Pradeep looked at him in desperation as they began to slow down. And then Pradeep's receiver beeped.

'Leila, Leila, there's no fucking way through!' Marchant shouted into the phone. His hands were wet with sweat and he gripped the receiver tightly as he ran, like a relay baton. He could hear her talking urgently to other people in the background. 'Jesus, Leila, we're slowing down with five hundred people backing up in front of us.'

'Head left, head left!' a voice was suddenly saying. It wasn't Leila's. Left? For a moment, all Marchant could think of was the blue tartan shoes he had as a child, 'L' and 'R' embroidered in red on the toes. Then Pradeep pointed ahead of them at a marshal who was beckoning frantically. He was trying to direct them over to the far side of the crowd, where marshals were pushing runners back, making a channel.

Marchant couldn't dredge up another word, let alone shout that he was a doctor, but in the end there was no need. They were suddenly through the roadblock, running on their own, the din of the crowd receding fast behind them. The marathon behemoth had spat them free.

Eight hundred yards ahead lay Tower Bridge, flags flying, eerily deserted. Marchant managed a faint smile, but not for long. Up until the roadblock, Pradeep's mission would still have had the appearance of viability to any observer. Now, as the two of them ran on alone up the empty road, the suicide operation was blown. All Marchant could hope for was that Pradeep's handler, if he had one out there, would wait until the iconic setting of Tower Bridge to cut his losses. The Ambassador wouldn't die, there would be no 'Carnage at the London Marathon' headlines, but a suicide bombing at one of the capital's most famous landmarks would still be worth something.

'Leila?' Marchant asked, still short of breath, struggling to grip the phone.

'We copy you,' an American man's voice said.

'Where's Leila?' he shouted. 'Put Leila back on the line, do you hear?'

'It's OK, Daniel,' a voice said. 'She's still here. We just patched you through directly to Colorado Springs. You're now talking to me, Harriet Armstrong, in London.'

The bitch, he thought, but he said nothing. He was too tired.

'They're going to slow you down in a couple of minutes,' Armstrong continued. 'We've got two from the Bomb Squad waiting on the north side of the bridge. As soon as you're walking, they'll move in. Try to get more out of Pradeep. Cell names, contacts, who's running him, anything. We'll call you back in two minutes.'

It felt strange to run the London Marathon through deserted streets. He had always liked empty spaces, big yawning skies, mountains, the open sea. In cities he felt trapped, but he could live here if it was always like this.

He suddenly thought of the Thar Desert, trudging over sand dunes with Sebastian on a camel beside him, their parents up ahead, smiling back at them.

As far as Marchant could tell, the police had cleared a corridor a hundred yards either side of the route. For a moment, he imagined that he was leading the field with Pradeep, having broken away from the leading pack in a ruthless final kick for home. Then his legs reminded him how tired he felt.

'Where are you from, Pradeep?' he asked. 'Which part of India?'

'How do you know I'm from India?'

'I used to live there.'

'Which place?'

'Delhi. Chanakyapuri.'

'Very nice,' Pradeep said, moving his head from side to side, managing a faint smile. Talk of home seemed to give him strength.

'All I remember is the yellow blossom of the laburnum trees. I was very young.'

For a few seconds their steps were synchronised, rising and falling together. They both noticed it, momentarily entranced. 'Are we going to die?' Pradeep asked.

'No. We're not.'

'My home place is Kochi.'

'Kerala?'

'My wife, she is also from there. We have one son, living with us in Delhi. They will kill him if I don't do this today.'

'Who's "they"?'

Pradeep didn't answer. Instead, he pulled out a small photo from a pouch at the front of the belt and showed it to Marchant.

Marchant looked at the young face that smiled back at him. This hadn't been a part of his calculations. Pradeep might have been a reluctant bomber, but he now had a motive to see it through. His heart sank. Pradeep had missed his target, the Ambassador, but he could still honour his word by blowing himself up at Tower Bridge to save his son. Marchant glanced at his watch: one hour thirty-nine minutes.

'But you don't want to go through with this, do you?' he asked. 'You don't want to die.' Before Pradeep could answer, Marchant's phone started to ring. It was Colorado Springs.

Again, Marchant imagined himself from high above, the bridge looking even more like a child's model than it did from the ground. He listened to the young American on the phone, calm and authoritative, talking to him, to Armstrong, to someone else. And then, at last, it was time to slow down.

'If the GPS makes any sound at all, increase your speed immediately, do you copy that?' the American asked.

'Copy that.'

'Now take it down slowly, sir. Your window is open. Two minutes and counting.'

Marchant looked at Pradeep, suddenly unsure of his cooperation. For so long he had wanted him to keep on running; now he was praying he would slow down. But Pradeep's pace remained constant, his eyes looking straight ahead. If anything, he was growing stronger. He was hanging on until they reached the bridge.

'Remember, you've got time to speed up again if the GPS doesn't like it,' the American said. 'Ease it down now. One minute forty-five and counting.'

Marchant moved closer to Pradeep and grabbed his arm. 'It's OK, we can slow down. We can stop. We've done it.' They were at the edge of the bridge, approaching the first tower, still not slowing. Marchant knew that tears were mixing with Pradeep's sweat as he tried to struggle on, for his young son, to the middle of the bridge. But his legs were beginning to buckle, first one, then the other, and soon he was in Marchant's arms, sobbing, as they slowed to a walking pace. Marchant glanced at his receiver to check their speed: it still said that they were running at eight minutes per mile.

Marchant never established the exact order of what happened next. He remembered two bomb disposal officers, weighed down with protective khaki clothing, running across from the far side of the bridge, shouting at him to remain where he was. And he later learnt that at the same time, somewhere in the skies above Heathrow, two passenger planes started their final approaches sooner than they should have, setting themselves on a collision course that was only averted by an extra-vigilant air traffic controller.

The double-tap gunshot that rang out on the bridge, jerking Pradeep's head back, must have been fired just before the bomb disposal squad reached them. Marchant remembered holding Pradeep's limp body for a second and then slumping down with him to the tarmac. The two dum-dum bullets had spread out inside Pradeep's skull, rather than passing through it. The back of his head felt like moist moss.

The belt was cut free and disarmed in the subsequent blur, but as Marchant was led away in a cacophony of sirens, all he could recall thinking about was Pradeep's son, and whether he would now be allowed to live.

4

Daniel Marchant looked out across the shallow valley and watched as a flock of Canada geese flew along the canal, rising from its surface to turn right towards the village. A faint mist hung above the water, streaked with blue smoke from the early-morning stoves of canal boats moored along the far bank. Beside the canal was the railway to London, and a small, three-carriage train was waiting in the station for the first commuters of the day. In the woods on the hillside beyond, a woodpecker was hammering in short bursts. Otherwise, there was stillness.

Marchant had slept only intermittently, despite his exhaustion, and he knew that another day of questioning lay ahead. At least he was now out of London, in a safe house somewhere in Wiltshire. After the marathon, an unmarked car had taken him from Tower Bridge to Thames House, where he had showered and changed into clothes brought over from his flat by Leila. He saw her briefly, gave back the mobile phone, but their conversation was stilted. The look on her face came as a surprise. He had been keen to meet, to thank her for helping him through the race, but he was grateful for her withdrawn manner; it had put him on guard.

It wasn't that he had expected to be fêted as a hero, but neither had he thought he would be led down into the basement of MI5's headquarters for hours of questioning in a small, airless room. A debrief in Legoland would have been more appropriate, given he was still on MI6's payroll. But it was clear, from the moment he had arrived at Thames House, that another agenda was being followed. He just wasn't sure exactly what it was.

His role in the marathon bomb plot was problematic for the intelligence community, he accepted that. It troubled him, too: why he had been there, why no one else had been suspicious of the belt. A have-a-go hero had saved the day, except that he wasn't an ordinary member of the public, he was a suspended MI6 officer; an officer whose late father had been suspected of treason; a son who wanted to clear the family name.

He knew MI5 was behind the decision to suspend him, just as it had been the driving force behind his father's removal as Chief of MI6, which had added an extra degree of tension to his interrogation in the basement.

'You can see how it looks from our point of view,' his interrogator was saying, as he walked around Marchant in the plain, whitewashed room, chewing gum. Marchant, sitting on the only chair, didn't recognise the man, who called himself Wylie. Shortly after his father's forced retirement, Marchant had been interviewed at Thames House by a panel of officers, but it hadn't included this man. Wylie was in his late forties, flat-footed with thinning red hair, his skin pale and too dry. If he passed you in the street, Marchant thought, you would guess he was an overworked police officer, or an inner-city schoolteacher, someone who saw more paperwork than daylight, knew his colleagues better than his wife.

'Two men, running together, desperate to reach Tower Bridge for maximum publicity. One of them fresh from the subcontinent, strapped up with explosives. The other –' Wylie paused, as if his disdain for Marchant had suddenly overwhelmed him – 'the other, a former member of the intelligence services with "issues", making sure he reaches his target.'

'Suspended, not former,' Marchant said calmly. 'His target was Turner Munroe, the American Ambassador.' Wylie, Marchant knew, was employing a standard interrogation strategy: push the less plausible of your two main theories (ex-MI6 man with a grudge) as far as you can, and see how much of your more plausible theory (ex-MI6 man saves MI5's skin) is validated by the interviewee's answers. He'd learnt it at the Fort, with Leila.

'When the order was given to slow down, you both kept on running at the same pace in order to reach your target, which was Tower Bridge,' Wylie continued, getting into his own stride, chewing faster on his gum. He spoke with an enthusiasm that drew Marchant in, until his ear became tuned to the underlying sarcasm. 'In fact, you

41

helped to keep this man going, at one point holding his arm to support him.'

Wylie tossed a black-and-white surveillance photo onto the table. It was of Marchant and Pradeep approaching the bridge, taken with a zoom lens. Marchant was shocked at how exhausted he looked: Pradeep seemed to be propping him up. His limbs felt weak again as he shifted his legs under the table.

'Why didn't you slow down, as ordered?' Wylie asked, standing behind Marchant now.

Marchant picked up the photo and took his time to answer, trying to get a measure of the person behind him as he ordered his thoughts. The exact events of the endgame were still not clear in his mind. Had they fired at Pradeep because he wasn't slowing down? He had thought the shots rang out afterwards, once they were walking.

'Pradeep was an unwilling suicide bomber,' Marchant said, talking over his shoulder. 'My own feeling is that he was coerced into the operation. When I first approached him, he was happy to be helped. It was a primitive response: "How can I stop myself from being killed?" Once his initial survival instincts had been addressed, he started to think of others, in this case his son, who would be killed if he didn't see his mission through. As we approached the bridge, this concern became paramount in his mind. He didn't slow down when I asked him to, and as you can see, I had to intervene to reduce his pace.'

Marchant dropped the photo back on the table. Both of them watched in silence as it spun around and came to a halt. Marchant wished there was a fan in the room.

'Did it ever cross your mind that you had no authority to take the actions you did?' Wylie asked, still behind him. 'You were suspended, after all.'

Marchant noted his interrogator's change of tack. 'I was behaving like a responsible member of the public.'

'Responsible?' Wylie laughed. 'Everyone knows you've gone to seed, Marchant.'

Marchant stared ahead, his tone even. 'I saw something suspicious, and in this instance, ringing the terrorist hotline wasn't really an option.'

'Why not?' Wylie barked, walking around in front of Marchant. His voice had an odd habit of cracking and rising in pitch when he was angry. The effect should have been funny, but it was unsettling.

'Why not?' Marchant echoed, louder now that he could see Wylie again. 'Because I didn't have a bloody phone with me.'

Marchant struggled to control his urge to shout. There was no reason to bring Leila into this. She would tell them about her TETRA phone in a separate debrief. He spoke slowly and clearly, emphasising the words as if speaking to a child. 'I chose to stay with Pradeep. I'm not sure it would have been that easy to identify him again. There were 35,000 runners out there.'

'Including some of our officers,' Wylie said.

Flat-footing it along at the back with the fifteen-minute milers, Marchant thought.

'This attack didn't come as a complete surprise,' Wylie added.

'I'm sure it didn't.' And if Marchant was writing the incident up, his report would have made that abundantly clear: MI5 saw it coming, and still screwed up.

'You knew about it in advance, then?' Wylie asked, his voice cracking again. This time he pulled out an asthma inhaler and sucked once on it, hard.

'I didn't say that.'

'But your former colleagues knew. They just don't like sharing information much, do they?'

Then Marchant thought he understood. Wylie was suggesting that his involvement was pre-planned: part of a conspiracy by MI6 to expose MI5's failings, to get his job back.

'I can't answer for MI6,' he said.

'No, you're right, you can't. But you'd like to. Working for Six kept you sober. We're seeing the real Marchant now, though, aren't we? Oh, come on, you were tipped off. One of your old "mates"' – he exaggerated the word derisively – 'chose to tell you rather than us. You went out there this morning looking for a man with a belt. You didn't just stumble across him, the one runner out of 35,000 who wanted to blow himself up.'

Marchant thought of Leila, what she'd said about Paul Myers picking up some chatter just before the marathon, and felt his palms moisten. Had someone logged the call from Myers to her? His chance encounter could begin to look anything but: Cheltenham tells MI6; MI6 informs suspended officer, who thwarts bomb attack under MI5's nose. Wylie, though, had no idea of the fear he was sowing in Marchant's mind.

'So what did this rag-head tell you about himself?' Wylie asked, changing tack again.

Rag-head? Marchant marvelled at how unreconstructed MI5 still was. He thought it had become more ethnically diverse. 'He said his name was Pradeep. He was originally from Cochin in Kerala. He called it Kochi, the local name, suggesting he was Indian.' Marchant had always liked data. Hard facts, unquestionable stats – they were reassuring in his shifting world.

'South India,' Wylie said. 'We all hoped that little terror campaign had gone away.'

Don't bring my father into this, Marchant thought. Last year's bombings, believed to have been run from South India, had stopped when his father stood down as Chief at Christmas, a point not lost on his enemies in MI5. 'Pradeep also had a good knowledge of New Delhi,' Marchant said, determined to remain calm. 'He was living there with his wife and son. He seemed to know Chanakyapuri, the diplomatic enclave in the south of the city.'

'An unusual part of town to know, where all the foreign embassies are.'

'Possibly. It's hard to tell. He revealed very little information about himself: spoke good English, with a heavy Indian accent. His child was four, maybe five, wearing a maroon school sweatshirt in a photo he showed me. If you hadn't shot him, he might have been able to tell you a bit more about himself.'

Marchant saw the punch coming – it had been coming ever since MI6 first looked down its public-school nose

45

at MI5 – and raised his left forearm quick enough to deflect it upwards. His instinct, honed at the Fort, was to strike back at the same moment with his right hand, but he resisted, grabbing Wylie's upper arm instead. Their faces were close before Marchant let him go.

'Next time we'll take you both down,' Wylie said, sucking deeply on his inhaler.

5

Paul Myers drew heavily on his third pint of Young's Special. 'Another thirty seconds and the planes would have collided,' he said. 'The CAA's lost the plot, wants to know how many other UK near-misses have been caused by Colorado tinkering with its atomic clocks.'

'And?' Leila asked, glancing around the pub. The Morpeth Arms, just across the river from Legoland, was a regular haunt for officers from MI5 and MI6. She recognised one or two colleagues at the bar, waiting to be served by the pub's Czech and Russian barmaids.

'Just don't rely on your Tom-Tom if there's a war on.'

Leila smiled, sipping at her glass of Sauvignon. She was tired. MI5 had let her go late in the afternoon, after a second day of interviews. The Americans had been present today: James Spiro, the CIA's London chief, had asked lots of questions about Daniel Marchant, but no one would answer hers. She wanted to be with him, talk through the events of the marathon, hear it from his side, but nobody would admit that they knew where he was. Myers was a consolation prize. He had played his part that day, was proof that it had all actually happened. But it was the chatter that interested her.

'It was good of you to call me yesterday,' she said, touching his freckled forearm. Myers was wearing a fleece too big for him, pulled up at the sleeves.

'We go back a bit, eh? I remember the first day you arrived at the Fort...'

'Do you remember exactly what you heard? The chatter?'

Myers sat back awkwardly. 'It was probably nothing. A South Indian we'd been monitoring. Talked about "35,000 runners". Did you pass it on to anybody?'

'Only Daniel. Briefly, just before the marathon started.'

Myers smiled, not sure where to look. Like most of the intelligence analysts Leila knew at GCHQ, he was socially dysfunctional, his head hanging too far forward over his pint, which he grasped with big nail-bitten hands. He was a good listener, though, not just to *jihadi* chatter, but to old friends like Leila. She knew that he still fancied her, partly because of his unsubtle glances at her breasts, but also because of the speed with which he had agreed to come up to London when she needed to talk. She knew, too, that it was wrong of her to exploit his enthusiasm; but she had no choice. The marathon had left her in desperate need of company.

'I'm still trying to work out how it all happened, why he was the one who spotted the belt,' Leila said, realising she shouldn't have another glass of wine.

'Come on, Leila, he's always been a jammy little shit. Some people land the best postings, win on penalties, get the girl.'

Myers lifted his head briefly, his thick glasses glinting in the light. He was always at his most lyrical when he'd been on the ale, he thought, stealing another look at Leila's heavy breasts.

'I'm worried about him,' she said. 'After what happened to his father.'

'He'll get his job back. He saved the day, didn't he?'

'I hope the Americans see it that way. They never liked Stephen Marchant, and they don't trust Daniel. I think it's best neither of us mentions the chatter. It might not look too good for him.'

'OK by me. I shouldn't have told you anyway. The guys in Colorado Springs thought he was a bloody hero,' Myers continued, draining his glass. 'Any chance of kipping at your place for the night? Missed the last train back to Cheltenham.'

'You can sleep on the sofa,' Leila said, surprised by his confidence.

As they walked out onto the empty Embankment, looking for a cab, Leila turned to Myers. 'You never thought it was true, what they said about his father?'

'No. We would have known. We hear about everything at Cheltenham, sooner or later. It was political, expedient. They didn't trust him. The PM. Armstrong. The whole bloody lot of them. Not because he was a traitor. They just didn't understand him. He was old school, not their type.'

'I sometimes wonder if there really was ever a mole,' Leila said, looking out across the water towards Legoland, lit up in the night sky like some sort of rough-hewn pyramid.

'It wasn't Stephen Marchant, that's all I know,' Myers said, momentarily unsteady as he took in her legs. 'Or his son. I can't understand why they suspended him. No, Daniel's one of the good guys. Good taste in women, too.'

Half an hour later, Leila lay on her bed, staring at the ceiling in her Canary Wharf flat, regretting that she had let Myers stay on her sofabed. He was already fast asleep, his body lying as if he had been dropped from a great height, and snoring loudly.

Leila thought again about her mother, how she had sounded on the phone the night before. The doctor who had first suggested a nursing home had told her not to worry, that she must expect her mother to sound increasingly confused, but it was still alarming. Sunday was not a day she usually called her, but the marathon that morning had left her frightened and tired. Alone in her flat, after four hours of questioning at Thames House, she had felt like a child again. When she was younger and needing to talk, she had never turned to her father, who had made little effort to know her. She had always confided in her mother, but now her voice had scared Leila even more.

'They came tonight, three of them,' her mother had begun in slow Farsi. 'They took the boy – you know him, the one who cooks for me. Beat him in front of my eyes.'

'Did they hurt you, Mama?' Leila asked, dreading the answer. The confused stories of mistreatment grew worse each time she rang. 'Did they touch you?'

'He was like a grandson to me,' she continued. 'Dragged him away by his feet.'

'Mama, what did they do to you?' Leila asked.

'You told me they wouldn't come,' her mother said. 'Others here have suffered, too.'

'Never again, Mama. They won't come any more. I promise.'

'Why did they say my family are to blame? What have we ever done to them?'

'Nothing. You know how it is. Are you safe now?'

But the line was dead.

Leila wanted to be with Marchant now, to hold him close, talk about her mother. If only they had met in different circumstances, other lives. Marchant had often said the same. But their paths had tangled and could never be undone, even though both had learnt to keep a part of themselves back that no one – agents, colleagues, lovers – could ever touch. Marchant, though, was unlike anyone she had come across before. He was driven, pushing himself to the limits of success and failure. Nothing in his life ever happened in half measures. If Marchant drank, he would keep drinking until dawn. When he needed to sleep deeply, he could lie in until midday. And when he needed to study, he would work all night.

She remembered the day, two weeks into their new entrants' course at the Fort, when she woke early after a fitful sleep. The wind had been blowing in off the Channel all night, and the old windows of the bleak training centre, a former Napoleonic fort on the end of the Gosport peninsula, were rattling like milk bottles on a float. The three female recruits were in a large, shared room on the north side of the central courtyard, while the seven men were in a block of separate bedsits on the east side, overlooking the sea. She went to the window and saw a light. She couldn't be sure it was Marchant's, but she pulled on a jumper, wrapped herself in a dressing gown and made her way quietly across the cold stone courtyard.

When she reached the row of men's rooms, she knew immediately that it was Marchant's weak light seeping out from under the old wooden door. She hesitated, shivering. The day before had been dedicated to the theory of recruiting agents. People could generally be persuaded to betray their country for reasons of Money, Ideology, Coercion or Ego: MICE. It had been a long day in the classroom, with only a brief drink in the bar afterwards. Marchant had studiously ignored her then, even though they had been in the same group all day, exchanging what she thought were meaningful glances.

She knocked once and waited. There was no sound, and for a moment Leila thought he must be sleeping; or perhaps he was partying down in Portsmouth and had left the light on as a crude decoy. But then the door opened and Marchant was standing there, in a faded surfer's T-shirt and boxer shorts.

'I couldn't sleep,' she said. 'Can I come in?' Marchant

said nothing, but stood to one side, letting her step into the small room. 'Aren't you cold? This dump is freezing.'

'It stops me falling asleep.' Marchant picked up a pair of trousers that were slung across the unmade bed, dropped them in the corner and sat back down at his desk. 'Make yourself at home. I'm afraid there's only one chair.'

Leila perched herself on the edge of the bed. A pile of papers was stacked up on Marchant's small desk, bathed in a pool of light from a dented Anglepoise. A half-empty bottle of whisky stood next to the papers. For a few moments they were silent, listening to the plangent wind outside.

'What are you reading?' she asked. He turned half away from her, flicking through the printed sheets.

'Famous traitors. You know Ames is still owed $2.1 million by the Russians? They're keeping it for him in an offshore account, should he ever escape from his Pennsylvania penitentiary. There was no higher calling, just the need for cash. His wife's shopping bills were more than his CIA salary. So simple.'

'It's four o'clock in the morning.'

'I know.'

'Why now?'

Marchant turned back to look at her. 'It's not enough for me just to pass out of here. I need to fly out of this bloody place with wings.'

'Because of who your father is?'

'You heard the instructor yesterday. It's quite clear he thinks I'm not here on merit. My dad's the boss.'

'That sort of thing doesn't happen any more. Everyone knows that.'

'He didn't.'

Marchant turned back to his desk and looked out of the deep, stone-lined window. In the distance, the lights of an approaching Bilbao-to-Portsmouth ferry winked in the dawn light. Beyond it, on the far side of the main channel, he could make out the faint silhouette of the rollercoaster they had all been on two days earlier, as part of a team bonding exercise. Leila stood up, came over to him and started to work his shoulders. It was the first time she had touched him. He didn't recoil.

'You should get some beauty sleep,' she said, close to his ear.

'I didn't mean to seem off with you tonight,' he replied, lifting one hand slowly to hers.

'You were with your friends, boys together. I should have left you to it.'

'It wasn't that.'

'No?'

He paused. 'I'm not going to be a particularly pleasant person to be around for the foreseeable future.'

'Isn't that for others to decide?'

'Perhaps. But we're spending the next six months learning how to lie, deceive, betray, seduce. I'm not sure I want what we might have mixed up with that.'

'And what might we have?' Leila asked. Her hands slowed.

Marchant stood up, turned and looked at her. His eyes were anxious, searching hers for an answer she could

54

never give. She leant forward and kissed him. His lips were cold, but they were both soon searching for warmth before Marchant broke off. 'I'm sorry,' he said, sitting down at his desk. 'I must finish this tonight.'

'You don't sound very determined.'

'I'm not.'

'Shall I go?'

'No. Stay, please. Get some sleep.' He nodded at the bed.

Ten minutes later, she was tucked up under his old woollen blankets, struggling to keep out the cold, while he continued to read about motives for betrayal. He had bent the Anglepoise lower, to reduce the light in the room. She wondered if he could feel any heat from the lampshade, close to his cheek. The sea air was freezing.

'What made you sign up?' he asked, glancing in her direction. She managed a sleepy smile.

'The need to prove myself, like you. Your father's the Chief, my mother was born in Isfahan.'

Later, she was aware of him in bed next to her, holding her for warmth as sleet lashed the windows. She hoped that he was wrong about them, that what they might have could somehow survive the months ahead.

6

Marchant watched from his bedroom in the safe house as the train pulled out from the village for London. He thought again of Pradeep dying on the bridge. For a moment he wondered if one of the two bullets had missed its intended target. Did they mean to shoot him as well as Pradeep? It was the right moment to fire – Pradeep collapsing in his arms – if they weren't bothered about collateral.

Below him a Land Rover was making its way along the road that ran along the valley. He assumed it was heading into the village, but the driver turned off onto the track that led up to the safe house. It was a tatty, dark-blue Defender, and as it bumped its way towards the house, Marchant could make out the local electricity board's logo on both sides. Downstairs he could hear movement. His babysitters were stirring, ready to confront the driver, play out whatever cover story they had been given.

Next to the safe house was a small electricity sub-station for the village, enclosed by spiked green metal fencing and with its own orange windsock, billowing gently in the early-morning wind. The compound also housed an old nuclear bunker. A small sign, put up by the local history society, explained that it was used by the Royal Observer Corps during the Cold War, and could house three people for up to a month.

The surrounding area was all fields. Marchant assumed that the Land Rover belonged to the electricity board's maintenance staff. It must be a routine check on the sub-station, he thought, but as it parked up below his window, he recognised the man who stepped out of the front passenger seat. It was Marcus Fielding, his father's successor.

From the moment he had joined the Service, fifteen years earlier, Fielding had been marked out as a future Chief. The media had branded him the leader of a new generation of spies, Arabists who had joined after the Cold War and grown up with Al Qaeda. They had learnt their trade in Kandahar rather than Berlin, cutting their teeth in Pakistani training camps rather than Moscow parks, wearing turbans rather than trenchcoats.

'I don't suppose anyone has actually thanked you yet,' Fielding said, as they walked down a path in the Savernake Forest. Marchant wasn't fooled by the bonhomie. Fielding had always been supportive of Marchant, dismissing his suspension as a temporary setback in the escalating turf war between MI5 and MI6. But the events during the marathon would have tested his loyalty, ratcheting up another notch the tension between the services.

All around them rainwater dripped off the leaves, resonating like polite applause through the trees. Marchant glanced back to where the Land Rover was parked. Two men from the safe house stood quietly at the foot of a monument to George III which rose out of a clearing in the woods.

'It was quite a show you put on,' Fielding continued. 'Saved a lot of lives. The Prime Minister asked me to pass on his personal thanks. Turner Munroe will be in touch, too.'

'He probably just wants his watch back. MI5 weren't quite so appreciative.'

'No, I'm sure they weren't.'

They walked on together for a while through the ancient wood, watched by its sentinel oaks. Fielding was lean and tall, professorial in appearance, with a high, balding forehead and hair swept back at the sides. His face was oddly childish, almost cherubic. To compensate, he wore steel-rimmed glasses, which added to his donnish air and broke up the expanse of forehead. Colleagues had been quick to dub him the Vicar. He had been a choral scholar at Eton, and it was easy to imagine him still in a cassock and collar. He didn't drink, nor was he married. Prayer, though, had played little part in his rise to the top.

'I'm sorry about Sunday,' he continued. 'We tried to get you out of Thames House as soon as we could, but, well, you're not strictly our man at the moment. MI5 insisted you were their guest.'

'You would have thought I was the one wearing the belt.'

'Nothing too unpleasant, I hope?'

'Six hours of amateur Q and A. First they suggested I was helping the bomber, then they thought it was a set-up by MI6 to get my job back. No wonder they didn't see it coming.'

'That's just it, I'm afraid. The whole incident doesn't reflect well on them. Or on us, to be honest. Everyone had assumed that last year's attacks were over. No one saw it coming. You're certain he was from South India?'

'Kerala, born and bred.'

'We were all hoping that threat was over. The one person to come out of this with any credit is you, and you shouldn't have been there.'

'Can't it be spun as a general intelligence-led operation?'

'The media's not the problem. It's the PM. He can't understand why a suspended officer was all that stood between a marathon and carnage. I'm not sure I fully understand either.'

That had always been Fielding's way: his subjects rarely realised that they were being interrogated, such was his seeming politeness. But just when you had dropped your guard, he hit you hard with a disguised uppercut of meticulous accuracy.

'Leila signed us up at the last minute. A friend of hers works for one of the sponsors. It was stupid, we hadn't done enough training. On race day, I saw a dodgy belt and did something about it. I'm beginning to wish I hadn't.'

'And you had no warning? You've heard that

Cheltenham picked up some chatter on the Saturday?'

'No warning, no.' There was little point in mentioning Leila, he thought. It would sound wrong, as if she had said more than she had, when in fact she had barely told him anything. It had been a passing remark, no hard information. It worried him, though, that Fielding also doubted that it had been an entirely chance encounter.

'I couldn't have done it without Leila,' Marchant added. 'You know that?'

'She did very well. A bright future should lie ahead of her. Ahead of you, too, if that's what you want.'

Marchant knew Fielding was referring to his behaviour of the past few months, when old demons had broken free again, unchecked by the discipline of intelligence work. Fielding stopped at one of the Savernake's oldest oaks. Storms had removed the upper boughs, leaving only the trunk, strained and contorted, as if in pain. He bent down to look at the base of the tree, putting one hand to the small of his back. Sometimes his pain was so severe that he would take to lying down in his office, conducting meetings supine.

'Spring morels,' he said, pulling aside some brambles to get a better look. Marchant stooped to study them more closely. 'Exquisite fried in butter.' Everyone in Legoland knew how seriously Fielding took his food. An invitation to one of his gourmet dinners at his flat in Dolphin Square was better than a pay rise. He stood up again, both hands now pressed against his back, as if he was about to address his congregation. They both stared out across the woods, the sun streaming through gaps in the canopy, forming spotlit pools of limelight on the forest floor.

'Tell me, are you still committed to pursuing your own inquiries into your father's case?'

Marchant didn't like his tone. In a quiet moment at his father's funeral, two months earlier, Fielding had told him to let his office know if he turned up anything. All he had asked was that he went about his inquiries quietly. Become another whistleblower like Tomlinson or Shayler and he would throw the book at him. His father would have said the same: he despised renegades too. Only once had Marchant lost it, at a pub near Victoria, when an evening had ended in a brawl. A junior desk officer had been dispatched to the police station to release him and smooth things over.

'Wouldn't you want to know what happened?' Marchant replied.

'I have a pretty good idea already. Tony Bancroft has almost finished his report.'

'But he's not going to clear my father, is he?'

'None of us wanted him to go, you know that? He was a much-loved Chief.'

'So why did we let MI5 get one over us? There was never any evidence, no proof against him.'

'I know you're still angry, Daniel, but the quickest way to get you working again is for you to keep your head down and let Tony finish his job. MI5 don't want you back, but I do. Once Bancroft is on record saying you pose no threat, there's nothing anyone can do about it.'

'But Bancroft won't clear my father's name, will he?' Marchant repeated.

They walked on, Fielding a few yards ahead of him. Marchant had met with Lord Bancroft and his team, answered their questions, and knew that he had no case to answer. He knew his father was innocent, too, but the Prime Minister had needed someone to blame. Mainland Britain had been subjected to an unprecedented wave of terrorist attacks during the past year. Nothing spectacular, but there was enough public fear to keep MI5 on a critical state of alert: electricity sub-stations, railway depots, multi-storey car parks. The evidence soon pointed to a terrorist cell based in South India, drawn from workers who had taken poorly-paid jobs in the Gulf.

The pressure to nullify the threat had grown, but the terrorists always seemed to be one step ahead. Soon the talk was of a mole, high up in MI6, helping the hunted. Daniel's father had become obsessed with the theory, but he had never managed to prove it, or to halt the bombings. Suspicion had finally fallen on him. When his position as Chief became untenable, the Joint Intelligence Committee, guided by Harriet Armstrong, MI5's Director General, recommended that he be retired early. The attacks had stopped.

Fielding paused at the point where their path met another. As Marchant joined him, they instinctively looked both ways before crossing, even though the forest was empty. A muntjac deer barked in the distance.

'Are you still drinking?' Fielding asked.

'When I can,' Marchant said.

'I'm not sure we can bail you out a second time.'

'How long will I be kept at the safe house?'

'It's for your own security. Someone out there's not happy you thwarted their attack.'

They walked on together, both at ease with the forest's noisy dampness. 'There are no surprises in what I've read of Bancroft's report, no moles uncovered,' Fielding said, as they began on a loop back towards the car. 'It's not Tony's style, not why he was appointed. Just a summing up of what happened on your father's watch and a measured assessment of whether anything more could have been done. There were too many attacks, we all know that.'

'And someone had to take the bullet.'

'The PM's a former Home Secretary. He was always going to favour MI5 over us.'

Marchant had heard all this before, but he knew from Fielding's manner that he was holding something back.

'Unfortunately, the Americans have been pushing for more, day and night, trying to establish that it was conspiracy rather than complacency on your father's part. We've resisted, of course, but the PM is indulging them. And now it seems they've persuaded him to hold back on the report's publication, saying the CIA have something specific.'

'On my father? What?'

'How much do you know about Salim Dhar?'

'Dhar?' Marchant hesitated, trying to think clearly. 'On the shortlist for masterminding last year's UK bombings, but no evidence to link him directly. Always been more anti-American than British. It's a while since I read his file.'

'Educated in Delhi, the American school, then disappeared,' Fielding said. 'The Indians arrested him two years later in Kashmir, and banged him up in a detention site in Kerala, where he should be now. Only he isn't.'

'No?'

'He was one of the prisoners released in the Bhuj hijack exchange at the end of last year.'

It wasn't his region, but Marchant knew the incident had been an almost exact copy of the Indian Airlines hijacking at Kandahar in 1999. Then, Omar Sheikh had been released, amid much international condemnation. It was never made public who was freed at Bhuj.

'AQ must have rated him,' Marchant said, wondering where his father fitted in.

'We had Dhar down as a small-time terrorist until Bhuj. They wanted something spectacular in return for his freedom. Within a month, Dhar was launching RPGs into the US compound in Delhi.'

Marchant had read about the attack, in the blur of grief. It had taken place just after his father had died, before the funeral. Nine US Marines had been killed.

'What's this got to do with my father?'

Fielding paused before answering, as if in two minds whether to proceed. 'The Americans would very much like to find Salim Dhar. After Delhi, he went on to attack their compound in Islamabad, killing six more US Marines And now the CIA has established that a senior-

64

ranking officer from MI6 visited Dhar in Kerala shortly before he was released in the hostage exchange.'

Marchant looked up. 'And they think it was my father?'

'They're working on a theory that it was, yes. I'm sorry. There's no official record of any visits. I've checked all the logbooks, many times.'

Marchant didn't know what to think. It wouldn't be unusual for the local station head from Chennai, say, to bluff his way into seeing someone like Dhar, but it would be extremely unorthodox for the Chief of MI6 to make an undeclared visit from London.

'In the context of MI5's own inquiries, I'm afraid it doesn't look good,' Fielding added. 'There are those who are convinced that Dhar masterminded the British bombings, despite his preference for killing Americans.'

'What do you think?' Marchant asked. 'You knew my dad better than most.'

Fielding stopped and turned to Marchant. 'He was under a lot of pressure last year to clean up MI6's act. The talk at the time, remember, was all about an inside job, infiltration at the highest level by terrorists with some sort of South Indian connection. Even so, why talk to Dhar personally?'

'Because he couldn't trust anyone else?' Marchant offered. For whatever reason, he knew that it must have been an act of desperation on his father's part.

'The good news is that details of this visit haven't crossed Bancroft's desk yet, and they might never,' Fielding said. 'His job was to draw a line under your father's departure, not to open the whole affair up again.

He'll need to be sure of the evidence before presenting it to the JIC, and there isn't a lot at the moment.'

'Is there any?'

'Dhar's jailer, the local police chief in Kerala. Someone blackmailed him to gain access to Dhar. It had all the hallmarks of an old-school sting.'

'Moscow rules?'

'Textbook. Indian intelligence found the compromising photos hidden in the policeman's desk drawer. They were taken with one of our cameras. An old Leica.' He paused. 'The last time it was checked out was in Berlin, early 1980s. Your father never returned it.'

7

Marchant knew that someone was in his room as he walked up the worn wooden stairs of the safe house. It was one of those intuitive things they couldn't teach at the Fort. After Fielding had dropped him off on his way back to London, Marchant had checked in with his two babysitters, who were watching porn in the small sitting room. They had hardly acknowledged his return, so he wasn't overly concerned as he turned the handle on the bedroom door. Besides, he could already smell Leila's perfume.

'Dan,' she said, getting up from the corner of the bed, where a newspaper was spread out across the covers: two pages on the attempted marathon terrorist attack. 'I was beginning to wonder what you were doing with the Vicar in the woods.'

They made love slowly, their limbs still tender after their morning on the streets of London.

'A proper debrief,' he smiled, as she slid his boxers off and eased on top of him.

Neither of them was ready to discuss what had happened at the marathon. When he had still been working they would meet up for snatched weekends whenever they could, in Berne, Seville, Dubrovnik, but never on their own patch. And they always had a rule of not talking about work, which meant they spent a lot of time making love, as they had little life beyond their jobs, only opening up to each other at the airport, minutes before they flew their separate ways. Today, though, would be different, they both knew that.

But first Marchant fell into a deep sleep, something he had rarely been able to do in recent months. His brain must have concluded that lying in a protected safe house in the depths of Wiltshire, with Leila by his side, was as secure an environment as he could hope for. Fielding had authorised her visit, she said, which added to the sense of sanctuary.

When he awoke, he felt less rested than he had hoped. No nightmares, but a nagging memory of Leila's hot tears, felt faintly through the layers of tiredness that had enveloped his aching limbs. He sat up, troubled that he had been unable to respond. Leila was taking a shower. The bathroom door was open, and from where he was lying he could see the brown haze of her breasts, a fuzz of pubic hair, blurred by the steamy glass of the shower cubicle.

As she tilted her head back, smoothing her long hair in the jet of water, he remembered the first time he saw her, when they were both waiting to be interviewed at

Carlton Gardens in London. There had been a mix-up over times, and he had sat next to her in the reception, suspecting she was there for the same reason as him, but unable to ask. Instead they had spoken with agonising formality about the weather, the architecture, anything but the one subject that was occupying both their minds.

When they had met again, on their first day of training at the Fort in Gosport, there had been a palpable frisson between them. The freedom to talk about whatever they liked was intoxicating. An instructor asked all of them to stand up and introduce themselves in turn. (MI6 was no different from the rest when it came to toe-curling corporate practices.) Leila spoke first in English, and then briefly in fluent Farsi, explaining that her father was an Englishman who worked as an engineer in the oil and natural gas industry. He had met and married her mother, a Bahá'í Iranian and university lecturer, while posted to Tehran. After the Revolution in 1979, they had fled to Britain, along with many other Bahá'ís, hounded out by the Revolutionary Guard, who had no time for unrecognised religious minorities.

Leila was born and brought up in Hertfordshire by her mother, while her father worked in various jobs around the Gulf, sometimes joined by his family. Her earliest childhood memories were of the fifty-degree heat in Doha. When she was eight, they all went to live in Houston for two years. For as long as the Ayatollahs ruled, however, there was never a chance of returning to Tehran, because the Bahá'ís remained enemies of an Islamic state that continued to persecute them.

She told the room, in English, how she had applied to the Service in her last year at Oxford, after the master of her college, a former Chief (Stephen Marchant's predecessor), had invited her for dinner. She feared the worst, not convinced she wanted to join an organisation that still seemed to recruit over a glass of Oxbridge Amontillado, but was surprised by his lack of pomposity, and by the vibrant mix of the four other young people who had been asked along to the same dinner. Only one of them was white, a demographic that was reflected in the room of aspiring spies that day at the Fort. It reminded her of the time she had visited the BBC's World Service at Bush House.

'Naturally suspicious, I went back to my room after dinner and sat up all night reading the website, about how people from ethnically diverse backgrounds would be welcome at MI6. I knew MI5 was recruiting multi-racially, but I thought the Service was the last bastion of the white, middle-class, safari-suit-wearing male. People like Daniel here.' Laughter filled the room. 'There was a catch, though, as we all know: you had to have at least one British parent. Luckily, my mother always had a thing about English men.' More laughter. 'The vetting takes an age, though, didn't you find? They interviewed my mother for weeks. It must have been the *shisha* pipe she kept offering round.'

'Have you ever been back to Iran?' the instructor asked. He was the only one not laughing.

'Back? I never lived there.'

'It must have sometimes felt like home, though,' the

instructor continued. The room's relaxed atmosphere tensed.

'I went there once, in my year off,' she said, fixing the instructor's eye. 'I assume everyone here was asked the same question in their first interview, whether they had ever persuaded someone to do something illegal. Well, I told them about my trip to Iran, how I talked a guard on the Turkmenistan border into letting me across to visit the rose harvest in Ghamsar for my PhD on perfume. The gardens were beautiful. I'll never forget – whole families picking roses in the dawn mist, the dew still wet on the scented petals.'

Marchant had spoken next, knowing that he could never match Leila for presence. Her sassy smile, the sexual poise, that worldly, cosmopolitan voice: sorted rather than arrogant. He explained that he had grown up abroad, moving from one embassy to another around the world until he had been packed off aged thirteen to a boarding school in Wiltshire. He had been told to be upfront about his father, who had recently taken over as Chief, so he joked about keeping it in the family. 'Spies are like undertakers, they run in families,' he continued. 'And I'm in good company, I guess. Kim Philby's father, St John Philby, had been a senior member of the Service.' It was a quip he later regretted.

'After Cambridge, I worked for a couple of years as a hard-up foreign correspondent, stringing from Africa for various British broadsheets and drinking too much cheap Scotch. I landed some of my best stories, including a splash about Gaddafi, thanks to a contact at the High Commission in Nairobi. It was only later that I discovered he worked for I/OPS in Legoland. I was young and naïve at the time, and didn't realise that it was his job to present the media with stories that helped the national cause. It was on his advice that I eventually returned to London to apply.'

He looked around at his new colleagues, gauging how honest he should be. The room had fallen awkwardly silent. 'I was in a bad way, to be honest. Rudderless. Broke. You know what hacks are like. There were also a few personal issues that needed resolving.' He paused again, deciding not to mention his brother. 'The bloke from I/OPS found me in downtown Nairobi one night, worse for wear. Told me to stop being in denial and apply. I'd always wanted to make my own way in life, not rely on my parents, my father, but I guess the family calling eventually proved too strong.'

Leila came back into the safe-house bedroom, a towel wrapped around her drying hair like a turban. 'Remember that first day at the Fort, when we all had to stand up and speak?' Marchant asked, putting on a cotton dressing gown.

'Yes, why?'

'We never did find out who was lying.'

After everyone had spoken, their instructor had announced that the life story of one person in the room was entirely false. They had each been told to write down who they thought it was, and why.

'I don't think it was any of us,' Leila said. 'The only one lying that day was the arsy instructor.'

'It wasn't you, then?' Marchant asked.

'Me? Is that who you wrote down?'

'All that Bahá'í back-story. I'm amazed they let you in.'

'It happens to be true, you cheeky sod,' she said, kissing his forehead as he lay there on the bed, watching her pull on some knickers. 'My mother's an amazing woman. The only reason I made it to Oxford. I actually found the vetting process very therapeutic, answering all those questions about her, learning more about the Bahá'í faith, her allegiance to Britain.'

'Were the vetters worried, then?'

'Not by the time they'd finished. She'd lived in Britain for twenty-five years.'

'You never talk about her any more.'

Leila fell quiet. He remembered her tears again and reached up to her waist, gently pulling her down to sit beside him on the bed.

'What is it?' he asked quietly.

'Nothing,' she said, wiping beneath an eye with the back of her hand.

'The marathon?'

'No. It's OK.' She rested her head on his shoulder, trying not to lose control, taking comfort in his warmth.

The only time Marchant had ever seen Leila cry was when she had come off the phone to her mother in their early days of training at the Fort. She hadn't wanted to talk about it. When he tried to raise the matter later, she had resisted.

'Is it your mother?' he asked. 'Have you spoken to her recently?'

Leila remained in his arms. She had once told him that

her mother often talked of returning to Iran one day. She wanted to be a widow amongst her own family, her people, and to care for her own, ageing mother. But Leila had told her that it was too risky for a Bahá'í to return to Iran while her religion was being systematically persecuted.

Instead, she had been admitted into a nursing home in Hertfordshire, after showing early signs of Alzheimer's. Leila said that she was bitterly unhappy there, and was soon complaining of being badly treated by the staff, but it was impossible to prove anything or to work out how much was a result of her confused state of mind. Marchant had offered to accompany Leila on a visit, but she didn't want him to form his only impression of her mother when she was not herself.

'You did well yesterday, I hope Fielding told you that,' Leila said, more together now, walking over to the dressing table. 'You thwarted a twisted plan.'

'I couldn't have done it without your help,' Marchant said, then paused. 'Pradeep had a son. He showed me a photo.'

The events of the marathon were finally catching up with him, too. Leila sensed the change in his voice. She came back over to the bed and stroked his neck. 'They were going to kill the boy if he didn't go through with it,' Marchant continued. 'Do you think they did?'

'He died trying to carry out his mission, and the London Marathon was cancelled for the first time in its history. Probably not.'

Leila had returned to her usual, unsentimental self. Marchant felt relief. Her professional manner put a distance between them, a reminder not to let her break his heart. He had been unsettled by her earlier display of emotion. It had made him want to talk more about the race, the incessant beeping of Pradeep's GPS, how such an innocent sound could have announced both their deaths, the exhilarating feeling of being on an operation again, the surprising heaviness of Pradeep's dead body in his arms. But her coolness now made him feel more detached from the events of yesterday. He knew it was the only way they had survived in their jobs.

'Fielding also talked about my father,' Marchant said, raising and lowering his aching limbs. 'My legs are killing me.'

'Anything new?' Leila stood up and went back to the dressing table, where she started to dry her hair.

'The Americans are leaning on Bancroft. Seems they might have something on him after all.'

'The Americans?' she said, turning to face him. 'What's it got to do with them?'

Marchant told her what Fielding had said, the pressure MI5 was putting on Lord Bancroft to identify his father as the mole, the Americans' belief that he had met Salim Dhar before last year's embassy bombings in Delhi and Islamabad.

'I remember the Leica,' Marchant continued. 'It was like a museum piece, beautifully made. He showed it to me once, at Christmas, just after I'd been accepted by the Service.' He paused. 'I'm not helping your case, you know that. I think you should keep your distance for a while.'

She glanced at him in the mirror, her eyes flicking down his body. 'I'm not going to stop screwing you because of MI5.'

'I appreciate the loyalty, but it's not going to do you any favours, that's all I'm saying.' He got up from the bed and stood behind Leila, cupping her bare breasts in his hands as they looked at their reflection. His chin rested on her shoulder. 'If they can suspect my dad, they can suspect me, too.'

'I thought the Vicar wanted you back,' Leila said, turning her face sideways to kiss him. 'Particularly after yesterday.'

'He does, but it might not be up to him if Bancroft finds against my father.'

'Your dad never really took to me, did he?' Leila said, unpeeling herself from Marchant's arms to apply some mascara.

'That's not true.'

'That time when we went to your home for lunch in the country, he was very ill at ease with me. Almost rude.'

'He was wary of all my girlfriends, suspicious of women generally. Two boys, you see, no daughters. And a distant wife.'

'Can't say it runs in the family.'

'What do you mean?'

'The Wariness of Women gene. I'm not sure he passed it on.' She smiled at him and he knew she was right, standing there in the evening light. He had never felt less wary of anyone in his life.

8

It was a long-held custom that the first half of the Joint Intelligence Committee's weekly meeting in the Cabinet Room at Downing Street was attended by senior officers from the American, Australian and Canadian intelligence services. The second half was only for the British. Marcus Fielding could barely wait for the foreign contingent to be shown the door, but for the next few minutes he would have to listen to James Spiro, the CIA's London chief, who had announced, with his usual hard-man hyperbole, that he had some 'weapons-grade HUMINT to bring to the party'. Fielding had already got the gist of it earlier that morning, thanks to one of several new listening devices installed at the recently opened American Embassy in Vauxhall (near Legoland), but he sat there, ramrod-straight, as if he was hearing it all for the first time.

'We are now certain that Stephen Marchant travelled to Kerala and met up with Salim Dhar in jail,' Spiro began, as ever liking the sound of his own voice. 'I appreciate Dhar's role in last year's UK bombings is far from clear, but there is absolutely no doubt that he tried to bomb the hell out of our embassies in New Delhi and Islamabad. Ask the families of the fifteen dead US Marines.'

So far, nothing new, Fielding thought, looking around the coffin-shaped oak table. The usual mix of Whitehall suspects were in attendance, including the heads of MI5 and Cheltenham, as well as mandarins from various departments, all presided over by the chairman of the JIC, Sir David Chadwick, who was sitting at the far end, in front of the double windows which had buckled when the IRA lobbed a mortar bomb into the Downing Street rosebeds. Everyone had flung themselves on the floor that day, the Cabinet Secretary lying next to the Prime Minister.

If it happened again this morning, Fielding idly thought, Harriet Armstrong, Director General of MI5, would do her best to prostrate herself next to Spiro. She glanced tersely at Fielding, as if reading his mind. They had never liked each other, their relationship chilling even further when she had enlisted Spiro's support to remove Stephen Marchant.

'What we do now know, however, thanks to Harriet here, is that Dhar was behind Sunday's foiled bombing of the London Marathon, an attack that I don't need to remind you was targeted at our Ambassador to London.'

Fielding looked up. This had not been in the transcript he had read in the car coming over from Vauxhall. He glanced across at Armstrong, who was studiously avoiding his eye. It was a stitch-up. Until now, any connection between Dhar and the London Marathon had been purely circumstantial, based on the nature of the target and Dhar's historical predilection for attacking Americans. If his involvement could now be proved, as Spiro claimed, it would cast Stephen Marchant and his son in a new and far more compromising light.

'I'll leave the domestic implications of this to the second half of your meeting, but clearly Dhar has just become a priority one target, and I'd be grateful if, on this occasion, the Service leaves him to us.'

'Marcus?' asked Chadwick, sounding as if Spiro had raised a mere technicality, rather than made it considerably more likely that the former Chief of MI6 had betrayed Queen and country. His clandestine meeting with Dhar had taken place two weeks before the attack on the American Embassy in Delhi.

'Dhar is of great interest to the UK, too,' Fielding said, buying time. 'Given his – apparent – role in the attempted London Marathon attack, I would expect a joint operation at the very least.'

'I'm sorry, Marcus, but this one just got personal,' Spiro said. 'Dhar's problem is clearly with us: the embassy attacks last year, now our Ambassador to London.'

'An attack which was foiled by one of our agents,' Fielding replied.

'With a little help from Colorado Springs, I gather,' Spiro continued, turning to Chadwick. 'Which brings me to my next point. Can we have a little chat with your suspended superhero?'

'Daniel Marchant? That shouldn't be a problem,' Chadwick said. 'Harriet?'

'Marcus?' Armstrong deflected the question.

'Is he not with you?' Chadwick asked.

'Right now, we're taking care of him,' Fielding interrupted. 'Given he's still on our payroll.'

'Well, Marcus, I'll repeat my question to you,' said Spiro. 'Can we have a talk with Marchant Junior? Preferably when he's not been on the sauce.'

'If we're working together on Dhar, I'm sure we can cooperate on Daniel Marchant,' Fielding replied coolly.

Spiro turned towards Armstrong for support.

'We'd clearly like to talk to Marchant again, too, in the light of Dhar's role in the marathon,' Armstrong obliged. 'Perhaps we could take care of him?'

'Our own debrief is still ongoing,' Fielding said.

'Shouldn't that read "detox"?' Spiro said, smiling around the table. Only Armstrong smiled back.

'We will, of course, circulate our findings once we're finished with him,' Fielding said. He had always known that there was little he could do about Stephen Marchant, whose reputation was ultimately in other people's hands, but he had hoped he could do something for his son. MI6 had fished Daniel Marchant out of the international pool of inebriated hacks, and turned him into one of the Service's best officers. Fielding wasn't going to let him go lightly, if only for his father's sake. Marchant's presence at the marathon, however, was beginning to look too much of a coincidence. He doubted whether Armstrong had any hard evidence – it was too soon –

but the link with Dhar had been made, and would be duly recorded in the JIC's minutes. In the light of his father's meeting with Dhar, Daniel Marchant's role looked less heroic by the minute.

After further curt exchanges and an offer from Chadwick to square Fielding and Spiro's differences, the foreign contingent left the room, leaving the British to assess Spiro's 'weapons-grade HUMINT'.

'Well gentlemen, Harriet, do we believe him?' Chadwick began, looking around the room, still sounding unruffled.

'There's no reason for them to lie about Stephen Marchant,' Armstrong said.

'Unless they want to go after Dhar themselves,' Fielding replied. 'Until we see the evidence, we have no way of knowing whether Stephen Marchant did or did not meet Dhar.'

'Let's be quite clear about this,' Chadwick said. 'If they do hand over the evidence, hard proof that Marchant met Salim Dhar, we would have to pass it on to Bancroft. His report would then become an investigation into whether the former head of MI6 should be posthumously investigated for treason.'

'The PM wouldn't buy it,' said Bruce Lockhart, the Prime Minister's foreign adviser. Fielding got on with Lockhart, liked his bullish Fife manner. 'I thought Bancroft was given this job to quieten things down, not stir them up.'

'The Americans aren't trying to make trouble,' Armstrong said. 'Quite reasonably, they want to stop

Dhar attacking their assets and to establish why the Marchant family seem to be helping him.'

'Helping him?' Fielding interjected. 'Let's not get carried away here. Bancroft has so far found nothing to substantiate any suspicion that my predecessor was anything other than complacent. For the record, I happen to think the Americans are right: Stephen Marchant probably did meet up with Dhar. I'm just not sure why. Until we find out, it remains idle conjecture, and Bancroft shouldn't touch it.'

'So we leave Dhar to the Americans?' asked Armstrong.

'We need to find him, too, given that he was behind the attempted attack on the marathon,' Fielding said, turning to Armstrong and adding quietly, 'Nice of you to pool that one.'

'I'd forgotten how much you liked to share information,' Armstrong replied.

'I think Marcus is right,' Chadwick said. 'We need to find Dhar.' He had always found that steadfastly ignoring tension between departments seemed to reduce it. 'Dhar targeted the London Marathon, Tower bloody Bridge, for God's sake. If that's not an attack on the fabric of this country I don't know what is. And it's also the only way we'll ever draw a line under Stephen Marchant. If the two of them did meet, which seems likely, we need to find out why, and what was actually said.'

'We're sure there's no record anywhere of Stephen Marchant or anyone else recruiting Dhar?' Lockhart asked. 'At this meeting or before? The PM wants specific reassurance on this point.'

'We've been through all Marchant's files many times,' Fielding said. 'Cross-referenced every database we have. Nothing. No one else in MI6 or MI5 has ever approached Dhar. We think the Indians once tried a deniable approach, but failed.'

Armstrong nodded her head in agreement, glancing at Fielding.

'And what about his son?' asked Chadwick. 'Do we let the Americans talk to him? You can see it from their point of view: Stephen Marchant meets Dhar, Dhar bombs US embassies; Daniel Marchant meets Dhar's running friend; Dhar's friend tries to kill US Ambassador.'

'And Marchant stops him,' said Marcus. 'That's the point here.'

But he knew the point was lost.

9

Later that day, Fielding accepted Chadwick's offer of a sharpener at the Travellers on Pall Mall. He was not a natural clubman, but in the past few years, as Stephen Marchant had begun to waver at the top, Fielding had been wined and dined by various senior Whitehall hands, including Chadwick, while his own suitability as Chief was assessed. He knew there was unease amongst the old guard that he was not married, but times were changing, and the general view was that the Vicar was celibate rather than gay. Fielding could live with that.

The Travellers used to double up as MI6's staff bar, in the days when the Service was situated in Century House, its drab premises in Southwark. Since the move to Legoland, with its plush second-floor bar and terrace overlooking the Thames, where people could drink outside in the summer, the Travellers had become less of a draw for junior staff. But old habits died hard for senior officers, and Fielding acknowledged a couple of familiar faces as he took his seat in the panelled library.

'I'm offering you a deal,' Chadwick said, swirling his Talisker around the glass. He was one of the safest pairs of hands in Whitehall, brought in at the end of a successful but unstartling career to steady the intelligence ship after the fiasco of Marchant's departure. Evidence, Fielding concluded, that mediocrity can take you surprisingly far in big organisations like the Civil Service.

'The Americans have agreed to drop their investigation of any meeting between Dhar and Stephen, providing they can have access to Daniel Marchant and we leave Dhar to them.'

'Access?'

'They want to sweat him.'

'Why?'

'Come on, Marcus. I know he was one of your best, but it's bloody odd he was there at the marathon. They think he might be able to tell them something about Dhar. And, to be honest, the idea of someone taking Marchant off our hands is quite appealing. We all know he's been drinking too much. The last thing the PM needs right now is another renegade spy on the loose.'

Fielding thought about defending Daniel Marchant again. Perhaps it was the effect of his gin and lime, but he was no longer as troubled by Chadwick's proposal as he might have been. A part of him resented having to protect Marchant any longer, given the headache his suspension had caused. Chadwick was right: Marchant had been the most promising case officer of his generation, just the sort of young blood the Service was trying to attract. But Fielding knew, too, that his suspension was entirely because of the accusations swirling around his father. And he needed those accusations to go away: they were continuing to cause too much damage to the Service. The sooner the Americans forgot about any meeting between the former Chief and Dhar, the better for everyone.

There was only one concern, and that was the 'enhanced' interrogation techniques favoured by the CIA. The new President might have banned torture, but old habits die hard in Langley. Despite everything, Marchant was still one of his own, and right now he was fragile.

'He mustn't leave the country,' Fielding said, finishing his gin. 'And I want him back alive.'

10

Leila headed back to London that night, leaving Marchant to dwell on Fielding's visit over a bottle of malt she had smuggled in with her. He knew he was drinking too much. The training runs with Leila, the impulsive decision to run the marathon, had been an attempt to impose some routine on his life, which had lost all shape since his father's death. He had never been fitter than when he was working for MI6. The drinking dulled the pain of loss, but it also dragged him back to another life, to dissolute, carefree days at the Nairobi Press Club.

The first weeks of his suspension had been the toughest. In his sober hours, Marchant had thought only of the mole who had supposedly penetrated MI6. It was his way of grieving, channelling his anger. Rising at dawn, head bursting, he had paced the empty streets of Pimlico, holding the rumours about his father up to the early-morning light, looking at them from every possible angle.

He would stand on Vauxhall Bridge, watching the barges pass below before turning to look up at Legoland and the buttressed windows of the Chief's office. Had the whole thing been cooked up as a Machiavellian way of removing his father, or was there a genuine possibility that Al Qaeda had infiltrated MI6?

The terms of his suspension meant that he wasn't allowed to step inside Legoland, or to talk with colleagues about work, or to travel overseas. All his cover passports had been seized. His mornings had been spent in internet cafés around Victoria station (he didn't trust the computer at his flat on Denbigh Street), going over each of the attacks again and again, looking for something that might link a cell based in South India to anyone in MI6, a Legoland colleague with connections to the subcontinent.

Now, at last, he had that link, but it was between his own father and Salim Dhar. Never once had it crossed Marchant's mind that his father had brought suspicion upon himself. Fielding was right: meeting Dhar privately was an irregular thing to have done. And Marchant knew, as Leila's whisky burnt his throat, that he too would have to meet him, wherever he was. It was the only way to clear his father's name. He needed to ask Dhar why the Chief of MI6 had run the risk of meeting with him. The consequences of such an encounter could prove equally disastrous for him, but the reality was that he didn't have much to lose.

As he gazed out across the Wiltshire countryside towards the woods beyond the canal, a grey heron lifted itself heavily from the water and rose into the air. His father used to say that they were like B-52s, but then he had always had a thing about bombers. During the Cuban Missile Crisis he had driven down to Fairford and watched them standing on the end of the runway, engines running, waiting for the order.

Marchant remembered the morning his father had called him with the news that he was to step down as Chief. The power and authority had gone from his voice, as if he had been using a megaphone all his life and someone had suddenly switched it off. Marchant had taken the call at Heathrow airport, on his way back from Mogadishu to London for Christmas.

'Have you cleared immigration?' his father had asked, almost absent-mindedly.

'I'm waiting for a taxi. Why? Is everything all right, Dad?'

'Take the Underground as far as Hammersmith, then a minicab from that place on Fulham Palace Road we used to use. Ask for Tarlton. They'll know.'

'Dad, what is this? Is everything OK?'

'I've been put out to pasture. Watch yourself.'

Marchant had immediately gone on his guard again, as if in a foreign airport. He moved swiftly down to the Underground, trying to work out the implications of their conversation, for his father, for him. He knew pressure had been building in recent weeks. There had been questions in the House about the incompetence of Britain's intelligence services, aggressive newspaper leaders about the wave of attacks and what more should have been done to prevent them.

His father paid off the minicab in cash, and insisted on taking his son's two bags. It was a cold December day, and the apple and cherry trees at the front of the house were laced with frozen cobwebs. A thin twist of smoke rose from the chimney. The house was in effect two Cotswold cottages knocked together, surrounded by lawns and a meandering drystone wall. It was a private location, half a mile out of Tarlton, a small hamlet near Cirencester. Marchant always felt strange when he was here. The house had been the only constant in his shifting childhood, a place where they came for brief respites from foreign postings, a home he had once shared with his brother. Its Englishness was overwhelming, not just because of its Cotswold prettiness, but because it had come to represent all that he missed about home: new-mown grass, autumn bonfires, orchards. And, of course, it had always disappointed, unable to live up to childhood dreams of Albion.

'Good of you to come,' his father said, walking through the back door in front of Marchant. 'Mind if we go for a drive?'

Ten minutes later, they were speeding through the cold open countryside in his 1931 Lagonda, barely able to hear each other above the roar of the two-litre engine. Frost had sharpened the hedgerows, and the road was black with hidden ice. But Stephen Marchant didn't seem to mind, wrapped up in a thick woollen scarf and gloves. Daniel sat next to him. He had forgotten how cold a car could feel.

'Can't trust the house,' his father said, changing down

the gears as they approached a junction. Home, Marchant knew, had been wired to a level of protection befitting the Chief's weekend retreat. Now that security was working against him.

'MI5?' Marchant asked, the smell of musty canvas and hot oil taking him back to another distant part of his childhood. He and his father had always been close, both of them at ease in each other's company, seldom needing to explain or open up. Even when Marchant had been expelled from school, his father hadn't been angry, just annoyed that he had been caught.

'I'm becoming a threat to national security,' he shouted, releasing the brake lever on the side of the car and accelerating away towards Avening. Marchant hoped he would age as well as his father, whose silver hair was blowing about in the strong breeze. He had thick, fair eyebrows and a compact, square face, like a barn owl, Marchant always thought. And then there were those famous family ears, which had only got longer, more distinguished, with age. Tribal lobes, his father had once called them.

After twenty minutes, Stephen Marchant pulled the Lagonda up in a lay-by at the top of Minchinhampton Common, on the brow of a hill looking west towards Bristol. He switched off the engine and they sat there for a few minutes in silence, absorbing the timeless landscape as steam rose off the bonnet. Below them the Cotswolds stretched out in a necklace of icy hamlets, threaded with quiet country lanes, each with its handsome manor house, enduring church, frosted green. Thin drifts of snow covered the shaded corners of fields.

'I look at this and wonder out of which pore of our beautiful country it's seeping from,' Stephen Marchant began. A bead of moisture had gathered on the end of his cold nose. 'Do you know what they said?'

'Tell me,' Marchant replied, noticing the emotion that had slipped into his father's voice.

'That they can no longer be sure my interests coincide with the country's.' He paused, struggling to keep control. 'Thirty years' service and I have to listen to a group of jumped-up pricks in shorts telling me that.'

'And it's all coming from the DG?' Daniel asked.

'Of course. Apparently I'm obsessed with the enemy within, and have taken my eye off the greater threat.'

'Dinner at the Travellers didn't do the trick, then.'

'God, no. Total disaster. She's not like the women you and I know, Daniel. This one's got balls, and I've been shafted, well and truly. They don't want me back in the office after Christmas. I'm afraid they're also talking about suspending you. Sins of the father. I'm so sorry.' Marchant turned away, his mind racing instinctively to calculate the threat, assess the damage. He hadn't expected it to affect him. Then he stopped, guilty that he had thought of himself rather than his father, whose career was in tatters after half a lifetime of service.

'Don't worry about me. You know I've never asked for help. I can look after myself.'

'The Service can't. If MI5 gets its way, Legoland will be sold off to the Japanese tomorrow and turned into a Thameside hotel. Come on, the idiots have arrived.'

Marchant looked behind them, and saw a white saloon car driving slowly up the hill.

'Do you know the best way to shake off a tail?' his father asked, firing up the Lagonda again in a plume of blue smoke. 'Better than anything they might have taught you at the Fort?'

'What?' Marchant said, watching the car in the mirror as it slowed to a crawl four hundred yards behind them, its exhaust loitering in the cold air.

'Drive faster than them.'

11

The gang of Year Five boys in the corner of the playing field knew all of the helicopters that flew through the Wiltshire airspace above their primary school: Chinooks were their favourite, flying low down the route of the canal, the sound of their twin blades reverberating like thunder in their tender eardrums. They knew their Merlins from their Sikorski Pumas, and barely commented these days on the black-and-yellow Wiltshire Police helicopter, which flew in every Friday for low-level practice over Bedwyn Brail. So when the boys saw the MD Explorer coming in towards the village from Hungerford, it was such a familiar sight that nobody noticed that it was a Thursday, not a Friday.

Half a mile south-west of the school, Daniel Marchant crossed over the two bridges and turned right onto the towpath of the Kennet canal. He smiled to himself as he remembered how his father had dropped down from

Minchinhampton at more than 90 mph, the Lagonda's low chassis threatening to shake itself apart as they raced through the frosty hedgerows without any real brakes, until their pursuers had finally given up.

Marchant wasn't sure if he could run faster than his minders, but he wanted to find out. The marathon was five days ago, and this was his first run since he had arrived at the safe house. He knew he couldn't keep going like this: the drinking followed by the guilt-runs. One of them had to prevail. The babysitters from MI6 had been replaced the previous evening by heavier-built types from MI5. Relations chilled accordingly, and conversation had all but dried up.

Marchant wasn't unduly worried by the change of guard. At worst, he assumed that he might be subjected to Wylie again, the man who had interviewed him at Thames House. More worrying was the silence from Leila. He had no means of contacting anyone in the outside world. There was no phone at the house, no computer or internet connection, and the babysitters kept their mobiles strapped to their expansive waistlines.

His plan this morning, as he gradually increased his stride, was to stretch the two from MI5, see how long they could cope with a six-minute-mile pace. They hadn't been keen on the idea of a run, but relented when Marchant agreed to show them on a map his exact route to the nearby village of Wilton and back. They preferred a shorter loop, along the canal towpath, up through the woodland known as Bedwyn Brail, and then back along the lanes into the village. Marchant agreed, tickled by the idea of pushing these two to their limits. The fitness levels in MI6 had always been greater than those of MI5, whose gym was no match for the one that glistened in the basement of Legoland, out of sight of Whitehall's bean counters.

But it was not proving nearly as entertaining as Marchant had hoped. His whole body hurt like hell. And both men from MI5 responded with unnerving ease to his initial kick, and he soon found them on his shoulder.

'Don't be a muppet, marathon man,' one of them said, barely out of breath.

Without answering, Marchant kicked again, turning off the towpath, as agreed, and carving out a diagonal route up the hillside towards the Brail. Near the top of the hill, he glanced over his shoulder and saw the lead minder floundering at the bottom of the slope. It looked as if he had slipped. Exhilarated to be alone for the first time since Sunday, Marchant upped his pace again.

It was as he crested the hill that he became aware of the black MD Explorer hovering in the field behind him, to his left. He slowed a little, taking in the scene, assessing the situation. His first thought, as he read the yellow police lettering on the side of the helicopter, was that he had stumbled on an incident of some kind. But seconds later, as his two minders drew level, the helicopter was no longer hovering, but tracking him across the field.

Marchant looked out across the stretch of farmland in front of him. It was at least two hundred yards to the woods on the far side, but he thought he could make it to the safety of the trees if he ran hard. He glanced above him and saw the face of the pilot in his helmet and visor, looking down at him with wasp-eyed indifference. At the same moment, he felt a minder on his shoulder and shrugged him off. The man fell away, swearing as he stumbled, but before Marchant could accelerate, the other minder was on his back, dragging him down.

They seemed to slow as they fell, Marchant rolling the man over so that they hit the ground with him on top. All around them, the flattened grass danced in the helicopter's downdraft. He grabbed the man by his hair and pushed his face hard into a flintstone lying in the earth. For a moment there was stillness. Marchant stood up and started to run, aware of the first man coming up behind him, the helicopter above. The woods suddenly seemed a mile away.

Twenty yards from the trees, Marchant began to believe that he could make it. Once he was inside the Brail, the helicopter would be useless, providing he kept to the cover of the trees. But he still had the man on his right. Five yards short of the trees, he saw a branch on the ground, heavy with the rain of winter. He veered off his path and picked it up, arcing the sodden log behind him in the same movement. As it collided with the side of the man's face, knocking him backwards, the blades above him seemed to grow louder, roaring their disapproval. Marchant sprinted into the dark woods, sidestepping through the trees like a street thief eluding his pursuers.

He had run barely thirty yards when the woods opened up into a small clearing. The helicopter swooped low overhead, touching down on the patch of grass in front of him long enough for two more men to jump out. Tired now, Marchant turned and headed back into the woods, but he was soon being dragged towards the helicopter, the smell of aviation fuel filling the air.

Marchant calculated that he had been in the air for fifteen minutes before the helicopter touched down, which made Fairford the most likely airfield. It was run by the Americans, who had spent $90 million extending the main runway for its B-2 Spirit Stealth bombers and the Space Shuttle. He suspected he would be travelling in something smaller. He couldn't confirm which airfield it was for himself because of the hood over his head, and he couldn't hear any cockpit talk because a pair of headphones had been slipped over the hood. His hands had been tied tightly behind his back, and his feet were bound together too. But he wasn't in any real discomfort, not yet.

Mentally, he was as together as anyone could be who knew he was in the process of being extraordinarily renditioned by the CIA. It was the only logical reading of the situation he found himself in, given that it was unlikely MI5 or even MI6 would use such extreme methods on one of their own. During his short flight he had concluded that Fielding, for reasons as yet unclear, must have agreed to hand over the keys of the Wiltshire safe house to MI5, who had duly allowed the Americans to remove him for their own questioning. What made his stomach tighten now, as he lay on the cold metal floor of the stationary helicopter, was the thought of the physical and mental pain that lay ahead.

12

The undisputed waterboarding world champion was Khalid Sheikh Mohammed. Marchant knew this thanks to a flippant email that had leaked its way from Langley to Legoland. The architect of 9/11, the Bali nightclub bombings and a thwarted attack on Canary Wharf, 'KSM' (as the CIA called him) deserved some silverware for his efforts, but instead Al Qaeda's number three had to make do with grudging respect from his interrogators. Two minutes thirty seconds – there were no officials, but that was the time clocked when he was waterboarded in early March 2003. At two minutes thirty-one seconds he broke, finally believing that he was about to drown. He screamed like a baby and filled his diaper. As the email concluded: the smell of victory is the whiff of excrement.

Marchant knew everything there was to know about waterboarding, a method of interrogation that had been favoured by the Gestapo and, thanks to the CIA, had been enjoying a revival in recent years, until the new President put a stop to it. The sensation of water being poured onto his mouth and nose convinced the victim that he was about to drown, triggering an immediate, involuntary gagging response. Because the feet were raised higher than the head, however, water did not flood the lungs, thereby avoiding death and allowing governments to categorise it as an enhanced interrogation technique rather than torture.

Marchant knew all about the three different levels, the same unrelenting message that each sends to the brain, the convenient absence of physical marks, the acute mental trauma that can be triggered for years afterwards: by taking a shower, washing up, watering the windowbox.

What his interrogators didn't know was that Marchant had broken KSM's record during his survival training course at the Fort. It wasn't official, because Marchant had been aware, at least before the water started flowing, that it was an exercise. KSM had thought he was about to die. But two minutes fifty seconds was still a record of sorts, good enough to make him the toast of the Fort. As Marchant was told afterwards, no CIA agent who had tested the technique on himself had lasted more than fourteen seconds.

Marchant liked to joke that his ability to endure waterboarding was honed at birth – he was born underwater. His mother had told him that he came out with his eyes open, looking around like a startled carp. Others, like Leila, said it was his Indian childhood: a case of Yogic mind over matter. As he lay in the dark now, his tightly bound feet raised above his hooded head on a cold metal table, he tried to recall the banter in the Portsmouth pub afterwards: his voice sounding funny because of the water still blocking his nose; Leila's tenderness beneath the bravura; her wet-mouthed kiss that he thought would asphyxiate him.

He suspected he was in Poland, or maybe Romania. The CIA had been ordered to shut down its network of black sites, but Langley was in no rush. It knew the bureaucrats would struggle to verify the closure of facilities that had never officially existed. After the helicopter had touched down, he had been escorted, still blindfolded, across the tarmac to another plane, a Gulfstream V, he guessed. Dubbed the Guantanamo Bay Express by enemy combatants, his flight had lasted two hours, although for Marchant, travelling in detainee class (complimentary boilersuit and adult nappies), it had felt like a lifetime.

He heard the two men enter his cell, closing the door behind them. Waterboarding was just a trick of the mind, he told himself, involuntarily flexing his fingers. They said nothing as they checked his wrists, bound tightly in shackles by his side, and pulled the cotton hood further down over his head. In a moment they would pour water continually over his porous hood.

When the water came, sooner than he expected, Marchant instinctively tried to turn his head away, but the man on his left held his jaw firmly while the other poured water onto his face, and then over his chest and legs, soaking his boilersuit. He could feel the panic rising.

There was his twin brother, lying at the bottom of the pool in Delhi, staring up at him through the clear water. He screamed for the *ayah*, jumped in and tried to grab his brother's arm. Sebastian, barely six years old, stared back at him, his hair floating like a rockpool anemone, unaware that he was about to drown.

The flow of water was constant, Marchant told himself, struggling to control his breathing. That suggested that they were using a hose rather than a watering can, the preferred method at the Fort. He screamed again, at his interrogators, at his mother, who had come running out from the house, but his cries were muffled by the damp cotton hood pressing down against his face. He could feel the water starting to seep through, running up his nose and into his mouth. It was warm, just as the training manual stipulated. This was an exercise, he told himself: they weren't going to kill him. The new President wouldn't allow it.

'Where's Salim Dhar?' one of the Americans shouted, twisting Marchant's jaw violently towards him. Marchant was shocked by how young the voice – Midwest – sounded. 'Tell us where he is and your brother will live.'

Marchant said nothing, waiting for Sebastian to start breathing, watching his mother bent over the tiny body. 'Is he OK?' he begged her. 'Is Sebbie going to be OK?'

His interrogator held the hose closer to his mouth. 'Where's Salim Dhar?' he repeated.

Why were they asking him? He wasn't his father. The water started to pour in through the cotton hood. Marchant kept his lips pressed tightly together, breathing

102

in slowly through his nose, but that was what he was meant to do: the water flooded up both nostrils. His lungs were bursting, desperate now for air. He tried twisting his head away, then he saw Sebastian spluttering back to life, vomiting the pool water, his tiny chest convulsing, coughing into his mother's perfumed embrace.

Marchant remembered what his trainer had told him: 'Your interrogator's greatest fear is that you might die on the board before you sing. Hold on to that. It's the only power you have over him.' He clutched this thought close to him as he lay still, feeling the water rise up through his nose and down into the back of his throat. The gag reflex kicked in as the water tumbled over his epiglottis. He knew it would sound as if he was choking. His interrogators pulled off his hood just as he vomited, turning away to conceal their faces. They cursed him: round one was his.

Waterboarding at level two required one airway to be sealed off. The taller of the Americans handed him a pair of tight swimming goggles and ordered him to put them on, all the time shielding his face. They must be embarrassed to be doing this to one of their own, Marchant thought. What about the real enemies? The West had enough of those without having to do this to each other.

The goggle lenses had been painted black, and he found the darkness a relief. The building they were in, wherever it was, was inhospitable, anonymous. He had glimpsed four dirty white plaster walls, a low ceiling, with some sort of crude plumbing running down one corner. Above the door was a small, reinforced aperture.

103

The room's ordinariness made Marchant feel alone, vulnerable, accentuating his sense that he could be anywhere in the world. His two interrogators were wearing regulation army fatigues, but the brightness of his own orange jumpsuit had surprised him.

He closed his eyes behind the goggles, but before he could seek solace in the blackness a piece of cloth was pushed into his mouth as far in as it could go. Marchant gagged as the cloth touched his epiglottis. The American, satisfied that the material was in place, pushed it in still further, working the cloth in a circular motion against the back of Marchant's throat, swearing at him all the time in his young voice. Marchant gagged again, and for the first time he thought he was going to die.

Instead, he forced himself to remember how his instructor had told them that there were only two types of people who could control the gag reflex: sword swallowers and deep-throat hookers. As Marchant gagged again, his stomach contorting, lifting the small of his back off the metal table, the hose was on him, more pressure this time, the water colder. Marchant could feel the cloth swell with water, pushing against the sides, the roof, the back of his mouth. He instinctively tried to breathe through his nose, only for his nostrils to fill up with water again. Panic gathered in the wings of his consciousness. He thought of his father polishing the Lagonda in the bright morning sunshine. As a child, he used to stand there watching him, one leg crossed in front of the other, a grubby hand leaning against the glistening passenger door.

'Get your filthy little hands off my car!' a voice shouted. 'Where's Salim Dhar?'

Marchant could feel round two slipping away from him. His nausea was now mixed with an intense claustrophobia, a sense that he would never be able to escape the cloth expanding down his throat, the water, the permanent imminence of drowning. He focused on his interrogator's questions, the reasoning behind them. There hadn't been a mistake. They were asking him about Dhar because somebody must have linked him to the marathon attack. 'Tell us about your fucking running buddy,' the shorter one was shouting, in between shoving the cloth deeper still into his mouth. 'How long did he know Dhar?'

The secret of surviving waterboarding, Marchant told himself again, trying to work through the consequences of Dhar's apparent role in the marathon attack, was not to fall for it. Because that's all waterboarding was: a trick of the mind. The body wasn't about to drown, the brain just thought it was. At the Fort, he was the only one who had remained cognisant of the training element. Now, as his entire upper body twisted with each new retch, he reminded himself that he was being interrogated in an equally safe context: the CIA wouldn't kill an MI6 officer, even if he was the suspended son of a suspected traitor. The struggle happening now was taking place in his head, not in the room: his amygdalae, the oldest, most primal parts of the human brain, were in a desperate dialogue with his more reasoning solar cortex. That's what the psychiatrist at the Fort had said, wasn't it?

Marchant's resilience was taking the two Americans to the limits of their trained self-control, and they were now swearing repeatedly at him. One of them finally flipped, ripped Marchant's goggles off and grabbed him by the back of his neck, lifting his head off the table. For a moment they looked into each other's eyes. Marchant saw more fear than he felt in the young CIA agent's face. He pulled the gag out of Marchant's mouth. Round two was also his.

'He's unreal, Joey. The guy's unreal,' the American said, tossing Marchant away, unable to cope with the eye contact. Marchant savoured the pain as the back of his head hit the table. He hung on to its sharpness, juggled with it in his hands as if it were a hot coal: it was real, physical; it would leave a mark, provide evidence that this had happened, and wasn't just taking place in his head. He turned to one side, spat out some phlegm and then managed a desperate cough of a laugh.

'Any chance of a drink of water?' he asked. 'My throat's a little dry.'

Marchant knew it was essential to maintain the pretence, however false, of being in mental control, without pushing his interrogators so far that they killed him out of frustration. He also needed to keep them interested: a balaclava-clad face had just appeared behind the bars of the small opening above the door, disappearing as soon as Marchant had seen it. He managed a smile for his interrogators, knowing the consequences, and hung out his tongue like a panting dog.

'You got something to say, save it for St Peter,' Joey

said, taking over from his colleague. He turned away, as if he had finished for the day, but Marchant knew he wasn't done yet. Joey swung his arm in a long loop, smacking the back of his hand across Marchant's face.

At the Fort, they had used clingfilm for level three, wrapped tightly around the face, making it impossible to breathe through the nose or mouth. A hole was cut for the lips, only it wasn't for breathing, but as a way to fill the victim with water. This approach, like waterboarding itself, was nothing new. They liked to cut straight to level three in the seventeenth century, swelling the bodies of victims to three times their normal size – without the clingfilm, of course.

But Marchant never reached level three.

13

Nine hundred miles west of Poland, Marcus Fielding took a deep breath and plunged into the seventy-four-degree water, his dive long and shallow. The pool in the basement of Legoland had been a source of contention in Whitehall when the headquarters was built, adding to the overspend by several million, like the adjacent gym, but it was worth every penny, Fielding thought, as he surfaced halfway down the pool, jetting water from his mouth. He never swam with his glasses, leaving them on his neatly folded towel, next to his phone. Blurred vision, focused mind, he found, and he did his best thinking in the pool.

The MI5 document which had crossed his desk at lunchtime made it clear that, much as he had suspected, Dhar's role in the attempted marathon bombing was far from certain. There was a South Indian element on the ground, as there had been in the previous year's attacks, but there was no direct evidence to link the planning of the bombing to Dhar, and there were any number of other suspects in the frame.

Reports coming in from Arabic specialists at GCHQ's sub-station in Scarborough were throwing up possible links to the wider Gulf region. In short, there was still not enough to nail the attack on Dhar, despite the South Indian connection and Dhar's anti-American crusade. Harriet Armstrong had been flying a kite, hoping to please the Americans. Fielding had no intention of sharing this information with anyone, not yet. It made him feel better about Daniel Marchant, but guilty that he had handed him over so casually to Spiro.

Staff knew not to disturb their Chief during his swim, taken without exception at 3 p.m. every afternoon, when the pool was clear of the workers who used it during their lunch break. (Fielding didn't realise it was actually empty because nobody wanted to be in the pool while the Chief was steaming up and down the fast lane.) Now, though, his phone was ringing with an internal tone. He headed for the steps and took the call, trusting that it was important. It was from Fielding's deputy, Ian Denton, a former head of the East European Controllerate and one of his closest allies. He wanted an urgent meeting. Dripping with water, Fielding told him to come up to his office and wait. He knew Denton tried to deal with as much of the Chief's day-to-day business as he could, never bothering him unless there was a serious problem.

'We've picked up an undeclared flight into Szymany, north-eastern Poland,' Denton said ten minutes later, as

Fielding looked out of his window at a solitary sand-piper bobbing in the Thames mud. Denton had spent much of his early career behind the Iron Curtain, where the fear of being overheard had become an obsession for Western case officers. As a result, his voice was so quiet that it was a struggle for anyone to hear him. But Fielding's ear was fine-tuned, and he prided himself on never once having asked Denton to speak up.

'Cheltenham's analysed the data strings,' Denton continued in a whisper. 'ADEP was Fairford, and multiple onward dummy flight plans were filed. It was operating under special status.'

'There's a surprise,' Fielding said, his back still to Denton, who was wrong-footed by the Chief's apparent lack of concern. Denton – northern grammar school, Oxford, keen on carp fishing – began to regret his request for a meeting. All undeclared CIA flights anywhere in Europe had become a priority for MI6, following a personal request from the Prime Minister, who wasn't as relaxed about them as his predecessor.

'What's strange is that it wasn't picked up here,' Denton continued. 'Usually MI5 . . .'

'I know.' Fielding turned and fixed Denton with a wry smile. 'Leave it with me, Ian. Thanks.'

Denton was so thorough, Fielding thought, as he left the office. He liked that in an officer. His big break had come in the 1980s in Bucharest where, as a junior officer working under diplomatic cover, he had spent every weekend fishing for carp and bream at a lake on the edge of the capital. Nobody knew why until, nine months later, he hooked the head of Romania's secret police, a fellow carper.

Fielding smiled. Maybe that was why Denton whispered: he didn't want to scare the fish. Below him a yellow London Duck emerged out of the Thames, water pouring off it, and drove up the slipway that ran alongside Legoland's outer perimeter wall. It was the only place the Second World War amphibious vehicle could get in and out of the water. Fielding had always wondered what the captain told the tourists as they passed by Legoland. One day he would take a ride and find out. Denton could come along too, with his rod.

Harriet Armstrong took Fielding's call in her official Range Rover, on her way to spend the weekend at Chequers. Fielding had heard about the invitation, one which had yet to be extended to him.

'Hope I haven't disturbed you,' Fielding began, failing to sound sincere.

'If you're calling about Marchant, I can't help you,' she said brusquely. 'We passed him on to Spiro.'

'I know. And I thought you should know, given you're seeing him this weekend, that we'll be filing a report to the PM on an undeclared CIA flight which left Fairford for Poland this morning. I seem to remember he was quite keen to know about such flights.'

'So keen, he signed this one off himself,' Armstrong said. 'I'll tell him you called.'

Fielding briefly considered phoning Sir David Chadwick, to remind him of their agreement at the Travellers that Marchant wasn't to leave the country, but other measures were now needed. Armstrong's increasingly close relationships with Spiro and the PM were beginning to irritate him. She might have removed Stephen Marchant from his post, but he had no intention of giving her the same satisfaction as far as he himself was concerned.

He called through to his secretary. 'Get me Brigadier Borowski of the AW in Warsaw on the line.'

14

Leila turned the key in the front door and slipped into Marchant's basement flat in Pimlico, across the river from Legoland. She was shocked by its untidiness, the unmade bed, clothes strewn across the floor, bottles spilling out of the wastepaper basket under his desk. Had the place been searched? She used to be a regular visitor here, and it had always been kept immaculate, almost too tidy. When he was suspended they had stopped staying over at each other's places, except for the night before the marathon, when she had insisted he stayed. Marchant was determined to limit the fallout from his father's departure to himself and no one else. They had stolen the occasional night away in the country, but Marchant had found it hard to relax. Until he had cleared his father's name, he couldn't be himself.

That self she had fallen for in those early days smiled up at her now from the photo of their final day at the

Fort, propped up on his desk in the corner of the room. A group of them were in the SOE memorial room, posing in front of the wall where previous members of the Service had been honoured. Marchant's arm was slung casually around her shoulders, like a college friend, giving no clue that they had slept together for the first time the night before. Already they were learning to deceive in love, mixing up their jobs with their private lives, just as Marchant had feared.

Next to the group photo was a picture of his father up a ladder in the orchard at Tarlton, in happier, idyllic Cotswold days. An eight-year-old Marchant in shorts was lying in a hammock strung between two apple trees, grinning confidently up at the camera. His twin brother, Sebastian, was lying next to him. They weren't identical, but they shared the same smile. Sebastian's face was turned towards his mother, who was standing at the bottom of the ladder, a basket of fruit in her arms. She was strikingly beautiful, confident, at ease with motherhood.

Marchant had only talked about the crash once, after they had both nearly drowned during survival training at the Fort. Sebbie, as Marchant sometimes called him, must have died a few weeks after the photo had been taken, in a traffic accident when they had returned to Delhi at the end of the English summer. Marchant had been in the jeep too when it collided head-on with a government bus, but he and his mother had survived unscathed.

Marchant's family had stayed on in Delhi until the

end of his father's tour, which surprised colleagues. Later, he told Marchant that he hadn't wanted to return home immediately because his family would have spent the rest of their lives hating India, and he couldn't countenance that.

Marchant's seemingly easy manner, Leila knew, dated back to those Delhi days. Everyone who met him now thought he was relaxed, charming, sociable (his *ayah* had described him as 'easy go happy'), but it was his way of protecting a place he wasn't prepared to go with anyone: a place where he was still an eight-year-old child, staring at his brother beside the wreckage of the car, watching the bus driver flee from the scene; a place she knew he had revisited when his father had died. His father's death had meant that Marchant was the only one left of his family. She sometimes felt like that too, her mother as good as dead to her, her father no longer alive. He had never been a happy presence in her childhood, either away on work or distant when he was at home, drinking too much at night and showing her mother too little respect.

Leila went over to Marchant's unmade bed and lay on it, turning her head to one side and inhaling his faint aroma on the pillow. He would try to make contact, let her know he was all right. The confinement of a safe house would drive him crazy, but he was better off there than in the outside world. He was now a marked man, wanted not just by MI5 but by whoever had sent Pradeep.

Sometimes, when they lay side by side after making love, in those brief moments before they headed back to the airport and their separate lives, they had talked about where in the world they would most like to be. Marchant always spoke first, about dreams of the Thar Desert, the African savannah – rangy, open spaces, wide skies – or sometimes the shady apple orchards of Tarlton in a Cotswold summer. When it was her turn, she would fall quiet, the memory of her one, all too brief visit to Iran silencing her with its beauty, before she began to speak of the bare mountains that circled Ghamsar's fertile plains, the scent of rose water, the village workers with cloth bags full of fragrant petals hanging from their necks.

Her mother had painted other pictures of Iran when she was younger, keen to keep the country alive for her daughter. She told her bedtime stories of Isfahan, homilies from the poems of Hafez, and, when she was older, tales of drinking Turkish tea in Tehran's cafés with elderly academics in berets and black suits. But it was always to Ghamsar's rose gardens that Leila's thoughts returned, an aching glimpse of what might have been.

Leila must have been asleep for at least an hour when her phone woke her. For a moment she expected it to be her mother, but it was Paul Myers, on an encrypted call from his mobile.

'The Americans have got Daniel,' he said.

'What?' Leila sat up on Marchant's bed, barely awake, confused by her surroundings and now by the sound of Myers's voice.

'I can't say any more,' he said, choosing his words carefully. Even on an encrypted call, he knew key words might alert someone. 'Seems he left on a flight to Poland.'

116

'When?' Fielding must have given in to the Americans, been persuaded of a link between the Marchant family and Dhar.

'Hard to say. Last couple of days?' Myers paused. 'It's not exactly a sight-seeing trip.'

'No.'

'He'll cope, right?' Myers said, surprising Leila with his sudden, urgent concern. 'He's tough as they come, doesn't everyone say that?'

Leila thought back to that night at the Fort when he sat beside her in the pub, still shaking, barely able to talk after his waterboarding training.

'I'll call you.' She paused. 'Paul?'

'Yes?'

'Thanks.'

Leila hung up and looked around the messed-up room. Her eyes rested on the picture of her and Marchant at the Fort. She walked over to the desk, knowing that she might never see him again. If Fielding had let him go, the Americans could hold him for years. She felt her eyes moisten. Leaning forward, she placed the photograph face down on the desk and slipped quietly out of the flat.

15

For a moment, Marchant wasn't sure if the explosion was part of the interrogation. His face had just been wrapped in clingfilm, so tightly that it had flattened his nose to one side, when he felt a loud blast to the left of him, followed by shouting in Polish. He couldn't see anything, because he was wearing the blackened goggles again, but he could hear the Americans choking. Moments later he was being unstrapped from the table, his shackles removed with bolt cutters, and the goggles and clingfilm removed.

He counted six men in the room, wearing gasmasks and army uniforms, all of them with semi-automatic weapons. One of them strapped a mask onto Marchant just as he was starting to taste the rancid tang of teargas, while another checked the two Americans for vital signs. Then he was bundled out of the room and into the back of a waiting black van.

'Hugo Prentice,' said a weatherbeaten man sitting opposite him. 'Warsaw station. Worked with your father in Delhi. Fielding sends his love, apologises for the slap and tickle.'

Fielding glanced at his watch, added an hour for Poland, and wondered how long it would be before Spiro was on the phone. Give him half an hour, he thought, looking at the files spread across his desk. HR had printed out the most recent employment profiles of Leila, Daniel and Stephen Marchant, and he had also requested the South Asia Controllerate's dossier on Salim Dhar. He glanced down the opening page, marked 'Confidential, For UK Eyes Only', and thought, not for the first time, that he was missing something, a piece of information that linked Dhar with his predecessor as head of MI6. What was it that had made Stephen Marchant fly five thousand miles to visit him in Southern India?

Dhar, according to the file, had been born Jaishankar Menon, to a middle-class Hindu couple in Delhi on 12 November 1980. His father worked at the British High Commission as an administrative officer. Shortly before Dhar was born his contract was terminated, but he soon picked up a similar job at the US Embassy. Dhar later attended the American School in Delhi – someone had handwritten 'employment perk?' in the file, below another mark that said 'bullied?' – but left at sixteen.

The next time Dhar showed up, two years later, he was in Kashmir, where the police arrested him for trying to blow up an army base. His charge sheet listed him as

'Salim Dhar'. Somewhere between Delhi and Srinigar, he had converted to Islam and become radicalised, focusing his hatred of the West on America.

At this point, RAW, India's Research and Analysis Wing, had stepped in and tried briefly to recruit him, sensing an opportunity to play him back into the Kashmiri separatist movement. But Dhar was having none of it. In another report, sent over from RAW as part of Bancroft's investigation into Stephen Marchant, it was concluded that Salim Dhar was 'utterly unpersuadable' and 'totally unsuitable' for recruitment. His commitment to the establishment of an Islamic caliphate, starting with the reunification of Kashmir and culminating in the destruction of America, was absolute. A year later, he escaped from jail and went to ground in Pakistan, later resurfacing in Afghanistan.

There was only one thing that caught Fielding's eye: in the psychological profile of Dhar, attention had been drawn to the poor relationship he had with his father, who unlike his son loved all things American, and hoped one day to emigrate to New York. It was cited as a possible reason Dhar had left school, and Delhi. If Stephen Marchant had tried to recruit Dhar, for whatever reason, had he held some information on Dhar's father? It was the one possible point of leverage Fielding could find in the file. Salim Dhar appeared to have led a clean life, his only points of conflict inspired by ideology rather than anything more basic. No women, drinking, stealing, corruption – nothing to blackmail him with.

In Fielding's mind, Stephen Marchant's tenure in Delhi

had been in the late 1970s, while Jimmy Carter had been in the White House. It was there, in the aftermath of 'Smiling Buddha', India's first nuclear test, that Marchant had made a name for himself. Few people in the Service hadn't heard of him. Partly that was because of his audacious recruitment of a senior player at the Russian Embassy in Delhi, who rose to great heights within the KGB when he returned to Dzerzhinsky Square, but also because of the family tragedy that had engulfed him.

Fielding reopened Marchant's file and looked through his postings. As he suspected, Marchant had arrived in India in August 1977, as a case officer, moving back to Britain in July 1980 for the birth of his twins (his wife had endured a difficult pregnancy and spent much of it in London, avoiding Delhi's oppressive heat). But Marchant had returned to India five years later, this time as station head and with his young family in tow. Then, in 1988, disaster had struck when Sebastian was killed in a car accident.

Fielding recalled it all more clearly now. Everyone in the Service had felt wretched about Marchant's loss, the subsequent deterioration in his wife's mental health, and his stoic refusal to leave Delhi until his tour of duty was over.

Fielding turned to Dhar's early life again, checking the dates of his father's employment at the British High Commission in Delhi. He had started in January 1980, which meant that Marchant and Dhar's father had overlapped for six months. Delhi was a big mission, second only to the British Embassy in Washington, but there was a chance the two might have come into contact with each other. It wasn't much to go on, but Fielding knew it was something. He picked up the phone and asked for Ian Denton.

16

After a bone-breaking, hundred-mile drive through the Polish countryside, Marchant found himself in the bar of the brand new British Embassy in Warsaw with a glass of Tyskie beer in his hand. He had been unable to speak for most of the journey, retching from the water still in his system and the potholed roads, drifting in and out of sleep. But he did register Prentice explaining that his interrogation had taken place at Stare Kiejkuty, a former outpost of the SS's intelligence wing during the Second World War.

Fifteen minutes from Szymany airport, the site had subsequently been used by the Soviet Army, when Brezhnev was planning to crush the Prague Spring. More recently it had been occupied by a secret division of the Wojskowe Służby Informacyjne, Poland's military intelligence service, who were more than happy to oblige the CIA's request for a secure facility in which to interrogate their High Value Detainees – in return for cash, of course. It was a canny, if ironic, choice by the Americans, Prentice had explained. The WSI wasn't subject to the same levels of public scrutiny as civilian agencies such as the new Agencja Wywiadu, and its officials, many of whom were survivors from the old communist era, could claim protection under NATO because of their military status.

'You're in good company – Stare Kiejkuty boasts some fine alumni,' Prentice had added. 'It's where they dunked KSM in 2003.'

The dank cell where Marchant had been waterboarded couldn't have been more different from the airy, glass and steel edifice he now found himself in. He knew that the sleek new building was a blueprint for British embassies of the future. Delayed and redesigned after the bombing of the consulate in Istanbul, it remained accessible to the public but was now built to withstand a major terrorist attack. It also incorporated a security feature required of all new Foreign Office buildings. In the event of a physical assault, an 'onion' layering of doors and walls protecting an inner sanctum that should take at least forty minutes to penetrate would allow sensitive documents to be shredded and hard drives wiped.

The bar was empty except for Marchant and Prentice and a couple of local embassy staff. They weren't sure what to make of the guest who talked strangely through his nose, and had left a pair of king-size, water-soaked nappies in the wastepaper basket of his guest room.

'Come, we need to have a proper chat,' Prentice said, stubbing out his Marlboro cigarette. Marchant followed him through the main atrium entrance of the embassy and down a series of pristine white corridors. 'This place has just been swept, but we should still use the safe-talk room,' Prentice said. All embassies had one, an interview room lined with lead beneath the plaster, which not even the most powerful bugs could penetrate. Marchant had spent a good deal of time in them over the past few years, and some were more basic than others. This one, with its crisp white walls and sunken lights, felt like a cross between a Swiss bank vault and a Harley Street consulting room.

'We're all still cut up about your old man,' Prentice said, gesturing at one of two chairs on either side of a rectangular glass table. There was a bunch of flowers in a vase on the table, a clear sign that waterboarding was off the agenda. Prentice closed the heavy door behind him and punched a code into the keypad by the handle, activating a further layer of electronic protection. 'The word in Warsaw was that the Americans were behind it. Armstrong wouldn't have got her way without their support.'

'Sounds about right,' Marchant said, still aware of his nasal tones. Despite the flowers, the two chairs and the table were strictly functional.

'So imagine our delight when the call came through from London,' Prentice said.

'And the Poles were equally overjoyed?'

'The new government's through with renditions, been waiting for an excuse ever since they pulled their troops out of Iraq. Stare Kiejkuty's run by the WSI, hardline communists who knew their time was up and were grateful for the dollars. What can the CIA do? Protest to the UN that one of their black sites has been blown? It was meant to have been closed down months ago.'

Marchant estimated that Prentice was in his late fifties. Chief of Station, Poland, at his time of his life was not immediate evidence of a brilliant career, but Marchant had heard of Hugo Prentice. Everyone who joined the Service had heard of him. Expelled from Eton for selling marijuana to fellow pupils in the 1970s, he had a rakish air, a full head of greying hair swept back and an expensive taste in platinum cufflinks and Patek Philippe watches.

He had never been a career officer, bent on promotion, but one of those rare people who had signed up to the Service because he loved the spy's life, wanted to be out there turning people on the ground, persuading the waverers of a greater good with a traditional mix of ideology, subterfuge and, even if not always necessary, brutality. For Prentice it was all about the expenses rather than the salary, the mistresses rather than the marriage.

'How's life in Legoland, anyway?' he continued, offering a cigarette to Marchant, who took one. 'Is it true the Vicar's banned fags in the bar?'

'Only inside. On the terrace is fine. It wasn't Fielding, though. It was the government.'

'We're all screwed if the spooks start listening to the politicians. Christ, who's going to check? Health and Safety? Your father would sooner have died than listen to the government.' The conversation stalled awkwardly.

'I'm sorry. Crass.' Prentice sat back and blew smoke into the air above them.

'It's fine,' Marchant said. 'Really.'

'You look a bit like him, you know – same jawline,' Prentice continued. 'I'll be happy if a quarter as many people turn up for my funeral. But what happened to the PM? Why wasn't he there?'

'Too busy, officially,' Marchant said, thinking back to the people spilling out of the small village church. He didn't recall seeing Prentice there, but staff had flown in from all over the world. There was, however, a noticeable absence of Establishment figures, a reluctance to honour a possible traitor.

'The bastard.'

'Are you sending me back to Britain?' Marchant appreciated Prentice's solidarity, but wanted to know where the conversation was heading.

'Not exactly, no,' Prentice said, his voice quieter, as if he had suddenly recalled a piece of bad news. Marchant picked up on the change of tone and shifted in his seat. The metal table had chafed his lower back. 'London sent you this,' Prentice said, pulling out a brown A5 envelope from his jacket pocket and handing it to Marchant. Marchant glanced inside: dollars, an Irish passport, airline ticket, some visa paperwork. 'We can't help you any more. You're too hot.'

'Meaning?'

'You tell me. You're the first serving MI6 officer I've ever come across who's wanted by the CIA and MI5. Watch your back. Give it a couple of hours and Warsaw will be crawling with Yanks looking for you. The WSI might like a little chat, too.'

'Any message from Fielding?' Marchant asked.

Prentice leant forward. 'Go get Salim Dhar.'

'Where is he?' Harriet Armstrong asked. Fielding sat back in his chair and looked down the river in the direction of her office at Thames House.

'Your guess is as good as mine,' he replied, talking on the speakerphone.

'I've just had Spiro on the line,' Armstrong said, 'threatening to go public about Dhar and your predecessor.'

'That could be embarrassing, but not as awkward as a member of the British intelligence services being renditioned by the CIA to Poland. Particularly if the PM nodded it through. I'd hate that to get out.'

'Where is he, Marcus? He's a threat to national security.'

'I'd question that,' he said. 'You saw my memo about Dhar? Seems like he had nothing to do with the marathon attack after all. But in answer to your question, I have no idea where he is. You had him last, no?'

Armstrong had already hung up. Fielding swivelled around in his chair, killed the speaker and read through the memo in front of him. The Polish economy would take a hit when the Americans started to pull business contracts. The confidential commercial information he was about to release to Brigadier Borowski, head of the AW, his opposite number in Warsaw, was the least he could do for a friend. The AW was involved in a fierce turf war with the old communist guard at the WSI. Borowski and others seemed to be winning, despite the best efforts of the CIA, whose dollars and High Value Detainees had done much to prolong the careers of its former Cold War enemies in Poland.

The information should give one of Poland's biggest IT companies the edge when it made its bid next month for a multi-million-euro e-government contract in Brussels. MI6's intelligence reports were still known as 'CX', after its first Chief, Mansfield Cumming ('Cumming Exclusively'). Fielding reached for the pen and signed in green ink, another Cumming touch. Borowski would like that.

17

Marchant knew that the best legend for a spy was the one that most closely mirrored his or her own life. After endless hours of interrogation, standing and sleep deprivation, even the mind of the toughest officer became confused and reverted to its default setting. The less that differed from the cover story, the better. Former girlfriends' names, sexual preferences, gap-year itineraries, favourite music, even the number of sugars in a mug of tea: all should be the same as the spy's own. As Marchant lay on his hostel bed in Warsaw and read through his new legend, he smiled to himself: he was heading back to India.

Prentice had dropped Marchant off around the corner from the Oki Doki hostel on Plac Dabrowskiego, in the centre of the capital. It was a popular haunt for backpackers, and a crowd of them – English, French, Italians – were in the bar when Marchant had checked in at the reception as David Marlowe, the name on his Irish passport. The hostel had a chic, hippy atmosphere, reminding Marchant of a place he'd once stayed in Haight-Ashbury. Each room or dormitory was designed by a different local artist. Prentice had booked Marchant into Dom Browskiego, the only single room, painted in the colours of spring. For a moment he wished Leila was here with him, but he pushed the thought away as fast as it had arrived, and swung his rucksack onto the foot of his bed. David Marlowe didn't know anyone called Leila.

He looked around the room and saw a basin in the corner. As he washed his face and glanced at himself in the mirror, drips of water falling off his unshaven chin, he was back at Stare Kiejkuty. He forced himself to think of something else. Clearly, he was the subject of a struggle between MI6 and MI5, who had handed him over to the CIA at the safe house. The arrival of Prentice at the black site meant that Fielding had not washed his hands of him altogether, which was encouraging. But Prentice had made it clear to him that MI6's help was limited. The passport, the money (a thousand US dollars), the ticket to Delhi, his legend: that was all Fielding could do. The rest was up to him.

He lay down on the bed, feet propped up on the rucksack, and looked again at his new life: David Marlowe (same initials as his own) was taking a year out to travel around the world, starting with Europe, after graduating with a degree in modern history from Trinity College, Cambridge, just as he himself had done. MI6, Marchant knew, had arrangements with various Oxbridge colleges and redbrick universities for phone enquiries and mail. If anyone rang Trinity to ask whether a David Marlowe had studied there, the porters would find the name on a list; if anyone wrote, the post would be forwarded to Legoland via its PO box address.

He had only briefly visited Poland on his own year out, and he needed to decide on where Marlowe had gone (the legend didn't go into detail): a week's stay in Krakow enjoying the jazz bars, followed by a few days in Warsaw. He had planned to travel further (the *Rough Guide to Poland* was noticeably well thumbed), but chose to head for India, fed up with the cold weather – the talk at the hostel bar had been of little else.

He sat up and looked at the rucksack, increasingly aware of the smell rising from it. Prentice had given it to him an hour earlier at the embassy. It was bulging and well-worn, with a bright orange sleeping bag sticking out from under the top.

'The thing's been knocking around here for months, you might as well take it,' Prentice had said casually.

'Whose is it?' Marchant asked, looking at the various badges that had been sewn on it: Paris, Prague, Munich.

'Student, on his gap year, travelling around Europe. Died six months ago.'

'Really?'

'Drug overdose. We flew his body back but the rucksack never made it. Held back as evidence. The police here thought he was a mule, part of a ring. Their dogs sniffed it, found nothing. You'd better check.'

'How old was he?'

'Bit younger than you, same height, not as handsome, but then I only saw him on the slab.'

'Any family?'

'Middle-class parents, Hampshire. They'd apparently disowned him. Never asked for any personal possessions to be returned.'

Marchant started to unpack the rucksack with the caution of a customs officer. As he suspected, the clothes were rancid, revealing little about the owner except that his year of travel hadn't taken in a visit to a launderette. He would ditch most of the fleeces and sweaters – he would only need thin clothes in India – but he would run the collarless shirts and cotton trousers through the hostel washing machine. The *Rough Guide to Poland* had to go, too. But the surfing bracelets would be useful once he was in India, although they weren't half as stylish, he thought, as the ones he had once worn himself.

He looked again at his passport, hardly recognising himself in the photo: shaved head, a saffron, tie-dyed T-shirt, stud in the left ear, shell necklace slung loosely around his neck. The cobblers in G/REP, the Legoland department that specialised in forged documents, had excelled themselves. His features had been aged a little, compared to the original photo, which had been taken during his gap year in India. In real life, he knew his features had aged even more, but he was confident that he could still pass himself off as a student. Deception was as much about gait, attitude and rhythms of speech as facial appearance.

His own gap year had been a carefree time of his life.

He had felt only relief when his mother had finally slipped away in his last year of school, her death allowing him to travel more freely than he might otherwise have done. For eighteen months she had suffered from cancer, but her health had started to deteriorate ten years earlier, when Sebastian had died. Severe bouts of depression blighted much of her subsequent life – and, he now realised, his own.

His father had almost sabotaged his entire year off on the night before he left. Sitting at the kitchen table of their London flat in Pimlico, he told him to let his hair down and live a bit. It could have been the kiss of death from any other father to a teenage son, but they had grown close during his mother's illness, so his father poured him another Bruichladdich and laughed.

'Just in case you should ever consider a career in the Service, there are only two things that make the vetters twitchy,' his father had continued. 'Heroin and whores.'

'Perfect qualifications for a journalist.'

'That's still the thing, is it?'

'Someone needs to expose all the Whitehall corruption,' he grinned.

'Your mother always wanted a doctor in the family, you know that.' Marchant watched his father knock back his whisky, a slight tremor in his usually steady hand.

'Because she thought Sebbie could have been saved?'

'The doctors were very kind, said there was nothing that could have been done, but she always blamed herself for the accident.'

The years immediately after Sebastian's death were

134

vague now, but he remembered them as a strange time, a part of his life that floated in limbo, separate from the rest of his past. The overt kindness of so many people, more time spent with his father, his oddly withdrawn mother, who missed Sebastian terribly. His father had once hinted at some kind of mental illness, but it was the one subject he could never talk about with him. His own grieving had played out in reverse; he missed Sebastian more as each year passed.

Marchant thought again about his brother as he read through more of his own legend: the family details (English father, Irish mother), schooling, everything the same as his own life, except for the decision to travel on an Irish passport, which he knew was for operational reasons (it would draw less attention than a British one). It frustrated him that he could no longer be sure which memories were his own and which had been shaped by family albums. He remembered Sebastian playing in the orchard at Tarlton, dropping apples on their father's sleeping head in the hammock; he could still see him sitting cross-legged with him in their room at the top of the cottage, trying to make as much noise as they could on their Indian *dholak* drums. There had been no photos of that.

His mother's death was there, so too was his father's, as well as a propensity to drink too much (a thoughtful gesture by the cobblers), but the career of David Marlowe's father had been with the British Council. It was Marlowe's first few years, though, that made Marchant curse them for not showing more imagination.

Marlowe had also lost his brother in a car crash in Delhi, where his father had been posted. The name, Sebastian, was the same; but had Marlowe ever felt his sense of loss, the sharp jabs from the shadows that came at any time of the day or night? Marchant screwed the paper up into a tight ball. If there was one thing he could have erased from Marlowe's past, it would have been Sebastian's death. But at least there would be no pretending.

He took the clothes downstairs in a plastic carrier bag and paid for some tokens and washing powder at reception. The young woman at the desk saw the bag and smiled at his domesticity. She had a flower tucked behind one ear, introduced herself as Monika, and joked that Irish travellers wore the cleanest clothes. Marchant knew conversation with anyone was a risk, but she had initiated the exchange, and it would arouse more suspicion if he kept quiet. Besides, Monika was good-looking, bohemian, early twenties – just Marlowe's type.

'Like the flower,' he said, smiling back at her. His accent was a soft Dublin one, like his mother's.

'Thanks.'

'My room's covered in them.'

'Oh, you're in spring. Do you like it? Dom is a friend of mine. The artist.'

'Groovy,' he said, hoping the irony translated.

Monika laughed lightly as he walked off down the corridor towards the launderette.

'Groo-vy,' he heard her repeat, saying the word slowly.

Under the heading of sexuality, David Marlowe had

been described as a 'promiscuous heterosexual'. He wondered if that's what it said on his own vetting file. In the early days at the Fort he had tried hard to prevent his relationship with Leila from becoming serious, deliberately dating other women. Spy school, he had joked, was no place to make an honest woman of her: it was where people learnt to cheat and lie, not to love. Marchant, though, had kept coming back to Leila, who seemed neither surprised nor resentful. At least until recently. In the months leading up to his suspension, just when he was finally ready to accept (and needed) their relationship, she had been hesitant to make the step up, oddly changeable in her emotions: one moment pulling him in, the next pushing him away.

As he emptied his bag of clothes into one of the hostel's empty washing machines, Marchant knew that it wouldn't require much effort for David Marlowe to pursue another woman. It would be harder for him, though, even if the hippy-chick charms of Monika held a certain nostalgic appeal. He must tap into his own past, rebuffing any pangs of guilt with the irritation he had felt at Leila's recent reluctance to commit.

It had been a few years since he had mixed with anyone like Monika, or stayed in a place like the Oki Doki, but he was encouraged by how easily old habits returned, once the mental switch had been flicked. He thought about rolling a joint again, something he hadn't done since joining the Service, and the joys of stoned sex.

His smile quickly faded, though, as he watched the load of washing turn and tumble. Wafting down the corridor from the hostel kitchen was the smell of Polish cooking: *bigos*, or maybe *flaczki*. His gag reflex twitched. Barely managing a nod at his new friend on reception, he headed outside to the street in search of fresh air. His stomach turned as he remembered the water, the panic.

He bent double over the gutter and vomited. Breathing in deeply, he stood up and walked down the empty street at a brisk pace, keeping to the shadows in the early-evening light. Then, a moment later, he heard a voice behind him. It was Monika's.

'Are you OK? You look terrible. Very un-groo-vy.'

The flower was now behind her other ear, but Marchant didn't say anything: Marlowe wouldn't have noticed.

'I'm fine,' he said, taking in her lissom figure for the first time. 'Is there a barber around here? Nothing fancy, I just need a crew.'

'Crew?'

'All off,' Marchant said, smiling. 'Buzz cut . . . wiffle . . . GI One.'

Half an hour later he was sitting on a stool in a bedsit flat, around the corner from the hostel, with a whisky in his hand. Monika leant in against him as she shaved the last remnants of sandy hair from his head, her bare studded navel pressed against his back. In one hand she held the razor, in the other a large spliff. Vashti Bunyan was on the CD player. Monika had offered to cut Marchant's hair herself, and he could think of no good reason to refuse. Her shift at the hostel was over, and he liked the anonymity her bedsit provided.

'I'm done,' Monika said, flicking away some loose strands. 'Can I rub in some moisturiser? Your skin, it's very dry.' As she said this she leant forward, her smiling face appearing in the mirror at the side of his own, and placed the spliff in Marchant's mouth.

'Sure, whatever,' Marchant said, assuming the dryness was down to something the Americans had put in the water. Before the weed dulled his senses he ran an eye around the room again, then went back over the last few hours, reassuring himself about her, their encounter. On balance, it was a good thing. The CIA would be looking for a single man, not a couple. Monika was in need of company, having recently split from her boyfriend, and she had already talked about spending the next few days together, looking at the antiques in Kolo Bazaar, drinking in the bars of Stare Miasto, although she knew he was booked on a flight the following morning.

'I wish you weren't going to India so soon, Mr Englishman,' she said, moving around and sitting on his lap, facing him. She took the spliff out of his mouth and placed it back in her own. Marchant curled his arms around her lower back, and pulled her closer to him. For a moment all he could see was Leila, naked in the shower, watching him. He closed his eyes, breathed in deeply and thought hard about David Marlowe.

He stroked her cheek as he tried to calculate the risks and benefits of delaying his flight to stay with her. His brain was easing up. It slowed even more as she leant forward and kissed him, her spliff-free hand slipping inside his Levi's.

'Stay here for an extra day,' she said quietly, holding him tightly. 'I'd like that.'

'What about my ticket?' he said, slowly unpicking the mother-of-pearl buttons of her shirt. Leila was stepping out of the shower now, hair wrapped in a turban of towel.

'What about it? I've got a friend, she runs a small travel agency not far from here. We send all our guests there. She can change it, she knows everyone up at the airport.'

But David Marlowe didn't give a damn any more about his ticket, or Daniel Marchant, or Leila, as he eased Monika out of her shirt.

18

Sir David Chadwick had spent a lifetime brokering compromises in Whitehall meeting rooms, but even he was struggling to keep Marcus Fielding and Harriet Armstrong apart.

'Before this gets referred to the PM, as it will, I need to know exactly what you're alleging here, Harriet,' he said, looking across his oak-panelled office at Armstrong, who was on the edge of her seat.

'The Poles must have been tipped off by someone,' Armstrong said, glancing at Fielding. He was sitting at a safe distance, equally upright though less on edge. On his lap was a clipboard, covered in a patchwork of blue and yellow Post-it notes. Armstrong had often wondered what Fielding wrote on them. No reminders to bring home dinner for his wife, because he had never had one, a fact that still intrigued her.

'Marcus?' Chadwick asked.

'I think we're underestimating our friends in Warsaw. The new government's been looking for a way out of these renditions for some time now. I imagine someone was keeping the airbase under surveillance and decided that they no longer wanted a corner of their country run by America.'

'Marcus, you rang me about the flight,' Harriet said. Fielding's poise riled her. Everything about him riled her: his equanimity, the Oxbridge intellect, those safari suits. And how could someone be 'celibate', as he had apparently defined his sexuality to the vetters, explaining that he was simply not interested in sex of any kind, with anyone? Her ex-husband had once accused her of something similar, but she hadn't consciously chosen to deny him; it had just gone with the long hours.

'True?' asked Chadwick.

'As you both know, we monitor all flights in and out of the UK, particularly ones that file dummy flight plans. To avoid confusion, I suggest that the next time the PM decides to authorise an undeclared CIA flight through British airspace, someone has the courtesy to tell us.'

'Harriet?' asked Chadwick, turning back towards her like a centre-court umpire.

'It was agreed that the Americans could talk to Marchant,' she said.

'Talk to him, not try to drown him,' Fielding replied. 'And I think we said it should be in this country.'

Fielding's last comment was addressed to Chadwick, who didn't care for the look that accompanied it. 'Oh, come on, Marcus,' Chadwick said, a nervous smile creasing his pale jowls. 'It must have felt like home from home, given the number of Poles over here.'

Harriet returned the smile, but Fielding stared out of the window onto Whitehall, watching an empty 24 bus make its way up towards Trafalgar Square. He didn't have time for cheap jokes about immigrants. He didn't have time for Chadwick, sitting behind his over-sized desk like a child who had broken into the headmaster's office.

'So where is he now?' Fielding asked him.

'I was rather hoping you'd tell us.'

'I want my man back alive. That was the other part of our deal.'

'If you haven't got Marchant, then who has?' Chadwick turned back to Armstrong.

'Spiro flew out to Warsaw this afternoon. They think he's still in Poland.'

'He lost him, he can bring him back,' Fielding said, rising from his seat. 'I've asked Warsaw station to keep a lookout.'

'Prentice,' Armstrong said coldly.

'You know him?' Fielding was now at the door, clipboard under one arm.

'Only by reputation.'

'Quite. One of the best in the business.'

'And once Marchant's found?' Chadwick asked, standing too, sensing another altercation.

'Then it's our turn to ask him about Dhar,' Armstrong replied.

Fielding opened the door to leave.

'Just make sure we don't lose him again,' said

143

Chadwick. 'Twice would be careless. Thank you, Marcus.'

Fielding closed the door behind him, leaving Armstrong and Chadwick alone.

'Whatever the differences between you two, I don't want it affecting operations on my watch, Harriet.' Chadwick had remained standing.

'Spiro's livid.'

'I'm sure he is. But it should surprise no one that the Service looks after its own. It always has done. Is this Hugo Prentice protecting him?'

'Quite possibly. We could throw the book at Prentice if we want. He's had run-ins with Spiro before. He's had run-ins with everyone. Any other agency would have got rid of him years ago.'

'I'll talk to Spiro.' Chadwick paused, shuffling papers needlessly on his desk. 'We want this contained, Harriet. The Americans need Marchant back.'

Fielding found Ian Denton, folder in hand, waiting for him in the room outside his office, making quiet conversation with his secretaries. The Chief of MI6 was entitled to three of them: his personal assistant, a letters secretary and a diary secretary. Anne Norman had been PA to the previous four Chiefs, all of whom had valued her brusque phone manner, particularly when taking awkward calls from Whitehall. She had resigned over the Stephen Marchant affair, only to be talked into staying on over a long lunch at Bentley's with Fielding. A formidable spinster in her late fifties, she was the archetypal bluestocking, except that she always wore bright red tights, usually with red shoes. Fielding had often meant to ask her why, but he was in no mood for small-talk after his meeting with Armstrong and Chadwick.

'Come,' he said, walking through to his office. Denton followed, closing the door behind them. 'What have you got?'

'Marchant's with AW,' Denton said, quieter than ever.

'And the Americans?'

'Spiro's turning Warsaw upside down. Prentice says they won't find him.'

Fielding hesitated a moment. 'What about Salim Dhar? Any progress?'

Denton pulled out a sheaf of papers from the folder he was holding. He, like Fielding, lived an ordered life, and he had grouped the sheets into clear plastic files. He handed the top file over to Fielding with the confidence of someone who knew he had done well. It was a printout of an old bank statement.

'Dhar's father, his current account in Delhi,' Denton said. 'This deposit here was his monthly salary payment from the US Embassy.'

'And this one?' Fielding asked, pointing to another payment that had been circled with red biro.

'As far as his Delhi branch manager is concerned, it was a regular payment from relatives in South India. Paid in rupees from the State Bank of Travancore, Kottayam. Works out at about £100 a month in today's terms.'

'Not bad for an administrative officer. You'd expect someone with a job in Delhi to be sending money back to his family in the south, not receiving it. So who was paying him?'

Denton paused for a moment, knowing that he would be blamed in some indirect way for what he was about to say. 'We've followed the financial trail back further.'

'And?' Fielding glanced up at him irritably.

'Cayman Islands, one of the Service's old offshore accounts.'

'Christ.' Fielding tossed the file onto his desk.

'Set up by Stephen Marchant in 1980.' Denton pulled out another file, made up of sheets more faded than the first, and handed it to Fielding, hoping that it would become the new focus for his anger. 'We found this in the FO's employment files. Seems like the first payment was put through shortly after Dhar's father was sacked from the British High Commission. There was a small disciplinary hearing, at which various references were read out, including this one from Marchant. He felt very strongly about it, thought the man had been shabbily treated.'

'So strongly he set him up with an index-linked agent's pension.' Fielding pushed his chair back towards the big bay windows that looked across the Thames towards Tate Britain. Denton was still standing. 'It doesn't add up. A junior member of the commission's admin staff – perfectly decent man, I'm sure, but not exactly a high-value intelligence asset. Is there any record of him providing information to the Service?'

'Nothing so far. For what it's worth, the monthly payment was roughly equal to the difference between his

146

British salary and his new, lower income from the US Embassy.'

'Very fair. Except that Marchant didn't have the authority to set up something like this. Even back then.'

'It never caught the eye of our auditors.'

'He always did know how to handle the bean counters. Are the payments still being made?'

'No. They stopped. 2001.'

'Why then?'

Denton shook his head. 'We don't know yet. But there's one other thing. We've found a second payment Marchant requested after he'd left India. To his driver, one Ramachandran Nair. Same account, gave him a pension of £50 a month.'

'And we're still paying him?'

'Seems so, yes.'

'Dear God, no wonder we're always over budget. Do whatever you have to, Ian. I need to know why Marchant was paying Dhar's father. What was it he did for him?'

19

Hassan was the only asset Leila had ever slept with. It wasn't usually her style, but at least he was young and good-looking. Most agents were paid, but Hassan had always been an exception, ever since he'd provided her with enough information to thwart an attack on a passenger plane over Heathrow. After that he could name his price, which in his case was hard sex rather than hard cash.

According to Fielding, fragments of intelligence in the wind pointed to some sort of Gulf connection to the attempted attack on the marathon. Word had gone out for all assets, however tenuous, to be harvested for HUMINT. Hassan knew more about what was happening in the Gulf than any Western analyst in Whitehall, drawing on his Wahabi roots to keep informed of the region's complex terror network. Ostensibly he was a travel journalist, writing for one of the many English-language newspapers in Qatar, but he didn't need the salary. His family was worth more than MI6's annual budget, which was why he was asking Leila if she could leave the media awards dinner early and host her first home match.

'You've always played away,' he said, topping up her glass of fizzy water. The dinner, in the ballroom of the London Hilton, was dry, which was why a herd of Western journalists was migrating steadily to the hotel's bars. It was a dry affair in other ways, too. There was little cross-cultural mingling, despite the evening's theme of global unity and despite the best efforts of the MC, a risqué, half-Iranian, half-British female comedian ('Whenever I tell people my biological clock is ticking, everyone ducks').

Leila had wanted to find her, say how much she had enjoyed her act, but Leila was acting too. She was attending the evening in the guise of a Gulf-based travel PR, one of her regular operational covers. It was the first time she had used it on British soil, and she felt more nervous than usual.

'I've booked a room here,' Leila said, wrestling with a sudden urge to join the hacks at the bar. She was used to having sober sex with Hassan, but tonight she felt the need for a drink.

'Leila, that's very thoughtful, but do you know what? The Hilton bores me. Hotels bore me. I spend all my life in hotels. Let's go back to your place. Why not? It's your first time on home soil.'

Hassan was proposing that she step over a line she

had never crossed before. Apart from the security implications of taking an asset back to her home, there were personal issues too. Sex in a hotel room was one thing, but at home, the place where she retreated from Legoland, the sanctuary she returned to after postings abroad? That was different.

'I'm sorry, Hassan. I've paid for the room. And it's a long way back to where I live.' But she knew, as soon as she spoke, that she had said the wrong thing.

'You've paid for a room?' he laughed. 'So what? I'll pay.'

She looked away at the myriad of tables, each with its candles and extravagant flower display, spread out across the ballroom floor like an illuminated orchard. She hated not being in control.

'It'll be worth it,' he said, leaning forward to touch her arm. 'I know who supplied the isotonics.'

Earlier that day, after her final debrief at Thames House, Leila had returned to her desk at Legoland for the first time since the marathon. The building was still buzzing with the attempted attack. In the canteen she noticed the glances, overheard people talking about her with an obviousness unbecoming of spies. The Gulf Controllerate, where she worked, was like a City traders' pit. There were no flickering international share prices, but the hum of ringing phones and the vast data-analysis charts on the walls, linking hundreds of names across the world, conveyed a similar chaotic urgency. Her line manager said it was even busier than in the days immediately after 9/11.

It had been a relief when Marcus Fielding had called Leila in to his office and asked about Marchant, how she had found him the day before. He had also praised her for the way she had thrown herself back into work, and repeated the need for her to be patient. Marchant, he said, was to be questioned by the Americans, which wasn't ideal, but he had every confidence he would be back in the fold soon. It was best, though, if he and she didn't see each other for a few days.

Leila didn't pursue what he meant by 'questioned', for fear of betraying Paul Myers, but there was also something about Fielding's manner that discouraged further discussion of Marchant. Instead, he wanted her to focus on Hassan, and to find out whatever he knew about the marathon attack. His intelligence had been accurate in the past.

'Squeeze the pips,' Fielding had said, in a way that made her doubt his reportedly celibate status. They both knew that she had never filled in a request form for Hassan to be paid, and the matter had never been discussed. Leila thought about that now as she tied Hassan's hands to the posters of her brass bed. It had shocked her how quickly she had got used to sleeping with a man she didn't love, and struggled to fancy. She had told Marchant after the first time, but he didn't want to know. It was her job: they would both have to sleep with other people occasionally, so they should just get on with it. The only reason for them to confide in each other, he said, would be if it meant anything more than sex.

151

Leila didn't find it so simple, and was annoyed that Marchant could be so matter-of-fact. She remembered when, towards the end of their six months at the Fort, a female instructor had taken her and the three other women in that year's intake for a drink one night, to pass on a few personal tips. She expected them all to deal with the health risks themselves. Her advice was solely about the emotional damage that professional sexual liaisons could result in. The key, she had said, was to think of themselves as actors playing out a scene in a film.

Leila tried to imagine the camera crew now, as she looked around her dimly lit flat. Hassan had hinted at less orthodox sex on their last meeting, in Doha, but she had kept their encounter firmly on the straight and narrow. Tonight would be different, something to trouble the censors.

'Leila, this is wonderful,' he said, lying face-up on the sheets. He was naked, his wrists and ankles tied securely with scarves to all four bedposts.

'It's what they call home advantage,' she said, picking up two large lit candles she'd been given by Marchant. She walked over to the bed with them. They were both brimming with beeswax, which burned hotter than ordinary candle wax. Still in her underwear, she placed them carefully by the bedside, then went over to her CD player and turned up Natacha Atlas. Outside, the lights of Canary Wharf Tower burned brightly as bankers worked late into the night. For a moment, she longed for a normal job. She drew the souk-bought curtains, sent by her mother, took another scarf from a drawer, and tied it over Hassan's eyes. He sighed with approval, mouthing a kiss at her. 'Darling Leila,' he whispered, but she put her finger to his lips.

'Ssshh,' she said, passing him the mouthpiece of the *ghalyun*, an Iranian hookah that she kept in the flat. Her father had brought it back from Tehran in 1979. As Hassan drew heavily on the mix of tobacco and hashish, she moved up onto the bed, straddling his chest, her back to him. Somehow it was more bearable if she couldn't see his face. Taking him in one hand, she reached across with the other to the candles on the bedside table.

'Are you ready?' she said quietly, working him firmly. She turned and removed the hookah pipe from his mouth.

'I've never been more ready in my life,' he said.

Hassan, Leila suspected, was a coward at heart, despite the bravado. Too much pain and he would cry for his mother. 'How brave are you feeling?' she asked, holding a candle six inches above him, then lowering it to three so the beeswax had less time to cool.

He screamed, as she knew he would, writhing for a few seconds as the near-boiling wax dripped onto his sensitive skin. But his smile returned as the wax hardened. Hassan, she realised, was weirder than she had thought. She caught the smell of his sweet cologne as she dripped more boiling wax onto him. Suddenly his presence in her home was overwhelming. She resented him, her job, the compromising position she found herself in; but then she thought of what they were doing to Marchant, wherever he was, and moved the candle even lower.

Half an hour later, Leila was running out of tricks, and Hassan still hadn't told her anything. Earlier, in the taxi from Park Lane to Docklands, he had insisted that his information was so potentially compromising, for him and for his country, that he would need something special to round off their home fixture. Only then would he talk.

She placed the hookah back in Hassan's mouth and told him to inhale deeply. For a moment she feared she had misjudged him, that he might pass out before telling her anything. But Hassan did as he was told, as he had done all evening, and gave her a stoned smile as she went over to her fridge and opened the fast-freeze compartment.

An air steward on a late-night flight back from Abu Dhabi had once told her how to make a man sob with pleasure. He was gay, but he reckoned 'the Narcissus' worked for most men. It tapped into their fundamental egos, he said, particularly if they liked blowing hot and cold. Which was why, after Hassan's initial cries of pain, Leila had moulded the solidifying wax around him. Once it had hardened, she had carefully slid it off and filled it with water. That water had now frozen, and was sitting upright next to a bag of peas. She peeled away the wax, looked at what she had in her hand with some satisfaction, and returned to Hassan in the bedroom.

'Turn over,' she said, unfastening his hand ties. It was time to find out what he knew about the marathon.

20

Spiro didn't like the CIA sub-station in Warsaw. He didn't like the coffee, he didn't like the tired, 1970s hellhole of an embassy in which the Company was housed (an opinion confirmed when his driver took him past the glistening new premises of the British Embassy), but most of all he didn't like the station chief. By rights, Alan Carter should have been fired years ago. He had messed up over the Agency's post-9/11 rendition flights to Stare Kiejkuty, a programme based on tight cooperation between the CIA and the WSI. Its basis was total denial, but word had got out, and Spiro blamed Carter.

Now he had messed up again. Marchant's release was in danger of sparking a three-way diplomatic row between Poland, America and Britain. Poland's new prime minister had already been in touch, saying it had been a case of mistaken identity. His office had received reports of a Westerner at the remote airport, and a team of special forces had been sent over to take a look. When the Poles had come under fire, they had returned the compliment, and the detainee escaped. Spiro had never heard such bullshit, but there was nothing he could do. His allies in WSI were becoming increasingly powerless, and the protocol simply didn't exist for lodging a complaint about a deniable project such as Stare Kiejkuty, particularly as it was meant to have been shuttered.

Spiro looked around at the bank of screens in the dimly lit room at the back of the US Embassy, a team of five junior officers keeping their heads down as he made his displeasure clear.

'Do we have eyes at the airport?' he barked at Carter.

'We've picked up a feed from CCTV in immigration,' Carter said. 'We'll see him if he's got a passport.'

'And the Brit Embassy?'

'Still trying. It's pretty secure over there.'

Unlike here, Spiro thought.

'We're also live at the station, and most of the city's malls,' said another officer.

'What have we got on him?' Spiro asked.

A photo of Marchant and Pradeep, running side by side in the marathon, was projected onto the wall in front of the computers. In the foreground, Turner Munroe, the US Ambassador to London, was clearly identifiable.

'Close to his target, wasn't he?' Spiro said. 'Too fucking close.'

'Sir,' one of the youngest officers asked tentatively, looking up at Carter for support. 'Shouldn't London be helping us on this one?'

'Don't even go there,' Spiro snapped. 'We're flying solo, that's all you need to know.' He turned to Carter. 'Where else might Marchant be heading? Krakow? The border? Why are we so sure he's coming to town?'

'We have an asset in a village four miles south of Stare Kiejkuty. He says an unmarked military truck drove through the village on the main road to Warsaw at fifteen hundred hours. Our guys at the airbase raised the alarm at twenty hundred last night, approximately five hours after Marchant was freed.'

'Five friggin' hours? What were they doing? R and R in the waterboarding pool?'

'Sir, they had been drugged, bound and gagged by the Poles – they were Grom, elite special forces. It's a credit to their training that they managed to free themselves at all.'

'Is that right? Well, it isn't a credit to your training that we have no fucking idea where Marchant is now.'

'We're into the city police's traffic cameras,' another officer announced, hoping to bail his boss out of trouble. They worked hard for Carter, and didn't like to see him humiliated.

'Screen one,' Carter said. A moment later, black-and-white images of slow-moving traffic were being projected onto the main wall.

'Gridlock,' Spiro said. 'Just like Route 28 after a Red Sox game.'

'If the truck was coming into Warsaw, it would have entered the city on the Moscow–Berlin road,' Carter said, looking over his junior colleague's shoulder at the

157

computer screen again. He was avoiding eye contact with Spiro as much as he could. The screen was split into three sections: the main traffic image, a city map, and a database displaying a list of camera positions throughout the city. 'Switch to camera 17,' Carter said. The junior officer scrolled down the list.

A new image, less grainy than the first, was projected onto the wall. The queue of traffic leaving the city was moving slower than the cars arriving.

'How long does it take to get from Stare Kiejkuty to Warsaw by truck?' Spiro asked.

Carter nudged the junior officer, who looked at his map again and zoomed out from the city to an image of the north of the country. A route highlighted in red wormed its way almost instantly from the airbase to Warsaw.

'Two hours fifteen,' Carter said, reading from the screen.

'Can you get us into traffic archive?' Spiro asked him.

'It'll take some time.'

'I want everything from eighteen to twenty-one hundred hours. Let's see if that truck showed up in the city last night. We also need passenger lists from Warsaw, Krakow and Gdansk airports. And I want the names of any Brits who are even thinking about flying out of Poland; then crunch them through Langley. How many have we got up at the airport?'

'Two units. We called in back-up from Berlin.'

'Marchant cannot leave this lousy country, is that clear?'

158

21

Marchant lay on the bed, watching Monika as she undressed and slipped onto the sheets next to him, at ease with her nakedness. Earlier she had offered to take his ticket to her friend, who could postpone his flight by a day. He had been more than happy to let her, falling into a surprisingly deep sleep while she was away. The less time he spent on the streets of Warsaw, the better, and they would be watching all the airports. Changing his flight departure might buy him a little time. The alarm would have been raised by now, and Prentice had made it clear that the Service's help was over.

Monika's kindnesses continued, but Marchant was far from certain that they were unconditional, particularly when she announced that she would be coming with him to the airport.

'India is calling you, I can tell,' she said. 'But first . . .'

She hooked a leg over his, but just as she started to kiss Marchant, he stopped her, noticing for the first time his rucksack in the corner of the room.

'Something wrong?' she asked.

'Did you bring my rucksack over?' he asked, propping himself up on one elbow.

'Of course. You're staying over, remember?'

'Did anyone see you, carrying it?'

'No, why? Is there a problem?'

He said nothing, and sank back on the bed. So far, he had avoided telling Monika anything that might arouse her suspicion, sticking as close as possible to his legend: he had been bumming around Europe, checked into the Oki Doki before flying out to India, but had been delayed by the bohemian charms of a beautiful receptionist. Par for the course for David Marlowe. But he knew he would soon have to say something more: their journey to the airport would need to be discreet. He decided to opt for the truth, give or take a few dollars.

'The Americans are looking for me,' he began, taking a pack of her cigarettes from the bedside table and lighting up. He had forgotten how it felt to embark on a lie, that exquisite moment when you step off from ordinary life into the shadows of deceit, where anything is suddenly possible. For a moment the thrill was intoxicating.

'Why?' She seemed genuinely surprised, resting her chin on both hands to listen.

'I needed dollars for India, the new bank at the US Embassy was offering the best rate, so I went along. But they wouldn't let me in without searching my rucksack.'

He paused, relishing the options, wondering which way to take his story. 'I had a row.'

'You should have left your rucksack somewhere, like at the station. It's the same everywhere.'

'I know. But I'd only just arrived in Warsaw. OK, I also had a bit of puff on board. I didn't want a scene.'

'Was it just a row?' Monika asked, putting one hand over her mouth to stifle a laugh.

'What's so funny?' he asked.

'Nothing. I just can't imagine you angry. Did you get very cross? Like really crazy?'

Her manner was coquettish, playful, and he wondered again whether she was playing a game too. 'There was a bit of mutual pushing. Your police were called, but they weren't interested.'

'But the Americans are?'

'Maybe I'm being paranoid. I had that rucksack with me, that's all. And they started to ask what was in it when I wouldn't show them.'

'No one saw me, Mr Angry-man. And you're with me now. I checked you out.' He stared at her through his smoke. 'From the hostel,' she added, kissing him.

22

Leila had met Jago, a tousle-haired six-year-old, once before, but this was her first time on the London Eye. Fielding had emailed her earlier in the day with the unusual time and place, explaining that he would have a godson in tow. Everyone in the Service knew the Vicar had an inordinate number of godchildren (fourteen at the last count). Less well known was how he found time to see them all. They were a lucky bunch, she thought, as Fielding led them through the shadows to an empty capsule, bypassing the long queue. He ushered Leila and Jago before him, nodding at an attendant as the doors closed. It evidently wasn't Fielding's first visit.

As Jago swung on the metal handrail, looking fearlessly at the Thames below him, Leila took in London from a new perspective. All around her, as they rose almost imperceptibly into the night sky, buildings coyly revealed parts that had seldom been seen by the public before: pointed skylights, roof gullies, curved domes.

'We always try to get a sunset flight,' Fielding said, looking west, where the high clouds were tinged with red. 'Don't we Jago?'

But Jago was too preoccupied by a passenger boat making its way up the river, its wake spreading like spilt salt behind it.

'He's grown up a lot since I last saw him,' Leila offered, doubting whether Fielding's effort to include his godson in their conversation was genuine.

'They do, you know,' he said, still looking out west. 'Sorry to bring you up here.'

'It's great. I've never been.'

'We just can't be sure about Legoland at the moment.'

'No?'

She presumed he meant MI5, but Fielding didn't elaborate. 'Stay away from the doors and these pods are almost impenetrable,' he continued. 'At least at the top. Curved glass, you see. Sometimes I reckon there are more of the world's intelligence services flying the London Eye than tourists. Word's got out.'

'Uncle Marcus?' Jago asked, not waiting for an answer. 'Are we moving faster than a clock?'

'A clock? Well, faster than the long hand, slower than the second hand.'

'What's the time now, then?'

'The time?' Marcus repeated, barely missing a beat. It was why he always accepted invitations to be a godfather: children's random thought patterns kept his brain nimble. 'Almost 12 o'clock,' he said, winking at Leila.

'When we reach the top it will be exactly midnight.'

'And then we'll all turn into pumpkins on the way down?'

'Every one of us.'

'Hassan was a disappointment, in many ways,' Leila said, checking that Jago was distracted again. The boy seemed to be deep in thought, contemplating his imminent transformation.

'Really?'

'I think he was just lonely.'

'Did you . . . ?'

'Squeeze the pips? Yes.'

'And?'

'When pushed . . . squeezed . . . he mentioned the Russians, said how they had liked the instability of last year, of seeing the Service wobble.'

'I'm sure they did. It wasn't the Russians.'

'No.' She paused, squatting down next to Jago. She had forgotten how brusque Fielding could be in his dismissals.

'What's that?' the boy asked, pointing almost directly beneath them.

'That's called a carousel,' she said, looking at a circular disc of colours far below them. They were almost at the top of the wheel now. Midnight was approaching. 'Horses and music and . . .'

'Oh yes, we saw it down there,' he said, already looking elsewhere, across the river towards Big Ben.

'There's something else I need to talk to you about,' Leila said. She stood up and walked over to Fielding, who was still looking upriver.

'Of course.'

'I need a break. From Britain, from everything that's happened.'

'As far as I'm concerned, you can have as long off as you want. Travel, see the world as a tourist for a bit. I thought HR had talked to you about this?'

'I don't want a holiday. I need to keep myself busy while he's away. But not here.'

'Your next foreign tour is, when, next year?'

'July.'

'I'm sure we could bring it forward.'

'I had something else in mind. The CIA's exchange programme. They've just advertised another position.'

He looked at her for a moment, studying her face. She was strikingly beautiful, he thought, particularly in the soft light of the setting sun. 'Is that what you really want? I'm surprised. Genuinely. Langley's no fun at all, you know that.'

'It's not in America. A three-month tour on the subcontinent. India, Pakistan, Sri Lanka. I'd start in the Delhi station.'

A thought crossed Fielding's mind with the fleeting transience of one of Jago's random musings; but it left a trace that was to linger much longer than he would have liked.

23

Spiro looked again at the grainy image of a two-tonne, dark-blue military truck, standing in heavy traffic on the northern edge of Warsaw.

'Grom. Polish special forces. When was this taken?' he asked, pulling hard on his cigarette.

'20.30 hours,' Carter said.

The room had gone quiet as everyone stared at the truck.

'Bring us in closer,' Spiro said, walking up to the wall as the image grew bigger and more blurred. 'This part here, the windscreen.'

The truck's windscreen was highlighted with an animated dotted line, before it expanded to fill the entire wall. The driver could clearly be seen on the right-hand side of the cabin, and the outline of another figure was visible in the passenger seat. But it was the profile of a third person between them that had interested Spiro.

'Can we rebuild this?' he asked.

The atmosphere grew tense as Carter and his team exchanged glances with each other, realising that Spiro was about to show them up. They had been more interested in establishing where the truck had gone next, and whether any of the city's other unreliable cameras had captured its progress.

In a few moments the image had been enhanced enough to reveal the blurred features of a familiar figure. Spiro turned to address the room, one side of the projected figure dappling his own. 'Hugo Prentice, employee of Her Majesty's Secret Service, Warsaw station. I guess his mother loved him. Langley wants him fried.'

Hugo Prentice wandered through Kolo Bazaar, aware of at least one set of watchers on his tail. He had already counted three of them, and spotted a fourth in the antique mirror on the stall in front of him. They had picked him up after he had left the embassy by car after lunch, following at a safe distance. He knew what their presence meant: they had spotted his image on the traffic CCTV. On the journey down from Stare Kiejkuty he had leant forward in the Grom truck at almost every set of lights, hoping that at least one of the ancient police traffic cameras had been working.

He walked down to the end of the market, stopping occasionally to look at items that genuinely caught his eye: Russian samovars, iron crosses, old leather sofas. It was important for his followers to believe that they had not been spotted. When he made his move, he must do it with the purpose of an intelligence officer who was taking the usual precautions before meeting his agent, rather than someone who was panicking under surveillance.

Spiro was agitated, watching Prentice on the main screen as he moved through the market in the fragmented images of the city centre's CCTV network.

'He's about to dry-clean,' he said. 'Moscow rules, British style. They should put this guy in a museum.'

Spiro knew what Prentice was up to. Marchant was too hot to be kept at the British Embassy – they needed to deny all involvement – so he had been secreted somewhere in the city. Prentice was now on his way to meet him. Spiro had asked old friends in the WSI for assistance, but he wasn't sure if they would be in a position to help after the Stare Kiejkuty fiasco.

'Eyes on the tram, unit three,' he said, as Prentice quickened his pace.

The number 12 pulled in just as Prentice reached the stop. He stepped aboard, glancing casually at his watch as he did so. The tram was crowded with afternoon commuters, and there were no seats available, but he wasn't going far. At the next stop he would get off, descend into the nearby underpass by a subway, and then leave from exit four, one of six possible exits, which was at street level. The street was one-way – the wrong way for any vehicle that might have been following the number 12 tram.

'Somebody better be following him,' Spiro said as Prentice disappeared down the underpass. 'He's in dead ground.'

'Unit four?' the junior officer said.

'The busker's playing our song,' a relaxed voice said on the intercom.

An image of a guitarist, sitting on the floor of the underpass, flashed up on the main screen. Carter allowed himself a nervous smile, pleased that his men were performing well on Spiro's watch. But Spiro wasn't impressed.

'Something's not right here,' he said. 'It's all too predictable, even for the British.'

'Exit four,' said the junior officer.

Spiro watched as Prentice sauntered up onto the street.

'We have a problem. It's one-way.'

'That's better,' Spiro said. 'The old soldier's warming up.'

Prentice slowed down to look in the window of a shoe shop, checking for trams as he did so. Number 23 was coming down the road, but was still fifty yards from the stop. If he increased his pace now, he just might make it. But he needed his tail to catch the tram too, and he was still packing up his guitar in the underpass.

The lights ahead changed, delaying the traffic enough for Prentice to walk slowly towards the stop. He didn't need to check that the busker was behind him. Prentice climbed on board at the front of the tram and worked his way down, searching for a seat. The busker was good, Marchant thought. He never once looked up to see where

Prentice had sat, which made him think he was wired. He would know in a few seconds. Just as the front and rear doors were about to close, Prentice slipped back out onto the street, synchronising his exit with the moment when the busker had a ticket in his hand.

The doors closed with the busker still inside.

'Textbook,' Spiro said.

'Unit 3's approaching now,' Carter said, watching the screen.

'Reminds me of my first surveillance op in London,' said Spiro. 'The Russian was sitting in the last carriage of the subway train, front end. When the train pulled into Charing Cross, Northern Line, he walked off just before the train left. I tried to follow, but the last set of doors don't open at Charing Cross. I must have been the only spook in London who didn't know. I swear the guy waved as the train pulled out.'

'Sir, target's on the move again,' one of the junior officers said. 'Boarding a 24, heading uptown.'

'Stay with him,' Carter said. 'These guys can take all day to clean up.'

Prentice, it was true, had been known to spend twenty-four hours establishing that he wasn't being followed, but he didn't have that luxury today. Instead, he took the tram towards the central railway station, getting off on the corner of Jerozolimskie and Jana Pawla II. The next ten minutes would be critical. He walked past the station's entrance and headed towards Zlote Tarasy, the latest in a series of huge shopping malls to have opened in the capital in recent years. Prentice knew the Varsarians loved to shop, but even he was surprised by Zlote Tarasy's opulence and range of familiar Western names. He could have been in Bluewater.

He headed for the escalator that would take him down to the lower ground floor. At the bottom, he moved confidently around to the base of the up escalator and rode back to the ground floor, glancing across at the escalator he had just come down on. He knew the Americans wouldn't fall for it, but today was about maintaining appearances. The CIA's watchers had never rated the Service's counter-surveillance skills, and he was more than happy to play down to their expectations.

He glanced at his watch and then headed for a café on the ground floor, where he ordered a black coffee, sat down at a small corner table, and started to read a copy of the *International Herald Tribune* that he had picked up from the counter. His table was discreet, with an empty seat opposite him.

For a few minutes he looked through the paper, concentrating on stories rather than just pretending to read them. He was always reminding his officers that the best counter-surveillance watchers were trained to spot eye movements. The vibration of his mobile phone interrupted a story on Belgium beer prices. Prentice reached inside his jacket pocket and read the text.

'This is it,' Spiro said. 'All units, I want Daniel Marchant brought in the moment he shows. Alive.'

24

Six miles south-west of the shopping mall, Daniel Marchant sat sipping a black coffee too. Monika was next to him, drinking mint tea in a tall glass and wearing a faded purple *salwar khameez*. A large rucksack covered in stickers was propped up beside her. The Terminal One departure hall at Frederic Chopin airport was crowded, and they had been lucky to get a table in the bustling café, but Monika seemed to know everyone, and after a brief chat with one of the baristas a reserved sign on the corner table had been removed.

If Marchant had had to select a spot that afforded views of the entire departure hall, and also offered the observer cover and protection, their table would have been his first choice. Their backs were to the wall, denying anyone the chance to approach them unsighted, the seating area was raised above the main concourse, and the entrance and exit onto the road outside was almost beside them. Anyone who entered the departure hall would have to pass beneath them, where they could be easily observed.

All of which made him genuinely drawn to Monika, because it confirmed what he had suspected: she was an intelligence officer, most probably with AW. The text she had discreetly sent while fetching the sugar had also smacked of the covert, but he had already begun to realise at her flat: her bringing his rucksack over from the hostel, his extreme sleepiness, the way she had confined him indoors, changed his flight. And then, finally, her announcement that she had managed to buy a ticket on the same flight and was coming to India with him.

He knew she wasn't, but he couldn't confront her, in case it jeopardised her operational cover: the Americans might have had them under surveillance for days. A part of him also wanted to believe that it was true. He was flattered that she trusted him to play the game, and he admired her thoroughness: he hadn't had such good sex since his own year off.

So he was still David Marlowe and she remained Monika, and together they talked about their shared love for the human drama of arrivals and departures, and whether India's airports would be any different.

'The queue for the check-in is short. We should go now,' she said, resting her hand on his.

'OK,' Marchant said, glancing across at the row of desks. He made a cursory sweep of the hall, but by now he was confident that his departure from Poland for India, via the Gulf, was in the safe hands of AW.

'Is there something wrong?' she asked.

'Nothing.' He paused. 'It's just the end of my European adventure, that's all. I've grown quite fond of Poland.'

'Really?' she said. 'Even after your experience with the Americans?'

For a moment, their separate masks slipped. As he looked at her, he wondered what her real name was, whether she had a boyfriend, if she made love differently when she wasn't in character.

'It's amazing how quickly you get over these things,' he said, thinking back to Stare Kiejkuty. 'Water off a duck's back.'

Spiro watched Prentice read his newspaper on the big screen, wondering from which direction Marchant would join him. He knew a part of him envied Prentice's reputation as a maverick; he could never have the confidence to disobey orders, to do his own thing in the way Prentice had done on numerous occasions over the years. The CIA didn't allow for freewheeling field agents, not any more. Gone were those glory days in Afghanistan, when he and others were dropped into Kabul with suitcases stuffed full of hundred-dollar bills and instructions to win the war on terror. Everyone now had to be accountable in a way that would have been unthinkable ten years ago. Did Prentice wilfully disregard his briefs from London, Spiro wondered, or had London learnt not to brief him too specifically, knowing that it would be futile?

Either way, Spiro knew Prentice had the better hand, which made what happened next all the more galling.

Prentice folded his newspaper, glanced at his watch and finished his coffee.

'This could be it,' Spiro said to no one in particular, but Carter concentrated even harder on the panel of visual feeds in front of him.

Everyone in the room watched as Prentice pulled a phone out of his jacket pocket and dialled a number.

'Did we get a shot of that?' Spiro asked.

The main screen changed to a close-up of Prentice, focusing on the phone in his hand. The images then played back in slow motion. Carter called out the digits as Prentice's fingers moved from one number to the next. But his voice started to trail off as the sound of Spiro's own ringtone filled the room.

25

Prentice sent the pre-written text while his hand was still in his jacket pocket, but neither Spiro nor Carter, or any of his team, suspected him of doing anything other than making a phone call. The only person who knew was Monika, whose phone buzzed in the back pocket of her jeans as they approached the check-in desk for their flight to Dubai.

Spiro didn't take the call immediately, letting the phone ring five times while his brain linked the image on the screen with the sound of his own phone.

'Prentice. What a pleasure,' he said at last, refusing to catch the eye of anyone in the room, although all of them were hanging on his every word. Prentice had humiliated him once before, in Prague a few years earlier, and he knew he was about to do the same again.

Prentice looked around the mall, as if trying to spot Spiro.

'I can offer you a deal,' Prentice said, not revealing that he knew he was being filmed. He had noted all the CCTV cameras as he came into the mall, and was tempted to face the one nearest to him, like a newsreader, but he didn't want to give an impression of being in control. Not yet.

'And there was I thinking we were on the same side,' Spiro said.

'It's a good deal.' Prentice paused, looking around the café again.

'Are all units in place?' Spiro asked briskly, muting his phone. Carter nodded. 'Try me,' Spiro continued to Prentice.

'You can talk to Marchant, but I need to be present,' Prentice said.

'He's a proven threat to America,' Spiro said.

'Who isn't these days?'

'The deal was that we could talk to him.'

'I know. And you can. Just without the watersports. Your new President banned torture, remember?'

'Where is he?'

'I'm at a café, ground floor, Zlote Tarasy.' Prentice knew he didn't have to tell Spiro, but he still wanted his old rival to feel empowered. 'When Marchant sees we're on our own – don't piss about, he's good – he'll come and join us for a latte.'

Marchant and Monika handed their passports over the airline counter. The luck of the Irish, he thought, as the check-in woman took his green passport and studied it.

He presumed Monika's passport had been cleared already. How far was she going to take this pretence? All the way to the plane?

He wasn't sure if she was on her own or had back-up. He still hadn't noticed anyone who might be AW, but they both clocked the man pushing a luggage trolley past them while their passports were being checked. Neither of them reacted when he looked in their direction for a moment longer than a stranger would, or when he reached for his phone, talked briefly as he glanced at Marchant again, and then quickened his walk to the main exit.

Carter looked hard at the image on his screen of Marchant and Monika as they waited for their passports to be handed back. There was something about them that troubled him: the lightness of skin around the man's hairline that suggested he had shaved his head recently; the pairing of Irish and Polish passports.

'Sir, I think you should take a look at this,' he said, turning to Spiro.

'Are all airport units on their way to the mall?' Spiro asked, ignoring him.

'They're mobile, sir, but I think you should . . .'

'Every floor, every exit. I want Marchant in a van before he's even smelled Prentice's coffee,' Spiro said.

As Spiro took his coat and strode out of the room, Carter hung back and looked again at the live feed from the airport. Marchant and Monika were moving out of the image towards passport control. Then his phone rang.

Operational cover was something that an agent never dropped, not until the job was done, but Marchant hoped that Monika might make an exception now. Their flight had been called, and they were queuing to board. He wasn't in India yet, but the dangers of the departure hall were behind them, and there was little that the Americans could do now. And he knew, from the way that they had hung back, waiting to be last in the queue, that she wouldn't be flying with him to India after all. These were to be their last few minutes together.

'I think we can drop . . .'

'Ssshh . . .' she said, putting a finger on his lips and nodding at the three check-in staff. There were still twenty people between them and the gate.

'Thank you,' he said, gently taking her hand from his face and holding it. 'I won't forget this, the time we had together.'

'Here, take this,' she said, pulling out a chrome pendant from her pocket. It was small and silver, attached to a piece of thread. She took it in both hands and slipped it over Marchant's head. 'It's an Om symbol, the sound of the universe. You can't go backpacking around India without one.'

As Marchant looked down at it she leant forward, kissed him on the lips, then hugged him. He wanted to taste her mouth again, but before he could, she was whispering in his ear, holding his head tightly in her hands.

'There's a man in Delhi called Malhotra. Ask for him, Colonel Kailash Malhotra, at the Gymkhana Club. Plays bridge there every Wednesday night. You may remember him; he knew your father. And he knows where to find Salim Dhar.'

Before he could reply, she peeled herself away, nodded at the check-in supervisor, and disappeared. Two minutes later, in the departure hall, she texted Prentice to tell him that he could finish his coffee and disappear too.

She didn't recognise Carter as she left the exit, but he noticed her, and reached for his mobile. Two thousand miles away, a phone began to ring in the crucible of a Delhi summer.

26

Daniel Marchant pushed open the blue door, not sure what to expect. There had been no *chowkidar* on the front gate, and he knew the house was deserted, but for some reason he hoped that Chandar, the family cook, would be in his little outhouse, on his *charpoy*, sleeping off the Bagpiper whisky of the night before. It was an absurd thought, he knew. He had last seen Chandar twenty years ago, all four foot nine of him, standing proudly in his baggy High Commission chef whites as he oversaw his Nepali cousins serving chicken curry to his father and mother for their sad, farewell dinner.

The small room was hot and empty. He had forgotten how stifling Delhi could be in May, or perhaps he hadn't noticed the heat when he was last here, as an eight-year-old child. A bare wire dangled from the ceiling, where once a lightbulb had hung. Apart from that, there was no evidence that anyone, let alone Chandar, had ever called the place home.

The other three staff rooms were similarly empty. Together they formed a single block, set apart from the main house. He struggled to recall who had lived in them all: the *mali*, he thought, or perhaps the *ayah*'s smiling brother, who sat behind a humming sewing machine all day in the searing heat. Chandar's room was the only one he and Sebastian used to enter as children. In the afternoons, when the twins were meant to be sleeping, they would slip past the dozing *ayah* and help Chandar roll the *chapattis* he made for his own late lunch. He could still hear the hiss of the blue flame, feel the comfort of the *chapattis*, folded like warm blankets. Chandar's wife sometimes came down from Nepal to stay in the tiny room too. The brothers' visits were never the same when she was around: she scolded Chandar for feeding the sahib's sons with cheap flour, and pinched their cheeks too hard.

Marchant walked over to the main house and peered in through a window which, like all the others on the ground floor, was protected with ornate metal bars. He remembered the cold marble hall floor, big and smooth enough for him, Sebastian and Chandar to play cricket on, although it was shiny when he lived here, not black and soiled as it was now. How long the house had stood empty he wasn't sure. The padlock and chain on the front door suggested it must have been for years.

Behind him was the swimming pool. Its bottom was caked with several seasons of big leaves, rotting in a few

182

inches of brackish water. The tiles, once blue and pristine, were chipped or missing, leaving a patchwork of decay. Marchant tried to force the thought away, but an image of Sebastian came into his mind, staring up at him from the bottom of the pool.

As he turned back towards the gate, he became aware of someone watching him, a figure beneath the neem tree on the far side of the lawn, where the generator used to belch out its black smoke. He walked across the brown, untended grass, reaching the trees just in time to see a young boy climb over the wall and drop down into the neighbouring garden.

'Hey, wait,' Marchant called, struggling to recall the correct Hindi. '*Suno, Kya Chandar abhi bhi yahan rahta hai?*' Does Chandar live here any more?

The name 'Chandar' seemed to have an effect, even if his Hindi didn't. The boy's black hair reappeared above the brick wall a few moments later.

'Chandar Bahadur?' he asked tentatively, still partly concealed behind the wall.

'*Tikke*,' Marchant said, smiling. The boy's whole face had now appeared, and Marchant knew from the glint in his eyes that he was looking at Chandar's son.

Ten minutes later, Marchant was sitting in the cramped staff quarters of the neighbour's house, eating *chapattis* and *dhal* with Chandar, his wife, who remained standing, covering her head with a scarf, and their only child, Bhim. Chandar's hair was still jet-black, but there was a tiredness around his eyes that betrayed the passing of twenty years. His English was still terrible (he said the same

183

about Marchant's Hindi), but the *chapattis* were as good as ever, and they were soon reminiscing about the baby cobra Chandar had once caught in the compost heap, the rides around the lawn on the handlebars of his ancient Hero bicycle, and the Christmas when he drank too much Bagpiper and forgot to cook the turkey.

Marchant asked about his old family house next door, once one of the grandest in Chattapur, a village seven miles south of New Delhi. His mother had insisted on living off the high commission compound because of the traffic pollution in the centre of the city, even though it had meant a hazardous daily commute for his father in an Ambassador. He knew, too, that his mother would never have made that fateful drive from Chanakyapuri if they had been living in the compound like everyone else.

According to Bhim, who translated his father's words into near-perfect English, the house had stood empty for a year after the Marchants left, then the landlord's only son, an IT graduate, had returned from California and moved in with another man. The landlord, a retired army colonel, discovered his prodigal son was gay, chucked him and his boyfriend out, and had let the house stand empty ever since as a symbol of his family's shame. A smile crept onto the boy's face when he relayed the last detail. Chandar had moved around Chattapur, cooking his famous chicken curry for various expats, and was now working for a young Dutch family who, by chance, had moved into the house next door.

'But my father says he will always remember working

for Marchant Sahib,' Bhim said. There was a pause in the conversation as Marchant looked around the tiny room, listening to the clatter of the water cooler by the window, the Bollywood film music coming from the over-sized radio-tape recorder in the corner. 'Is sir still alive?' Bhim asked, with a sensitivity that suggested he already knew the answer.

'No, he's not,' Marchant said. 'He died two months ago.'

There was no need for Bhim to translate. Chandar bowed his head for a few moments, staring at the dusty concrete floor, and then started talking animatedly to his wife, who went over to the *charpoy* and pulled out a metal trunk from underneath it. Marchant watched as she opened the trunk lid and rummaged around inside. A moment later, she handed Chandar a handwritten letter, which he looked at for a token moment, as if reading it, and then passed to his son.

'My father received a letter from Ramachandran Nair, your father's driver. He used to live here. Now he is back in Kerala, his home place.'

Marchant remembered the driver's name – they used to call him Raman – but he couldn't picture his face. Bhim started reading the letter, his father barking incongruously fierce instructions at him in a way that Marchant suddenly recalled. His memories of Chandar were faint, but he could still remember that sense of contrast: one moment the subservient cook in the company of his father and guests, the next bossing everyone around in the kitchen, where Chandar was king.

'Ramachandran says your father visited him last year, in the monsoon,' Bhim said, his eyes scanning down the letter. Marchant felt an imperceptible drying of his mouth. Suddenly there was a new connection between this place he was in and the past of twenty years ago, like the ignition sparking in his father's old Lagonda.

'Does he say why my father was there?' Marchant asked.

There was another pause as Bhim carried on reading.

'He says he was worried about Marchant Sahib. He looked very tired. He didn't eat his wife's curry. "I asked him why he had come to Kerala"' – Bhim was translating directly from the letter now – '"and he told me he had come on family business."'

Marchant smiled to himself. His father would never have disclosed what he was doing, of course, even to his faithful old driver. He had heard the words 'family business' more than once in his childhood, an expression that his father's generation had used whenever they were referring to state secrets.

27

'It was a precaution, Marcus, nothing more,' Sir David Chadwick said, watching Fielding carefully as he poured them both a gin. 'She was never working for them as such. Ultimately she answered to you, to us.'

Fielding remained silent, looking out through French windows at a posse of female statues in the garden. There were three of them, their crude curves lit up by spotlights sunk around an ornamental pond. Chislehurst seemed to be full of naked garden statues, Fielding thought, at least on the private road where Chadwick lived. Statues and speed bumps and video-linked doorbells. Even Fielding's driver, parked outside in his official Range Rover, had been taken aback by the ostentation.

'The Americans insisted on it,' Chadwick continued, filling the silence. Fielding made him nervous when he was in this sort of mood, his reticence impossible to read.

'Unfortunately, we weren't in a very strong position to argue. You know as well as I do how things were. We were in turmoil. No leads on the bombing campaign, the Chief of MI6 under suspicion.'

Fielding still said nothing as he turned to take his drink. He had asked to meet outside London, and Chadwick had thought that inviting him to dinner at home would be the perfect solution, particularly as his wife was out at choir practice for the evening. The informal setting would allow them to talk properly about the future of the Service, how it might start to rebuild itself after the damage inflicted by the Stephen Marchant affair, and what the hell he had done with Daniel Marchant. Did he also want to show off the Edwardian-style orangery that had been added since he took over as Chairman of the Joint Intelligence Committee? Perhaps. But now he was regretting it, because Fielding somehow knew about Leila.

'I need reassurances that there's no one else,' Fielding eventually said.

'She was the only one,' Chadwick replied, joining him at the window. 'No one was happy about it, Marcus.'

'Except Spiro. And Armstrong.'

'We needed to know if it ran in the family.'

'Which is why I suspended Daniel Marchant.'

'And that was the right and proper thing to do. But it wasn't enough, I'm afraid. Daniel began to go a little off-message when Stephen died, started to show all the signs of a renegade.'

'He knew the rules, that we'd go after him if he became another Tomlinson.'

'The Americans wanted more assurances – not a bad call in the light of the marathon attack.'

Fielding laughed dryly. 'Which Daniel Marchant thwarted.'

'Leila's account of the incident is a little more ambiguous.'

'Not in the debrief I read. No doubt she told others what they wanted to hear.'

'You've approved her three-month attachment?'

'Of course. With a proviso that she never returns.'

'How did you know, by the way?'

'How do any of us know anything in this business? We join the dots, squint a little, turn things on their side and try, with a lot of luck, to see the bigger picture.' He paused. 'She didn't debrief properly, after meeting one of her best Gulf contacts. I knew the CX had gone elsewhere. She knew I knew. Then she asked for a transfer.'

Chadwick said nothing, matching Fielding's silences with one of his own.

'There's something else you should know,' he said. 'MI5's had a breakthrough on the running belt. As we suspected, there was a remote-detonation option from a mobile phone. But it was configured to work only on the TETRA network.'

Chadwick sensed that, for the first time that evening, he had unsettled Fielding. TETRA was only used by the emergency services and the intelligence agencies. Terrorists would love to have access to TETRA – it would allow them to detonate a bomb even if the main mobile networks had been knocked out – but its use was tightly restricted (although not tightly enough for Fielding's liking).

'And?'

Chadwick went over to the mahogany sideboard, where a brown A4 envelope lay next to the silver drinks tray. He pulled out a photo, glanced at it and walked back over to Fielding by the window.

'Take a look at this,' he said, handing it over. The photo was a grainy image of the London Marathon, a screen-grab from the BBC's helicopter camera. In the middle of the picture was Daniel Marchant, surrounded by other runners, and holding a mobile phone in his right hand. The unit had been circled in yellow marker.

'You can just make out the short aerial,' Chadwick said. 'MI5's certain it's a TETRA handset. Motorola.'

'Of course it bloody is,' Fielding said. 'How do you think we were able to talk to him out on the course? I understood he borrowed Leila's.'

'Apparently not. He brought his old one along, according to her. The one he should have handed in when he was suspended. We've checked the phone records at Thames House, and she's right. She rang him on his old encrypted number.'

Fielding wasn't convinced. He knew Marchant's suspension hadn't been as thorough as it might have been, partly because of his own reluctance to withdraw one of his best agents from the field; but failure to return an office phone, particularly an encrypted one, would not have been missed by even the most routine of Legoland's security checks. He needed to make his own enquiries.

'Has it ever occurred to you that someone might be setting Daniel Marchant up here?' Fielding asked, looking at the photo for a few seconds before passing it back. 'Knowing what a weak case there was against his father?'

'Setting him up? Why?'

'Oh, come on, David. You know as well as I do that there are plenty of people who would rather the Service didn't dine at top table any more.'

'I'm not sure even the Americans would risk the life of one of their own ambassadors to frame an MI6 officer.'

'I don't know.'

'Is that why you're protecting Daniel? You still believe he's innocent?'

'We're not protecting him, not now.'

'Prentice gave Spiro the runaround in Warsaw. You know Langley's recalled him?'

'The man's a fool.'

'Where is Daniel, Marcus?'

'I've no idea. Clearing his father's name, I assume.' Fielding finished his drink. 'And if you really want to see the Service's reputation restored, I suggest we let him.'

28

After twenty-four hours in India, Daniel Marchant concluded that he wasn't under surveillance, but he still took no risks as he was driven in a cream-coloured Ambassador taxi, ordered by Chandar, from Chattapur up into the centre of New Delhi. At Qutb Minar, in Merauli, he asked the driver to pull into the dusty car park, near the landmark monument, where they waited for ten minutes under the shade of some trees, engine and air conditioning still running.

The driver stood beside the car in his white uniform. It was obvious that he was having a smoke, but he still tried to conceal the cigarette, cupping it in his hand as he shifted from foot to foot. A tour guide handed him a leaflet and glanced hopefully in at the window at Marchant, but moved on when the driver swore at him. Marchant wound down the window, felt a wave of hot air, and took the leaflet from the driver. A few sweltering

Western tourists were drifting around the complex, being informed about the tower's 399 steps, how it had been begun in 1193 by Qutb-ud-din Aibak, the first Muslim ruler of Delhi. No one mentioned the stampede in 1998, when the lights went out in the tower and twenty-five children were crushed. Marchant remembered reading about it at the time. Visitors weren't allowed up the tower any more.

Marchant watched as the party of tourists climbed back into their minibus. The place was now empty. Nobody seemed to have followed him. Monika and her colleagues had given him a head start, but it would only be a couple of days at most. He also assumed that Prentice had done his best to hamper the Americans on the ground. But he knew it wouldn't be long before the connection was made between David Marlowe and Daniel Marchant. The CIA had a big station in Delhi. He wondered what the CX from Langley would be saying once they had worked out he was in India: suspended MI6 officer on the run, suspected of trying to eliminate US Ambassador.

Why did they still think he was behind the attempted marathon attack? How could anyone interpret his actions that day as anything other than loyal? Only he and Leila knew what had happened out there on the streets of London, how he had come to be propping up Pradeep as they stumbled towards a deserted Tower Bridge. He wanted to talk to her now, go through the events again to find any ambiguities; and yet, for the first time since they had met, a new emotion had crept imperceptibly over the horizon.

Perhaps it was the change of continents, the physical separation that had been imposed on them. But he knew it wasn't that. They had been apart before. Again he asked himself, how could the Americans view his actions as suspicious, even through the warped prism of his father's guilt? Leila was the only other person who knew what had happened. Her explanation should have clarified his role, spared him the waterboard; but it hadn't, and he couldn't help resenting her for that.

Before his resentment grew into something more troubling, he realised that he was looking at it all from the wrong end. It didn't matter whether the Americans thought he was guilty or not. They *needed* him to be guilty, to damn the father through the son. And in order to do that they had either distorted the evidence, wilfully ignoring the debriefs, or the whole thing had been an elaborate set-up. That would explain why he and no one else had spotted the belt. He knew, though, that the Americans would be unlikely to sanction such a risky plan. Either way, Leila was the one person who could have proved his innocence. Why hadn't she cleared him?

He sat back in the taxi and closed his eyes. He hadn't had time to think since he had touched down in India, a land that was so full of conflicting memories for him. His arrival at Indira Gandhi airport late the night before had been much more stressful than he had expected. Passport control hadn't questioned his Irish passport or the tourist visa in the name of David Marlowe, but the security measures at the airport had surprised him. There had been police officers everywhere, randomly checking luggage. Outside, army trucks lined the main approach road to the city, soldiers sitting in the heat.

The scene reminded him of Heathrow in 2003, when Scimitar and Spartan reconnaissance vehicles had rolled in to guard the terminals. He had been an undergraduate in Cambridge at the time, and had read the chilling newspaper reports: it had been one of those exhilarating, self-affirming moments when he knew what he wanted to do with his life. If only he had acted on it then, been honest with himself and his father, rather than wasting years pretending he wanted to be a journalist, trying to do something – anything – other than follow in his father's footsteps.

For a moment at the airport, Marchant thought the Indians had been tipped off about his arrival, but then he discovered the reason for the heightened security. According to a newspaper stand, the US President was due to arrive in Delhi in four days' time. Marchant felt a surge of unease at the news, at the thought of Salim Dhar being in the same country at the same time. The visit was part of a four-country tour of the subcontinent. Arms deals would be signed between Washington and Delhi in a bid to shore up India's defences against China.

The capital had set about cleaning its streets and white-washing its walls in febrile anticipation of the visit. The road from the airport to the Maurya Hotel, where the President's entourage would be staying, was being transformed into a corridor of cleanliness. The city of Agra was also sprucing itself up. Thousands of litres of cheap perfume had been reportedly emptied into the Jamuna

195

river, beside the Taj Mahal, in an effort to reduce the smell of the city's effluent. Tigers, too, had been corralled into a corner of Ranthambore wildlife sanctuary to ensure a presidential sighting. Marchant knew he did not have long to find Dhar.

After collecting his tatty rucksack from the luggage carousel, Marchant had taken a deep breath and walked out of the arrivals hall into a wall of heat, knowing that, as a backpacker, he wouldn't have the budget for a taxi. (The thousand US dollars given to him by Hugo Prentice was carefully split between his money belt and a purse strapped to his shin beneath his cotton trousers.)

A horde of shouting people, mostly in white *kurta* pyjamas, had jostled for his custom, tugging at his backpack, calling out snatches of German, French and Italian as well as English. He had eventually settled on a Sikh auto-rickshaw driver, for no other reason than that he was bigger and more dignified-looking than his rivals. After an early, unpromising stop for fuel, the driver smiled in the wonky rear-view mirror and drove down the main highway into New Delhi, turning to make inaudible remarks about American presidents.

On either side of the road, road sweepers pushed their straw brushes idly in the heat while painters daubed thick yellow emulsion on the railings that ran down the central reservation, removing shirts and saris that had been hung there to dry. Occasionally, parts of the road itself had been cordoned off for potholes to be filled and new tarmac laid, tribal women trailing damp rags on the big wheels of the steamrollers to keep them moist.

The rickshaw took Marchant all the way to Pahaganj, north of Connaught Place, where his *Rough Guide* promised cheap accommodation and the company of other backpackers. The Hare Krishna guesthouse wasn't exactly the Oki Doki, but with its permit room ('for quenching thirst') and rooftop restaurant overlooking the bazaar, it was perfect for David Marlowe. His flight from Poland, with a four-hour change at Dubai, had been tiring, and he slept deeply, despite the heat of the night and the rhythmic rattle of the ceiling fan.

Now, as he watched an orange sun set behind Qutb Minar, he knew his search for Salim Dhar must begin. He was wearing the least tatty clothes he could find in the rucksack, and he hoped that the taxi, an extravagance for David Marlowe, would not attract attention when he arrived at the Gymkhana Club.

As he was driven into town, the flow of traffic was busy on the other side of the road as commuters streamed out of the scrubbed-up city towards the suburbs. The sight of an elephant, ambling along in the slow lane, brought back memories of childhood birthdays at the high commission, always shared with Sebastian. He turned back to look at the animal, admiring the unrushed fall of its padded feet. An elephant used to be obligatory at expat parties, a telephone number for bookings written in chalk between its eyes. Children would be lifted up onto the unsteady palanquins to ride around the commission compound, thrilled and scared by the muscular sashay of their mount's huge haunches.

Marchant remembered the time he fell out of love with

the birthday elephant, or at least with the *mahouts* who brought them up from the slums by the river. He and Sebastian were sitting at the front of a gaggle of children, directly behind the *mahout*, when he saw the metal spike that had been driven deep into the animal's thick and bloodied neck. The *mahout* twisted the spike whenever he barked an order, desperate to assert his waning authority over the animal.

The Gymkhana Club felt as if it had been waning for the past hundred years. A *chowkidar* at the gate searched under the car with a mirror before waving them on. Marchant told the driver to wait for him in the car park to the side of the whitewashed Lutyens building, explaining that he might be back in five minutes, or maybe an hour. '*Koi baat nay*,' he replied, rocking his head gently from side to side before driving off.

Marchant paused beneath the large porch, catching the perfume of bougainvillea tumbling over the nearby perimeter wall. Above him, crows were roosting, their cries faintly eerie. He hadn't been here before, but his father often used to talk about the place. Under British rule it had been known as the Imperial Gymkhana Club, but the Imperial had been dropped after 1947, and now its tennis courts, Lady Willingdon swimming pool, library and bridge drives were for the exclusive use of Delhi's social elite, many of whom had waited thirty years to become a member.

Non-Indian guests were welcome, but Marchant remembered his father telling him of an unsettling custom at the bar that if a 'Britisher' bought a round of drinks, he couldn't expect the favour to be returned. Marchant's father had liked his Kalyani Black Label beer, but had found that the only way to quench his thirst was to keep standing rounds for everyone. Buying a drink solely for himself would have caused offence, and given that British diplomats often ventured to the Gymkhana Club to gauge the military's current level of hostility towards neighbouring Pakistan, a subject about which they were especially prickly, it was important to keep the members onside.

'I've come to talk to Kailash Malhotra,' Marchant said to the khaki-uniformed man at the colonnaded reception.

'*Colonel* Malhotra?' the man checked him.

Marchant nodded, taking in the colonial setting – high ceilings, the whiff of floor polish, a sign saying that 'bush' shirts were prohibited – as the man looked through a list on a clipboard. Marchant could detect cigar smoke coming from somewhere, and it took him a few moments to realise that a distant clinking sound was the noise of billiard balls colliding. Marchant would be back at his Wiltshire boarding school if he smelt boiled cabbage for dinner.

'He's playing bridge in the card room,' the man said finally.

'I thought they didn't get underway until eight.' Marchant had made a call earlier.

The man looked at Marchant's crumpled shirt for a moment, unable to conceal his disdain, then glanced at a large clock on the wall to his right. 'Right now they are having sundowners in the bar. Is he expecting you?'

'Yes. Could you tell him David Marlowe's here?'

Ten minutes later, Marchant was sitting opposite Colonel Malhotra in a corner of the bar, sipping a '*burra peg*' of Chivas Regal.

'When you were a naughty little boy – my God, you were so naughty – you used to call me "uncle",' the colonel said, laughing, one hand patting Marchant's knee. 'You can still call me uncle. Uncle K. It's the name your dear father always used.'

Marchant had only very distant memories of Uncle K: watching *Mother India* and other old Hindi movies on a Sunday afternoon at his house, where he and Sebastian would eat pistachio *kulfi* and be told off by their mother for complaining that it didn't taste like real ice cream. Uncle K used to sing along to all the songs, tears often streaming down his face. Afterwards, he would retire with Marchant's father to another part of the house and talk in low voices while his mother fielded the children.

When Monika had mentioned the name Malhotra at the airport, he couldn't be certain it was the Uncle K of his early childhood. It was only when the colonel had walked towards him in reception, open-armed, that Marchant knew for sure it was the same man. Now, as they talked, more memories came back: the discreet acceptance of a gift of Scotch brought over from Britain; the blunder-buss on the wall, once used for shooting tigers; the *touché* shaking of hands after cracking a gag; Uncle K's avuncular kindness when Sebastian was killed.

'Your father was very keen that you didn't grow up

200

resenting India because of the traffic accident,' he said. 'It could have happened anywhere.'

'He did a good job. It's great to be back.'

Marchant didn't tell him that he hadn't visited Delhi since they had left as a grieving family twenty years ago. He had backpacked through India in his year off, paving the way for David Marlowe, but he had made a point of travelling through the south, and then up into the Himalayas, consciously bypassing Delhi.

'I fear your mother never got back her health, though,' Uncle K said.

'No,' Marchant replied, but he was no longer listening. His attention had been distracted by a man who had walked up to the bar, briefcase in hand.

'I still feel bad about your father's funeral. It just wasn't possible.'

'No. Can we talk about our mutual friend?' Marchant asked, turning back to Uncle K. 'We might not have much time.'

'Tell me what you want to know.'

'Why did my father visit him?'

Uncle K paused, glancing around the bar. 'I tried to recruit him once, a couple of years back. I was called out of retirement especially, told the whole thing was deniable. There was some sympathy there, but his hatred of America? It was too much. We had to drop him.'

'Was my father trying to recruit him too?'

Uncle K lost his smile. 'There's something else you should know about Salim Dhar, but I'm not the person to tell you. It can only come from him.'

Marchant glanced again at the man at the bar, who was looking back at them. He was still holding his briefcase, gripping the handle too tightly.

'Can you show me around this place?' Marchant asked the colonel, interrupting him.

'What, now?'

'I need a bit of fresh air.' He gestured at the table next to him, where a brigadier was drawing on a large cigar.

'Of course,' Malhotra said, picking up on Marchant's anxiety. 'It's safe to talk here, I know them all,' he joked, nodding at the brigadier as he rose from his chair. 'They're all far too busy discussing today's hodgepodge with the cricket to listen to us. But why not? Let me show you round.'

Marchant knew they were too late when the man at the bar looked at them again. All he had time to do was duck.

29

It was Alan Carter's first visit to Legoland, but after the events in Poland, he knew it wouldn't be his last. Spiro had been recalled to Langley after he lost Daniel Marchant. The DCIA was furious. Carter had taken over, fast-tracked to the head of the National Clandestine Service, Europe. It was a personal success for him, but he also knew it was a victory for the new thinking that was sweeping through the Company as it tried to refocus on its core business of espionage, following the intelligence disasters of 9/11 and Iraq.

Carter had been present at the interrogation of KSM, and also of Zayn Abu Zubaida, the first of the big-name AQ detainees to be dunked. But waterboarding wasn't his style. Nor were the freelance deniables who made up the rendition teams. Carter had joined the Agency with a vulpine belief in espionage, that the best way to beat the enemy was to infiltrate its leadership, rather than drown a few hoods. Spiro used to tell him not to worry, that renditions should be judged not by whether they were right or wrong, but by what the President thought. And their former President had preferred not to know.

So when the backlash came, as Carter knew it would, he didn't feel so bad about having leaked details of Stare Kiejkuty to a few handpicked Washington journalists. And now, with a new President in office, he had no regrets at all about hastening Spiro's demise. Langley might have spared him if Carter had stopped Marchant's departure on an international flight out of Frederic Chopin airport. But Carter had said nothing, and Spiro sank.

Instead, he rang the CIA's station head in Delhi, then put in a call to Langley, recommending that Marchant was followed rather than pulled in when he reached India. Langley told him to talk to the Vicar. It was Carter's belief that the renegade MI6 officer would try to make contact with Salim Dhar, a far bigger prize for the CIA than Marchant. Then they could both be brought in; but he wouldn't tell Fielding that, not yet.

'We're not interested in Daniel Marchant,' Carter said, sipping a Bourbon. He was sitting opposite an upright Marcus Fielding in the dining room that adjoined the Vicar's spacious office. The place had style, he thought, more than he would have guessed from its unpromising location on a busy traffic junction. And he began to understand why they called Fielding the Vicar. Music was playing quietly in the background somewhere: Bach, maybe his second Brandenburg concerto. He even had his own butler, which struck him as very English (even if the butler wasn't), not to mention a fifty-something PA who wore red pantyhose.

'Spiro wanted Daniel Marchant's balls,' Fielding said. 'Is he suspended, or just taking a long holiday?'

'Let's call it a blood substitution.'

'It's never easy when one of your players is withdrawn from the field.'

Carter looked at him for a moment. 'Marchant was good, I know that. It wouldn't have been my call.'

'Nor mine. What about Leila? Was that Spiro too? Did he recruit her personally?'

'Of course. And I have similar regrets about her.'

'Don't we all. Where is she now?'

'New Delhi station.'

'I thought she was Spiro's asset. The Agency's planning on keeping her, then?'

'She may prove useful if Marchant forgets the script.'

'I'm assuming Spiro asked her to set Marchant up,' Fielding said. 'Handing him his old TETRA phone during the race.'

'I'm afraid I don't know the exact details of her recruitment or her role within the Agency, Marcus. Let's just say her debrief with Spiro after the marathon included some very leading questions.'

'She told him what he wanted to hear, in other words. That Daniel was as guilty as his father.' Fielding paused. 'For the record, who made the first move? Spiro or Leila?'

Carter had been told to take the rap for the Leila operation, but he hadn't expected someone so apparently cerebral as Fielding to come over all emotional. He was starting to ask questions a husband would put to his cheating wife.

'Spiro was on the lookout for someone close to Daniel Marchant,' he said, hoping to move on.

'Moscow rules?'

'Money. Her mother wasn't in the best of health, needed expensive medication. And we're very keen to support people like Leila's mother. She's a Bahá'í, one of the persecuted good guys in Iran.'

'And you trust Leila?'

'You obviously did. I've read the reports. Copper-bottomed. Only problem was, your vetters never figured her mother had moved back to Iran. Of course Leila should have told you, but she feared for her job. Spiro found out, used it as leverage when he recruited her.'

Carter didn't want to fall out with Fielding. That wasn't why he had come. He'd been keen to meet a man who enjoyed something approaching the status of a legend at Langley. Fielding was a very different kind of spy from Stephen Marchant. A fellow believer in espionage, he had the intellectual arrogance shared by all the MI6 officers Carter had ever met, but he had unquestionable form, too: Fielding had helped them to talk Muammar Gaddafi out of his nuclear ambitions, drawing on his enviable knowledge of the Arab world to defuse a delicate situation. If only their previous President had deployed the same tactics with Saddam Hussein.

'Does our profession ever surprise you, Alan?' Fielding asked. He had stood up from the table, and was now looking out of the buttressed bay window, his back to Carter. A couple of staff were taking a cigarette break on the open terrace below, the Union flag billowing above them.

'Every day.'

'It often appalled Stephen. He despised the people he turned, the people who made his reputation. Loyalty was something he valued higher than anything, which made traitors the lowest of the low, even if they were betraying the enemy.'

Carter stood up to join Fielding at the window. Outside, in the dark London night, the lights of a passing party boat sparkled on the Thames. It was nearly midnight. Legoland, like Langley, never slept. Up on the roof, the array of aerials and satellite dishes Carter had seen from Vauxhall Bridge linked the building with every time zone in the world.

'Shall I tell you why I think Stephen took that flight to Kerala?' Carter asked.

'Please.'

'He went out there because I think in Salim Dhar he saw what we're all after: a senior AQ operative who might just be turned. Sure, we could have brought him in, knocked him about a bit in a remote detention site, found out what he did or didn't know on the water-board. That's what Spiro wanted. But Stephen Marchant had other ideas.'

'To be honest, I think he just wanted a name – the name of the mole in MI6 who had been making his life a misery.'

207

'Come on, Marcus, he wanted much more, you know that. He wanted his own man high up in AQ.'

Carter had read all the files on Stephen Marchant, and knew that one of his biggest regrets was that MI6 had never infiltrated Al Qaeda on his watch. He was a Chief, after all, who had built a brilliant career on penetrating Dzerzhinsky Square, in the days when intelligence officers didn't dunk the enemy, they blackmailed them with sordid photographs taken in seedy motel rooms. Far more civilised.

'It became an obsession for him, didn't it?' Carter continued. 'Someone on the inside. Particularly after 9/11. But we were going the other way. Round them all up rather than recruit them. It's why the Company grew so suspicious of MI6. We thought you'd fallen asleep at the switch. What were you all doing, for God's sake?'

'Finding the intelligence to justify your wars,' Fielding said.

'But you weren't beating up the bullies. Americans are a very simple people at heart. Somebody hurts us, we want to hurt them back. Publicly. It's not subtle. And we sometimes hurt back the wrong people. It also puts those of us who believe in more covert methods out of a job.'

'Salim Dhar would never work for the Agency.'

'I realise that.'

'So why do you think you might be able to turn him?'

'I don't. But he might respond to a British approach.'

'Why?'

'You tell me. Stephen Marchant knew something.' Fielding walked away from the window, one hand on the small of his back.

'Do you mind if I lie down?' he asked.

'Go ahead,' Carter said. He had heard about the Vicar's back problems. 'Lower lumbar?'

'All over.'

Carter watched as the Chief of MI6 calmly lay down on the floor of his dining-room suite, seemingly unaware of the figure he cut. Or perhaps he just didn't care.

'Do go on,' Fielding said from the floor, but the wind had been taken from Carter's sails. Had Fielding known what he was about to say?

'Salim Dhar's father worked in the American Embassy compound in the early 1980s,' Carter continued, not sure where to address his comments. Looking down didn't feel appropriate. 'After he'd been sacked by your high commission. We've run some checks. It seems that someone was conduiting him a little bit of extra pocket money every month.'

Carter became aware of some activity outside the dining room, where his lady in red was working late.

'The money came via one State Bank of Travancore in South India,' Carter continued. 'At least, it was meant to look that way. Seems like the rupees might have started life as greenbacks in the Cayman Islands. Or maybe even sterling in London.' He paused. 'I've got only one question, Marcus. Why were the Brits paying a salary to Dhar's father?'

'The payments stopped in 2001,' Fielding said calmly, his eyes closed.

'Twenty-one years after he'd quit working for your high commission.'

It should have been a bombshell, enough to make the British hand over Daniel Marchant, but the Vicar couldn't have seemed less troubled.

'We only discovered the payments ourselves a few days ago.'

'Let's hope it's just you and me who know, then.' Carter was suddenly annoyed that Fielding had managed to defuse his story by the simple ploy of lying on the floor. It had the effect of belittling everything he said. 'I hate to think what Lord Bancroft would make of one of the world's most wanted terrorists drawing down an MI6 salary.'

'While you were funding a generation of mujahideen in Afghanistan.'

'That was Spiro too, as it happens.'

'We really don't know where Daniel Marchant is,' Fielding said. Outside the dining room, voices were getting more agitated.

'We do.'

'He needs to be left to find Salim Dhar. And with the greatest respect for your people's tradecraft, he's not going to do that with a ten-strong surveillance team on his case.'

'I'm offering you a deal, Marcus. We keep quiet about the Cayman trust fund and let Marchant find Dhar, but when he does, we share the debrief.'

'You're assuming that Dhar will talk to him?'

'Aren't you?'

Carter knew that he was. MI6 must be staking everything on it. The discovery of the payments would have changed everything. Salim Dhar really might be one of theirs, one of Stephen Marchant's most breathtakingly prescient signings. More likely he just got lucky. No one had seen Islamic terrorism coming in the 1980s. Dhar must have been a punt, one of the many people signed up by intelligence agencies around the world on the off-chance of coming good later. But in Dhar, Marchant had come up trumps, one of those breaks that happened once in a career. Would he have risked running him, though? Dhar's track record of violence against the Americans would have made him a high-risk asset, particularly when the CIA was leading calls for Marchant to stand down as Chief.

Carter paced around the room, finding it easier to look at Fielding's long, supine figure from different angles. 'You don't have to tell me if it was Stephen Marchant who personally authorised those payments, but I'm working on a wild guess here that it was. I'm also jumping to the crazy conclusion that you don't know if all that money was well invested or not, which god Dhar prays to at night. From a ringside seat, it doesn't look too good.'

Fielding's eyes remained shut.

'He has, however, only ever targeted Americans, which must give you people hope that he has the good manners not to bite the hand that fed him for the first twenty-one years of his life. And if that's the case, there's only one person he might possibly trust to run him: Stephen Marchant's son, Daniel. We want some of that, Marcus. Salim Dhar could be the best penetration of AQ the West has ever had.'

211

There was a pause, Carter's words hanging in the air, followed by a knock on the dining-room door.

'Come,' Fielding called out.

'I'm sorry,' Anne Norman began, glancing at Carter, then back to her boss on the floor. 'We've just had Delhi station on the line. There's been a bomb at the Gymkhana Club.'

30

Leila took it as a very public expression of gratitude that the CIA had assigned her to its team in Delhi who were liaising with the Secret Service in advance of the US President's visit to the city. One of the agents had heard first-hand from a colleague at the London embassy about her role during the London Marathon, an event that seemed to have sealed her reputation as a player. 'Though Turner Munroe never did get his fancy running watch back,' he had joked on her arrival in Delhi that morning. 'Good to have you on board.'

Neither side was calling it a defection, but relations had sunk so low between Britain's and America's intelligence communities that Leila had been told to treat officers from MI6's Delhi station with the same caution as she would those from more traditionally hostile countries such as Iran and Russia. The paperwork called it a three-month exchange, but she knew there was no chance of her ever working – or living – in Britain again. She told herself that she had always preferred life abroad, and it was true that the sense of not being rooted anywhere was not a new one.

As she looked out of her room in the American Embassy, taking in the yellow of the laburnum trees lining the roads of Chanakyapuri, she forced herself not to think about Daniel, whether they would ever see each other again. For the past two years she had known that the day would come when she would have to confront the choices she had made in her life. Those choices had become much harder in recent months, but that day had not arrived. Not yet. For the time being she was able to keep his photo face-downwards on the table, to consign their life together to another place, where it could be guarded by the traditional sentinels of the spy's conscience: if you live the lie, expect to be deceived, just as he had warned.

In those rare moments when her guard did drop, she could console herself that honesty of a kind had played its part, despite the deceptions. Her mother's welfare had always been paramount in her life. She just wished she had been asked to get close to someone else, rather than a man she was struggling not to fall in love with.

Earlier that day, after an introductory meeting with her new colleagues, she had slipped out of the embassy compound and walked through the 40-degree heat of the May morning to a taxi rank. She had seen a public phone booth there when her car from the airport had driven past at dawn. As she dialled the number in Tehran, she glanced across at the taxi drivers, lying on string *charpoys* in the shade of a large canvas canopy, limbs hung listlessly as they listened to All India Radio blaring out from a nearby car, its doors flung open.

'Mama,' she began. The line was faint. 'It's Leila. Things will be better soon.'

But it wasn't her mother's voice that replied. 'Your mother's in hospital,' a man said in Farsi. Leila's stomach tightened. For the past year her mother had been in and out of the Mehr, a private hospital in Tehran, her treatment paid for by the Americans. Each time the doctors had prepared her for the worst. Normally, though, her neighbour had sent a text to tell her that she had been admitted to hospital.

'Who is this?' she asked. His voice sounded familiar.

'A friend of the family,' the man said. She could hear other male voices in the background. 'She's fine and, *inshallah*, will have the best treatment dollars can buy.' The mocking tone was thinly disguised, his words addressed to the others in the room with him.

'I want her looked after, that was always the deal,' Leila said, trying not to raise her voice. A man outside the telephone booth glanced up at her. She knew she should be at her mother's bedside, but that was impossible.

'I will tell her you called,' the voice said, then paused. 'And that her health rests in your hands.'

The sun was at its highest as she walked back towards the embassy. In the distance, an unseen nutseller was rattling his spoon rhythmically against a frying pan.

Otherwise there was a stillness in the midday air. Even the traffic police at the junction near the embassy had retreated to the shade, where they snoozed on flimsy wooden chairs. She had never minded dry heat. It somehow made her feel closer to her mother, who she knew needed her now more than ever.

She had just turned nine when she first sensed that all was not well between her parents. They were living in the expat community in Dubai, where her father was working, and he had come home late, as he often did. But this time she was awake. There had been a problem with the electricity in their apartment block – there was not enough power to run the air conditioning, and the sudden warmth had woken her. One of the staff had placed an old fan in the room and she lay there mesmerised by the way it turned as far as it could one way, before sweeping back in the other direction. But above its hum she gradually became aware of shouting downstairs, and then screaming, followed by slammed doors and silence.

She had found her mother curled up in a corner of the kitchen, their Indian maid holding a bloodied cloth to her forehead. Her mother smiled weakly when she saw Leila, but the maid gestured crossly for her to go back upstairs.

'It's OK,' her mother had said, beckoning Leila towards her. She walked tentatively across the kitchen and sat down beside her mother, watched anxiously by the maid. 'It's OK,' her mother repeated, putting a shaking arm around Leila as the maid retreated.

They must have stayed like that for most of the night, hunched together on the marble floor in the heat of a Dubai night, the weak yellow lights flickering. Her mother explained how her father was under a lot of stress at work and sometimes drank too much whisky, hoping that it would make him feel better. But it just made him angry, and when he was angry he wasn't himself, and did silly things.

In the years that followed, Leila and her mother learnt to be out of the way when he was not himself, but Leila knew that he continued to vent his whisky-fuelled fury on his wife. Not even a *burqa* could disguise the black eyes. Her father's long hours and frequent trips abroad meant that she had always been closer to her mother than to him, but his violence bonded them further, uniting them in a mixture of shame and solidarity. She had never forgotten that night, the sight of her mother crying, and could never forgive her father, whose light in her life went out.

All she could do now, slumped on the floor of her bare embassy room, was to fulfil her side of the deal and hope that the voices at the end of the phone in Tehran would honour theirs. But before she could think what that deal might bring, the evening stillness was split by a sound that she knew at once was not thunder.

31

Marchant felt the weight of a body lying on top of him, but he didn't realise it was Uncle K until he tried to move out from under his heavy frame. Other people were stirring on the bar floor all around him. For a moment, in the dark silence, Marchant was back at the marketplace in Mogadishu. But then the moaning started, guttural cries of primitive pain, and he remembered the quicksilver shards dicing the air, the compression, the chilling cacophony of disintegrating glass.

'Uncle K, are you OK?' Marchant asked, trying to shut out the sweet smell of cauterised flesh. It was a smell he hated more than any other, one that had never left him. Now, five years later, the same nagging thoughts were suddenly back once again: could he have done more about the man at the bar?

He was kneeling beside Uncle K now, checklisting his own body as he spoke. He put a hand briefly to his face, touching warm blood as he bent over the colonel. The old man's features were still intact, the plump, putty-faced cheeks and pursed, rosebud mouth, but the angle of his lower body was too jack-knifed for a seventy-year-old.

Marchant looked at the debris all around him, the lights torn from the ceiling, the upturned tables, shredded curtains. He saw a plastic bottle of mineral water on the floor, a few feet away from him. Reaching over, he dribbled some onto the colonel's dusty lips, spitting grit out of his own mouth. Slowly, the colonel's lips began to move. Marchant leant closer, cupping one hand behind his head.

'You must go,' the colonel whispered. 'They will try to blame you for this.'

'Who will?'

But the colonel had lost consciousness again. Marchant put the bottle to his mouth, spilling water over his lips and chin. Blood was seeping now from the corner of his mouth. The colonel opened his eyes, coughing feebly.

'You must go,' he urged. 'Om Beach, near Gokarna. Ask for . . .' The next word was lost in the blood and saliva. '. . . brother Salim at the Namaste Café.'

'Leila, I want you to get down to the club and slip inside the cordon, assuming the Delhi police have put one up. It's usually a free-for-all at these things. They might do Golden Temples, but crime-scene golden hours? Give me a break.'

A ripple of polite laughter moved around the room as

219

Monk Johnson, head of the Presidential Protective Detail, addressed a room of ten officers, a mix of Secret Service and CIA. Behind him, a large TV screen was showing library footage from NDTV of the Gymkhana Club before the blast. Cameras had yet to reach the scene. Leila had been tempted to head out into the Delhi evening as soon as she heard the explosion, but she had been summoned to the meeting within minutes. The station was already on a state of high alert: in seventy-two hours the new President of the United States would be flying in to Palam military airbase, five miles from Delhi, as part of his four-country tour of South Asia.

'I've just come off the phone to the Director of the Secret Service,' Johnson continued. 'He says POTUS is adamant the tour is still on. The best we can do is buy ourselves a little time: the Islamabad leg could be brought forward, but the Indians won't like it – they've insisted all along that they go first. They tested their nukes before Pakistan, and they want to make damn sure they're the first to shake the new President's hand.'

'You're assuming this is a Pak thing, right?' asked David Baldwin, head of the CIA's Delhi station. He was sitting behind Leila.

'You tell us. It's got to be an option. The Gymkhana Club is a colonial hangover, full of army brass.'

'First up is Salim Dhar. General Casey was due to go there tonight, but cancelled.'

'Thank God,' Johnson said.

'Vivek?' Baldwin said, ignoring Johnson.

'Dhar's exact location on the grid is still to be

220

confirmed, sir,' Vivek Kumar said, 'but it has all his hall-marks, particularly if Casey was the target.'

Leila had already been introduced to Kumar as a fellow newcomer. One of the Agency's brightest analysts, he had been flown in from Langley earlier in the week, and knew more than anyone about Salim Dhar. He knew all about Daniel Marchant, too. Marchant, he said, had left Poland and was already somewhere in India.

'Widespread military collateral, high-profile US target,' Kumar continued. 'We can't rule out Daniel Marchant either. Right now, that whole situation's a little compli-cated. He's just become the subject of an ongoing level-five covert run by Clandestine, Europe.'

'Tell me about it,' Baldwin said, glancing at Leila. 'I'm speaking to Alan Carter in ten.'

'OK, let's re-meet in two hours,' Johnson said. 'Unless another bomb goes off. What's wrong with Texas? Why can't POTUS go there and shake a few hands?'

Marchant didn't know who he was fleeing from as he picked his way through the wreckage of the bar and climbed out of a large broken window. It went against every instinct to leave Colonel K, but there had been an urgency to his voice that persuaded Marchant to leave.

He stumbled across the lawn, still dazed, glancing back at the wounded building, curtains lolling from its windows like lacerated tongues. No one could blame him. The Gymkhana Club reception would confirm that a respected Indian colonel had signed him in. But Uncle K was an old friend of his father. He was also travelling as David Marlowe, not Daniel Marchant. Uncle K was right. Daniel was on the run, and once his presence at the club had been discovered, his name would be in the frame. If he could be blamed for the marathon, they would try to pin this one on him too. He thought of the look the man at the bar had given him, purposefully catching his eye. Who was he? Who had sent him?

Marchant had walked through an unmanned side gate and was now on a main road, but the traffic was not as noisy as it should have been. He could barely hear a passing goods lorry, its horn eerily muted. It was then that he realised his ears were resonating with a high-pitched tone that didn't stop when he shook his head. He looked back towards the club building again, black smoke threading up into the Delhi sky. A rickshaw slowed, its driver eyeing him with a mixture of hope and wariness. Marchant slumped into the back seat and asked for Gokarna.

'Gokarna?' the driver asked, smiling in the rear mirror as he throttled the tiny two-stroke engine. 'Too far, sir, even for Shiva. Airport?'

'Railway station.'

'Gymkhana, firework problem?'

Marchant nodded, gripping the side bar of the rickshaw to stop his hand shaking. 'Big problem,' he said. On the opposite side of the road, a diplomatic car drove past at speed. Marchant turned back to look at the blue number-plate. It was American. For a moment he thought he recognised the female figure in the back of the car.

32

'Can we assume that Marchant was at the club?' Fielding asked, off the floor and back sitting upright at the dining-room table.

'It's a Wednesday night,' Denton said, glancing at the flat screen mounted on the wall. It was now relaying Sky images of a burning Gymkhana Club. 'We've spoken to Warsaw. Bridge night was all he had to go on.'

'Are you saying you knew where Marchant was?' Alan Carter asked. He had joined them again after stepping outside the Chief's office to make a couple of calls to Langley. At Fielding's request, Anne Norman had reluctantly connected him on a secure line.

'I thought you knew too,' Fielding replied.

'We knew he was in India.'

'He was to make contact with a colonel who used to work in Indian intelligence. Kailash Malhotra, former

223

number two at RAW. He played in a bridge drive at the Gymkhana on Wednesday nights.'

'I'm sorry,' Carter said. 'The DCIA wants Marchant brought in. I've just spoken to his office. He'll be patched through shortly on the secure video link.'

'I thought you were more interested in Dhar.'

'We are. But we've also got our new President flying into Delhi Saturday.'

'We must let Marchant find Dhar.'

'The timing of this bomb couldn't be worse, Marcus. I'm not going to be able to hold the hawks back if Marchant was at the club. Spiro isn't completely out of the picture. The Director and him go way back. It's a Marines thing. After this, Spiro will be telling him to go after Dhar with everything we've got. And it's hard not to agree with him.'

'Except that you don't know where Dhar is.'

'But the colonel did. He could have told us, told you, saved a lot of time, a lot of lives.' Carter glanced again at the TV screen. Burnt and blistered bodies were being lined up beneath the club's Lutyens porch.

'He would never have told us,' Fielding said. 'Our relationship with Delhi is better than yours, but Dhar's an embarrassment to them. RAW tried to recruit him once.'

'But he was happy to tell Marchant of Dhar's whereabouts.'

'We hoped he might be. He was once very close to his father. But we don't know what he said. Right now, we don't even know if Marchant and Malhotra are alive.'

Carter paused. 'It doesn't look great, does it? Daniel

Marchant, suspected of trying to kill the US Ambassador in London, now at the scene of a bomb blast in Delhi, three days before the President arrives there.'

'Except that you and I both know that Daniel Marchant wasn't behind either of those incidents.'

'He just happened to be present at both. I'm losing my nerve here, Marcus. Remind me why Marchant's on our side?'

'Because he's being set up. And if it's not by you, then someone's got us both by the balls.'

'What makes you so certain?'

'I knew Stephen Marchant. And I know Daniel. If he's still alive, he'll make contact with Dhar.'

'Who's walking around Delhi blowing up clubs.'

'This wasn't Dhar, Alan. Trust me on this one. Whoever planted this bomb was after Marchant.'

There was a knock on the door, and Anne Norman's head appeared. She looked straight at Fielding, ignoring Carter. 'Sir, I've got Langley on the line. The DCIA's ready to join you.'

'Screen two,' Fielding said. 'Thank you, Anne.'

'Mind if I take the lead on this one?' Carter said as she closed the door.

'He's all yours,' Fielding said. William Straker, Director of the CIA, flickered into life on a screen next to the one that showed a smouldering Gymkhana Club.

Daniel remembered the red-shirted porters from his last visit to India, when he had travelled the length and breadth of the subcontinent by rail. But he had never seen so many of them before, bobbing through the crowded concourse of Nizamuddin station with suitcases on their scarved heads, sweating, sometimes smiling, always shouting, followed by anxious tourists trying to keep up. For once, nobody pestered him. Porters approached and then melted away, clocking that the *farangi* had no bags. Or was it the blood and soot on his clothes? They probably thought he was a drug addict, one of the many Westerners who end up begging on the streets of India for enough money to fly home.

He had washed as best he could when the rickshaw dropped him off at the entrance to the station, buying some bottled water at a food stand on the main concourse. It had been the right decision to come straight there, rather than try to pick up his rucksack from the guesthouse. His room would have been searched and ransacked by now. Marlowe's passport and money were strapped safely to his leg. He would buy new clothes when he was safely out of Delhi. His ticket, third-class, to Karwar, near Gokarna, was in his pocket. All he had to do now was find platform 18, where the Mangala Express to Ernakulam would be leaving in half an hour, twelve hours behind schedule, which wasn't so bad for a seventy-seven-hour journey.

As he made his way across the concourse, stepping over sleeping bodies and broken clay *chai* cups, he became aware of a commotion ahead of him, alongside a train that seemed to stretch forever in both directions. Two Western backpackers, both of them young women, were being harangued by an Indian businessman. Marchant slipped into the large crowd that had gathered to watch.

'How dare you come to our country wearing your next-to-nothings and skimpy whatnots, and complain that our men are Eve-teasers,' the businessman was saying shrilly. The argument appeared to have been running for several minutes.

'The guy pinched my bloody arse,' the younger of the two women said. Marchant detected a faint Australian accent, adopted rather than native, as he glanced at her figure. What little clothing she was wearing wouldn't have looked out of place on a caged go-go dancer. The elder woman was dressed more modestly. Marchant pushed through the crowd, sensing an opportunity. The cover of travelling in a group would be useful. The women were trapped. When the elder of them told the other one that they should go, the crowd pressed together, preventing them from moving. 'Out of my way, will you?' the woman said, panic rising in her voice. 'I need to get on this train. Hey, stop it! Get off me!'

'*Kareeb khade raho*,' the businessman barked as the crowd pressed against the women. 'Close in, close in. We keep them here until the police arrive. These Western harlots must be taught a lesson.'

'*Kya problem, hai?*' Marchant said as he reached the businessman. 'Is there a problem?' He could smell alcohol on his breath.

'And who are you?'

'They're travelling with me,' Marchant said, glancing at the two women, who were now visibly frightened. Something in his eyes must have told them that he was on their side.

227

'So you must be their pimp.'

'Kind of,' Marchant said, resisting the temptation to punch him. 'We've just come from filming the new Shah Rukh Khan movie,' he said, his voice loud enough to be heard by the crowd. Marchant was thinking quickly. While waiting for Uncle K to meet him at the reception of the Gymkhana Club, he had read in the *Hindustan Times* how the US President had hoped to visit a Bollywood film set while he was in India, but his itinerary was preventing it. Shah Rukh Khan was making a film at the Red Fort in Delhi, a joint production with a Western company. The star had extended a personal invitation to the President to watch the filming while he was in town.

'Shah Rukh?' one of the crowd asked excitedly.

'Sure. We were only extras, though,' Marchant said.

'Did you meet him? My God, you met him, didn't you?' said another member of crowd. 'He met Shah Rukh!'

'Only to say hello to,' Marchant continued, looking at the businessman, who clearly didn't believe a word of what he was hearing. But the less educated crowd, as Marchant had hoped, was already beginning to turn.

'What was he like?' someone else called out. 'Did you hear him sing?'

'No, we didn't hear him sing. They add the soundtracks later, you know. But we did see him dance.'

'With Aishwarya? Did you see her dance, too?'

'Of course. We were in a large fight scene, playing dirty, filthy Westerners of low moral standing. And I apologise for our appearance now. We had no time to change. The sooner we can board this train the better, then we can dispose of these offensive garments.' Marchant turned towards the two women. 'Follow me towards the train as soon as the crowd starts to back off,' he told them quietly.

'How can you prove this fanciful story?' the businessman asked, as Marchant put his head down and made for a carriage door. The crowd, as he had calculated, started to part for the Westerners, ignoring the businessman, who found himself being carried away in the tide of people. 'And why didn't these two women mention any of this before?' he called out after them.

Marchant let the two women climb up into the carriage first, then followed them, before turning to wave to the crowd.

'You're not fooling anyone,' the businessman persisted, pushing his way to the edge of the platform. Marchant was aware that the public scene he had created needed to end quickly. The police would arrive soon, questions would be asked, statements taken. Up until now he had avoided using force, hoping to defuse rather than exacerbate the situation. But the businessman had a doggedness about him that troubled Marchant.

'Drugs only deceive yourself, my friend,' the businessman said. 'You don't fool me.'

'I know I don't,' Marchant said, leaning down towards him, his mouth close to the man's ear. 'But what I do know is that if you try to come after us, or talk to the police, or identify us to anyone, I'll personally break your neck, just like Shah Rukh does in the film.'

33

In another life, a different time, Marcus Fielding and William Straker might have been close. American intelligence officers everywhere had cheered when Straker was appointed Director of the CIA. He was a spy's spy, a HUMINT man through and through, rising to head the Agency's Clandestine Service before taking over as its Director. His appointment had softened the blow of the CIA suddenly finding itself answerable to a higher authority, the new Director of National Intelligence. But working for a DNI suited Straker fine. It helped to deflect some of the unwanted publicity.

Not many clandestines made it to the top of a bureaucracy as big as the CIA. Straker was good for the spy's soul at a time when Congress was questioning the Agency's very existence. And his Marines background played well with the paramilitaries, too. He was less popular in London. Straker had personally led the drive to remove Stephen Marchant, which, given Fielding's loyalty to his predecessor, made for a far from special relationship between the two intelligence chiefs.

But Fielding had been suspicious of Straker long before he helped to remove Marchant. He knew that they should have been allies rather than antagonists. Straker couldn't be more different from the previous Director, a showman who had somehow emerged from the harsh, post-9/11 spotlight as a celebrity clandestine, savouring the international limelight before retirement and memoirs. Straker was different, more like the British. He had always preferred the penumbral. And as such he was a greater threat to the Service, because he played by the same rules.

'Sirs,' Straker said, his manner drilled, precise. 'There's not a lot of time. One of our top generals was almost killed tonight. I need to know everything we have on the Gymkhana blast. Was Marchant involved?'

Red lights on three small cameras, mounted on a terminal in the centre of the table, glowed discreetly. Carter glanced at Fielding, who nodded and then looked up at the video screen. 'Sir, as you know, Marchant's become the subject of a level-five covert. MI6 think he was at the club, but that he wasn't responsible.'

'I thought you'd say that. Just like he wasn't trying to take out Munroe. Marcus?'

'Will, I know how this must appear, but we're convinced Marchant's being set up here.'

'Not by us he isn't,' Straker said.

Fielding read the subtext – Leila hadn't been used by the Americans to frame Marchant – and ignored it. To look at, Straker reminded Fielding of one of the thickset rugby players his college at Cambridge used to admit, the promise of an impressive performance on the field outweighing any academic shortcomings off it. Only he knew that Straker was the sharpest officer of his generation. Both fluent Arabic-speakers (Straker spoke Russian and Urdu too), their paths had crossed when he and Fielding had talked Gaddafi out of his nuclear ambitions. For a while there had been a healthy intellectual rivalry between the two of them, until Langley claimed all the credit for castrating Gaddafi.

But what bothered Fielding now was the knowledge that the Leila plan would have been personally signed off by Straker, even if it had been Spiro's operation. A line was supposed to have been drawn after Stephen Marchant's resignation, but relations between the CIA and MI6 had remained resolutely sour.

'I've got POTUS touching down in Delhi in seventy-two,' Straker said, 'and right now I need a very good reason not to bring Marchant in and lean hard on the Indians to take Dhar out.'

'It would be better to let Marchant find him first,' Fielding said coolly. He didn't care for Straker's bullying impatience.

'I appreciate that's an option, Marcus. It's why I pulled Spiro and put Alan there in charge. But I was hoping Marchant would lead us to Dhar, not try to take out General Casey at the Gymkhana Club.'

'We think Dhar might be a potential asset,' Carter said, glancing at Fielding, who was happy for him to

232

take the lead. Since the discovery of the payments to the Dhar family, Fielding had been wondering how to break the bad news to the Americans. Letting one of their own be the messenger seemed as good a solution as any.

'An asset? Am I missing something here? Right now, Salim Dhar's our new Ace of Spades.'

'Sir, we think he could be turned.' Carter looked back again nervously. Fielding gave the discreetest of nods.

'Is that right?'

'MI6 have turned up some interesting CX on Dhar,' Carter continued.

'Will, we think he might be one of ours,' Fielding said, acknowledging Carter, who had drawn enough of the Director's fire. He would take it up from here.

'You think?'

'Stephen Marchant set up a retainer for his family back in 1980, when he was posted to Delhi.'

'Christ, Marcus, why didn't you mention this sooner?'

Fielding pointedly ignored the question. 'Monthly payments to his father, following his dismissal from the British High Commission.'

'Didn't he once work at our embassy?'

'For a number of years, yes.'

'So why was Marchant paying him? Dhar was just a kid.'

'I know.' It was the one question Fielding didn't have an answer to.

'But you think this makes Dhar a good guy, rather than confirming our worst fears about Stephen Marchant? Forgive the Monday-morning quarterbacking, but from our point of view this doesn't exactly look like asset cash well spent: two US Embassy attacks, the London Marathon.'

'No one's saying he's ours, sir,' Carter said. 'But we think he might be persuaded to work for the British.'

'And Daniel Marchant is the only person who can find out,' Fielding added. 'Dhar would be the highest ranking member of AQ the West has ever run. We'd be prepared to pool on this one.'

There was another pause, and for a moment Fielding thought the link with Langley had dropped. But he knew the plan would appeal to the clandestine streak that ran deep in the Director.

'I can't have Marchant and Dhar running around India when the President arrives. The DNI just wouldn't buy it. And I wouldn't blame him.' He paused again. 'You've got twenty-four to figure out which side Dhar's on, then we're bringing them both in.'

The two women, Kirsty and Holly, had tickets for three-tier A/C on the Mangala Express, which was considerably more comfortable than Marchant's bare-benched economy carriage. Their entire compartment was open plan, but it was loosely divided up into separate areas by curtains. The lights had already been turned down, even though Delhi was only an hour behind them, and the atmosphere was like that of a well-behaved school dormitory, a faint murmur of snoring rising above the rattle of the wheels. Marchant's carriage, by contrast, was a seething mass of people who were clearly intent on eating, burping and arguing all the way to Kerala, 1,500 miles south. There were no beds, just hard wooden seats.

The two women's area consisted of a pair of three-tier bunks facing each other. They were sleeping on the top two bunks, and a Keralan family, with one child, occupied the lower decks. The bunk directly below Holly was empty, and it was on this that Marchant was now lying, talking up to Kirsty.

'You can stay there the night, if you want to,' she said, glancing across at Holly. 'She's already asleep. There were three of us, but Holly and Anya had a bit of a falling out, so Anya stayed in Delhi. You're on her bed.'

'I'll see if the ticket guy'll upgrade me,' Marchant said. He could hear the inspector making his way down the carriage. Earlier, a member of staff had eyed him suspiciously while he distributed sheets and blankets around the carriage.

Holly and Kirsty, both English and in their early twenties, were going to Goa. They were on a six-month world tour and had been travelling in India for two weeks. Holly, the younger one, was already at war with the subcontinent, railing at its food, the weather, the men, her bowel movements and the state of the public lavatories, before falling asleep. The argument at the station had clearly exhausted her. Kirsty had a more relaxed manner, and was obsessed with neither the weather nor her bowels. Something about her laid-back approach to life reminded Marchant of Monika, and they had immediately hit it off.

'D'you hear that?' Kirsty asked, nodding down the carriage. Marchant listened as someone protested about not being allowed to stay in an empty seat. The inspector explained about waiting lists, three-month advance bookings, the police. Marchant's and Kirsty's eyes met.

'Quick, come up here. You can hide under my blanket.'

Marchant looked below him. The man from Kerala, an engineer who had earlier given him his business card, was snoring. The woman was also sleeping, but the toddler, who was cradled next to her, had his big brown eyes open and was staring up at him. Marchant smiled, putting a finger to his lips. 'Sshhh,' he said, stretching his leg across onto the edge of the opposite bunk, where the Keralan family had stowed some of their luggage. Then he heaved himself up onto the narrow top bunk. Kirsty giggled as she shuffled across to the edge, trying to make some room for Marchant beside the wall.

'They're tiny, these beds,' Marchant whispered, feeling her body warmth as he pulled the wool blanket over him. Its coarseness reminded him of school.

'The man's coming,' Kirsty said, pulling her rucksack up from her feet to provide a screen. Marchant lay still, listening out for the ticket collector. He heard him stir the family below as Kirsty reached across to wake Holly.

When the inspector had gone, Marchant stayed where he was for a few moments, lulled by the carriage's rhythmic motion. The last time he had been on a train in India, in his gap year, he had travelled to Calcutta on what had once been known as the Frontier Mail.

'David?' Kirsty said quietly. 'He's gone now.' Marchant

came up for air, and the two of them lay there, looking up at the metallic-blue 1950s interior, with its rivets, brass switches and bakelite fittings. The style reminded Marchant of the inside of an old naval ship.

Earlier, they had talked about the incident on the Delhi concourse. Both women thanked him for his gallant rescue, asking if any of what he said had been true. Marchant chose to maintain the deceit, a harmless one for once, and told them that he had spent two days working as an extra up at the Red Fort, and that Shah Rukh was shorter in the flesh. He needed to keep his liar's hand in.

Holly had sensed the chemistry between Marchant and Kirsty, and had retreated to her bunk in a sulk, leaving the two of them to sit on the open doorstep of the train, watching Delhi's suburbs slide by. Their conversation had been unforced, as if they had known each other for years. No questions or accounting for lives, which suited Marchant.

He learnt little about Kirsty, except that she wanted to practise Ashtanga on a beach in Goa, and had the lissom figure of a yoga babe. All Kirsty thought she knew about him was that his name was David Marlowe, his rucksack had been stolen from a guesthouse in Paharganj, and he was originally from Ireland. They were strangers, in other words – much more so than Kirsty would ever know.

But Marchant felt there was something about their carefree encounter, lying on the narrow top bunk bed of a night train to Goa, listening to the long, droning horn of the engine, somewhere far ahead of them, that made it inevitable she should link a leg over his. He was about to reciprocate the gesture when, below them, the child from Kerala coughed. Marchant smiled as Kirsty moved her leg away. Instead, they lay there together, their colliding worlds moving apart from each other again, as the Mangala Express pushed on through the darkness towards the Arabian Sea.

34

Paul Myers had been drinking heavily all evening in the Morpeth Arms, watching the lights of Legoland across the Thames burning brightly into the night. He knew that what he was about to do could lead to his dismissal. It was also a betrayal of Leila, one of the few people he had been able to call a friend. But she had betrayed him, and he now realised that he was left with little option. Draining his fifth pint of Young's Special, he stood up and walked outside, making his way across the Embankment to the pavement by the river.

He watched the dark water running silently beneath him as he dialled the personal mobile of Marcus Fielding. Very few people knew the number, and even fewer were allowed to ring it. But when you worked at GCHQ, with the security clearance of a senior intelligence analyst, there were ways. Myers looked up at the Vicar's office as the number began to ring.

'Who's this?' Fielding said.

'Paul Myers, senior analyst, Asia desk, Cheltenham,' Myers said, aware of a slight slurring of his words.

'This is neither an appropriate channel of communication, nor an appropriate time,' Fielding said. 'Who do you report to?'

'Sir, it's about Leila. I need to speak to you tonight.' Despite the alcohol, Myers detected a missed beat at the other end of the phone. 'We've intercepted some of her calls. I think you should see the transcripts. I've got them with me.'

A pause. 'Where are you?'

'Just across the water.' Myers glanced up at the buttressed bay window at the top of Legoland. He couldn't see anyone, but imagined the Vicar looking out into the darkness.

'I'll pick you up in my car,' Fielding said. 'I'm on my way out.'

Ten minutes later, Myers was in the back of a Range Rover, next to Fielding, as they were driven down the Thames towards Westminster. Myers was much as Fielding had imagined: few social skills, heavy-rimmed glasses, little personal hygiene, drink problem, and an IQ off the scale. A typical Cheltenham data cruncher, in other words.

'The first call showed up on the grid a few hours after the marathon,' Myers said. 'We were listening to everything, desperate for a lead. It was mayhem, a bit like 7/7. South India was obviously in the frame, so we were scanning for Malayalam, Tamil, Telugu. But we were on the lookout for Farsi, too. I picked up this. I knew it was Leila's voice straightaway.'

He passed Fielding a printout of a phone transcript.
Fielding read it through carefully.

Mother (Farsi): 'They came tonight, three of them. They took the boy – you know him, the one who cooks for me. Beat him in front of my eyes.'
Leila (Farsi): 'Did they hurt you, Mama? Did they touch you?'
Mother (Farsi): 'He was like a grandson to me. Dragged him away by his [feet?].'
Leila (Farsi): 'Mama, what did they do to you?'
Mother (Farsi): 'You told me they wouldn't come. Others here have suffered, too.'
Leila: 'Never again, Mama. They won't come any more. (English) I promise.'
Mother (Farsi): 'Why did they say my family are to blame? What have we ever done to them?'
Leila (English): 'Nothing. (Farsi) You know how it is. Are you safe now?'
[Line dropped.]

Fielding passed the transcript back.

'Did you log this, give it to anyone else?'

Myers was silent for a moment, bobbing his head.
'No. I know I should have done. Leila and I were friends.
Good friends. I thought nothing of it. She had talked to
me before about the nursing home, the way the staff
mistreated her mother. To be honest, I felt a little awkward
listening in. Felt like family business.'

'What made you change your mind?'

'Well obviously the news that she was working for the Americans. I hated her for that when I heard. It felt very personal, a personal betrayal. I went back to the transcript, read it through again.'

'And?'

'I'd overlooked the most important part of it, the transmission data. Leila had always talked about her mother as if she was in a nursing home in Britain. When I heard her talking about a cook, the beating, I assumed it was just about the nursing staff. The call had been made to a UK mobile number, but I checked back through the intercept log and realised that it had been routed via a mobile network in Tehran.'

They had all missed it, Fielding thought. Everyone except the Americans, who had not only learnt that Leila's mother had moved to Iran, but had used that information to turn Leila. More worryingly, it meant that the Developed Vetting system had failed, the first casualty of the Service's new policy of casting its recruitment net wider. How many more would slip through in the future?

'We used to look out for each other,' Myers continued.

'In what way?'

'The odd thing, here and there.'

'Go on.'

'At Cheltenham we heard some chatter on the morning of the marathon. I passed it on, told her to be careful.'

'Did you tell anyone else?'

'No. At the time I thought it was nothing. I just knew

she was running. She thanked me, said she would pass it up the line, but I know she never did.'

'And you think that's important now?'

'Yeah, I do.'

'Why?'

'My line manager recently received instructions from MI6 to focus solely on the Gulf. We picked this up on today's grid. It's from a phone booth in Delhi. Leila's voice again. I've run it through profiling. She's trying to talk to her mother – in Tehran.'

He handed Fielding another transcript.

Leila (Farsi): 'Mama. It's Leila. Things will be better soon.'

Unidentified Male (Farsi): 'Your mother's in hospital.'

Leila: 'Who is this?'

Unidentified male: 'A friend of the family. [Male voices in background] She's fine and, inshallah, *will have the best treatment dollars can buy.'*

Leila: 'I want her looked after, that was always the deal.'

Unidentified male: 'I will tell her you called. And that her health rests in your hands.'

[End]

'Do we know who the male voice is?' Fielding asked, passing the transcript back.

Myers paused. 'Ali Mousavi, a senior officer in VEVAK, the Iranian Ministry of Intelligence and Security.'

'I know him,' Fielding said. 'Takes personal pleasure in persecuting Bahá'ís.'

243

'Does he also enjoy masterminding marathon attacks?'

'Why?'

'I've listened again to the chatter I picked up that night, before the race. All we got was one side of a conversation, London end. South Indian accent, clean mobile.' Myers handed Fielding another transcript. 'But the call came out of Iran. This afternoon I finally managed to trace the phone. It was used once earlier this year by Ali Mousavi.'

Fielding looked up at Myers. Like everything in intelligence, it wasn't conclusive, but it was enough for him. He read the transcript:

Unidentified male (English, South Indian accent): 35,000 runners.
Caller: [no data, encrypted, out of Iran]
Unidentified male: Acha. 8 minutes 30.
[End]

Fielding asked for the other two transcripts back, and studied them again.

'Thank you for showing me these,' he said, sifting through the pages. 'I appreciate the risk.'

'We heard that the Americans were paying for Leila's mother's healthcare in return for her working for them. Her mother was a Bahá'í, so they were more than happy to support her.'

'That's what we heard, too.'

'VEVAK believe all Bahá'ís are Zionist agents, get wind of this, turn up at her mother's house, answer Leila's call when she rings.'

'That would be the logical explanation. But if the arrangement between Leila and the Americans was secret, as we must assume it was, then why would she say to an unknown Iranian who answers the phone in her mother's house: "I want her looked after, that was always the deal"?'

Myers sat quite still, staring at the footwell of the car. For a moment Fielding thought he was going to be sick. Then he looked up and turned towards Fielding.

'Leila wasn't working for the Americans, was she?'

'No, she wasn't.'

'And there wasn't an American mole in MI6.'

'No. There wasn't. There was an Iranian one, who is now working for the CIA in Delhi, seventy-two hours before the new US President touches down. I think I need to drop you off.'

35

Marchant heard the police before they reached his carriage. He lay there, eyes open, Kirsty by his side, listening to the sounds of sleep all around him. In the background he could detect the faint but urgent voices of authority. He disentangled himself from Kirsty's limp embrace and swung down to the floor of the carriage, making sure his footfall was silent. He knew he had to move quickly. Police were working their way through the train from both ends.

Marchant stepped out of the sleeping area and into a small space at the end of the carriage, where it was joined to the next one. In a cubicle marked 'Laundry', a junior-looking train official slept on a fold-down bed, pillows and blankets stacked neatly on shelves above him. The door was ajar. Quietly, Marchant pulled it closed. Then he pushed down on the handle of the outside door and swung it open. The night air was warm, the surrounding countryside flat: paddy fields. Marchant estimated that the train was travelling at 30 mph – not quick, but too fast to jump.

Beside him was a small metal cupboard marked 'Electrics'. He pulled at its dented front panel. The lock had long since broken, and it opened easily. Voices were now getting louder behind him. He looked up and down the train, then flicked all those switches in the cupboard that were in the up position. Two lights above him went out, along with the dim night lights in the main carriage. It would buy him a few seconds. Checking that no emergency lighting had come on, he stretched down onto the step outside the train's open door, holding onto the handle beside it. He then put his left foot up onto the door, and lifted himself upwards, glancing at the printed list of passengers that had been glued to the outside of the train in Delhi: name, sex, age.

For a moment, suspended horizontally above the moving ground, he thought he was going to fall, but with his left hand he managed to grip the top of the door, and pulled himself up further. A second later, the train passed a concrete signal post, which brushed against his billowing shirt. The surge of adrenalin made his legs heavy, and he knew he was losing strength.

Glancing both ways, he grabbed onto the lip of the train's roof, then lifted himself upwards again, pushing with one foot on the small light above the passenger list. The next moment he was lying flat on the roof. He thought of Shah Rukh Khan dancing on the top of a train in *Dil Se*, but he didn't feel like a film star as he pressed himself against the dirty train roof, looking out for bridges.

He knew he wasn't safe yet. Leaning over the side of the train, he grabbed the heavy door and swung it shut. The door clicked closed, but not properly. There was no time to push it flush with the side of the carriage. He started to shuffle back down the roof of the train, towards economy class, keeping his body as flat as he could.

Below him, a posse of policemen entered the carriage from the far end, making their way through the sleeping families, looking for someone. They didn't disturb passengers unless they couldn't see their faces. When they reached Kirsty's and Holly's cubicle, the policeman in charge deferred to a female colleague, who moved forward. Holly's face was clearly visible, but Kirsty's was hidden beneath her blanket.

'Yes please, wake up madam, we need to see your passport,' the policewoman said, tugging on Kirsty's blanket. She then spoke to Holly, whose eyes had opened. 'Passport, madam? Police check.'

Holly sat up and fumbled sleepily through her rucksack, which was at the end of her bed. 'Kirsty, wake up,' she called across to her friend, who was still asleep. 'Kirsty?'

Kirsty stirred, blinking at the policewoman, whose head was just below the level of her bunk. Instinctively, she turned to where Marchant had been lying, and then looked back at the woman.

'Lost something?' she said to Kirsty.

'Just my bag.'

'Is this it?' the policewoman said, tapping the rucksack at Kirsty's feet.

Kirsty nodded, then pulled out her passport from the money belt around her waist, sweeping back her hair, still half asleep. Where had David gone? She hadn't heard him leave. As the woman inspected both passports, then passed them to her senior colleague, Holly glanced quizzically at Kirsty, who shrugged.

'Is there something wrong?' Kirsty asked.

'We're looking for an Irishman, David Marlowe,' the senior officer said, a bamboo *lathi* in one hand. 'He was seen embarking this train in Delhi with two female foreign tourists. Have you seen anyone of this name?'

Kirsty glanced at Holly.

'Yes, he's travelling in economy,' Holly said. 'We only met him on the platform at Nizamuddin. Bit of a loser.'

Kirsty threw her a reproachful, confused look. She knew she should have stayed in Delhi with Anya.

'Which place was he heading?' the policewoman asked, making notes on a small pad.

'Why don't you ask her,' Holly said. 'She knew him better.'

'He helped us out in a difficult situation on the platform in Delhi,' Kirsty said, addressing Holly as much as the policewoman. 'I think he said he was going as far as Vasai.'

Whatever David might have done wrong, Kirsty thought, he had still gone out of his way to help them in Delhi. Holly seemed to have forgotten that.

'Vasai? He wasn't travelling to Goa then?'

'He didn't have enough money.'

'Did he say anything else?'

'No.'

'And he was travelling alone?'

'I guess so.'

'Any luggage?'

'I don't think so. Why are you asking me so many questions?'

'Can you recall what was he wearing?'

'I don't know.' Kirsty suddenly felt very tired. 'Jeans?'

'He smelt, that's all I remember,' Holly said. Kirsty didn't even bother to look at her this time. She just wanted to go back to sleep, and wake up in her own bed in Britain.

'A word of advice, madam,' the policewoman said, handing back both passports to Kirsty. 'Stay away from ne'er-do-wells like David Marlowe.'

'What's he done?' Holly asked.

'You'll read about it soon enough in today's papers. He's dangerous, a slippery fellow.'

36

Fielding had ordered his driver to turn round and head back to the office after dropping Myers in Trafalgar Square, where he said he would pick up a night bus to a friend's flat in North London. Legoland was reassuringly busy as Fielding took the lift up to his office. It troubled him when the place was quiet. He left a message on Denton's mobile, asking him to get in early the next day, and then settled back down at his desk to read through Leila's Developed Vetting report, which he had called up from the night duty manager. At about 3 a.m. he asked for the latest files on the Bahá'í community in Iran, Ali Mousavi, and the London Marathon attack, which needed to be delivered by trolley.

By the time dawn broke, a vivid orange warming the dark Thames beneath his window, Fielding had a better understanding of the threat posed by Leila, and the implications of her unprecedented triple-agent status for the

Service, for Stephen Marchant, and for his own career. The Americans would have to make their own assessment, based on a briefing he would give Straker in a few hours. She was their problem now.

The implications for MI6 were still catastrophic, though, if Leila, one of the Service's star recruits, had been working for VEVAK, Iran's Ministry of Intelligence and Security, from the day she arrived at Legoland. Developed Vetting, introduced ten years before, was meant to guarantee the highest level of clearance, far superior to routine counter-terrorism and security checks. Such vetting was more important than ever now that the intelligence services were recruiting from such diverse ethnic backgrounds, but in Leila's case it appeared to have suffered an unprecedented failure.

A wide-ranging interview had been carried out with Leila shortly after she first applied to the Service, followed by two further interviews before she began training at the Fort, nine months after her initial application. The last of these had been conducted in the presence of a senior vetting officer, and triggered an 'aftercare' concern about family ties to Iran.

A more junior vetting officer was dispatched to interview Leila's mother at her home in Hertfordshire. Widowed two years earlier, she had been a resident of the UK for more than twenty-five years, after fleeing her job as a university lecturer in Tehran at the time of the Revolution. She was a devout Bahá'í, and had continued to follow her religion in England, joining a small local group.

The subsequent DV report raised no security objections, describing Leila's mother as a fully integrated member of British society. Along with other Bahá'ís who had left Iran to live in Britain, she was vehemently opposed to the current regime in Tehran, but she was a low-key member of the expatriate Bahá'í community. Significantly, she had not been associated with any of the various political campaigns around the world that called for religious freedom in Iran.

Two months before Leila began her training at the Fort, her mother was interviewed for a second time. She was still at the same address, but there was talk of her moving out to a nursing home in Harpenden. The interview came back clean, and a handwritten note had been added to the file suggesting that further interviews should be avoided if they were not strictly necessary. Much of what she said appeared muddled, and it was concluded that she was presenting signs of early onset Alzheimer's.

What troubled Fielding was the vetters' complete failure to pick up on the mother's move back to Iran, which must have taken place shortly after her last interview. As far as the vetters were concerned, she was still residing in Hertfordshire. It would have been Leila's responsibility to inform MI6 of any change in her family circumstances, particularly given the West's sensitive relationship with Iran, but she had clearly chosen not to tell a soul. Within Whitehall it was acknowledged that Developed Vetting relied too heavily on the responsibility of the individual to report such changes, but the system's fundamental flaws had never been so exposed.

Fielding tried to take the charitable view. If Leila had been aware of her mother's plans in advance, she would have opposed them, knowing that they could potentially expose her to blackmail. But once she was back in Iran, what could Leila do? She was fiercely ambitious, and her promising career in MI6 would have been over before it had started if she had told the authorities what had happened.

Fielding decided she probably had no warning, just a call from her mother explaining what she had done: instead of moving into a nursing home, she had taken a flight back to Iran. Had the mother's muddled manner in her last interview been a bluff? Once she was settled in Iran, Leila's worst fears would have been confirmed. Her mother was soon being targeted because of her faith, and VEVAK came knocking at Leila's door in London, knowing that she was about to embark on a career with MI6.

Two hundred Bahá'ís had been killed in Iran in the early 1980s, and many thousands had been arrested. In recent years, the Islamic government had renewed its campaign to eliminate all Bahá'ís from the country. Leila must have been given a stark choice: work for VEVAK, or her mother dies. She wouldn't be the first or the last Bahá'í to be executed.

For a brief moment, Fielding felt sorry for Leila. The files suggested a touchingly strong bond between mother and daughter, made even stronger by Leila's father's drinking. They had been united against his excesses, which included violence towards Leila's mother, but not towards her, although their relationship was far from close. One entry in her file suggested that there was a complete breakdown of communication between the two after Leila had started at Oxford University. She had told her vetting officer that the tears she shed at her father's funeral, in her final year, were solely for her mother.

Fielding stood up from his desk, stretched and looked out of the window as the first planes into Heathrow stirred London from sleep. There was a knock on the door, and Otto, who had served as a butler for three Chiefs, brought in a pot of Turkish coffee, a small basket of warm flat breads and some *labneh* cream cheese. Fielding's tours of duty had left their mark on his palate.

'You must take some time off, Otto,' Fielding said. 'Working late last night, here so early today.'

'It's no problem, sir. The duty manager called me. He said you had been up all night and so forth.'

'The difference is that I'm paid enough to work through the night, you're not,' Fielding said, pouring a coffee. He knew that many of MI6's new recruits bridled at the notion of a butler working in Legoland, until the practicalities of the Chief dining with anyone of importance were pointed out to them. On most days of the week, he lunched with politicians, senior civil servants and colleagues from other agencies, but their conversations were too sensitive for even the most trustworthy restaurants (MI6 had a number of small, security-cleared establishments in central London on its books).

Otto was originally from Yugoslavia. He had arrived in London in the 1960s, having learnt his English entirely

255

from reading 1950s spy novels. The dated turns of phrase had gradually disappeared over the years, but he still surprised people with the occasional 'ruddy' expletive, a 'chin chin', or even, the office's favourite, 'We meet again.' Fielding often wondered what the outside world would once have made of the Chief of MI6 employing a butler from Eastern Europe. Now, of course, there was nothing unusual about his nationality, but at the height of the Cold War it must have raised a few eyebrows in Whitehall.

'Family keeping well?' Fielding asked, as Otto cleared away some cups from the night before and headed for the door.

'Yes, sir. Thank you. Mr Denton is here. Be seeing you.'

Fielding's brief moment of sympathy for Leila passed as quickly as it had arrived when Ian Denton, unshaven and carrying a coffee from the canteen, reminded him of what her work for the Iranians might have entailed: not only betraying her country by facilitating a wave of terrorist attacks, but personally destroying his predecessor's career.

As Fielding filled Denton in on the night's developments, he became increasingly certain that Leila was the mole who had done so much to destabilise the Service in the past year, leading to Stephen Marchant's early retirement, ill health and death. Britain had made no secret of its opposition to Iran's nuclear programme, and although the government had fallen short of supporting America's calls for a military invasion, Fielding was only too aware of the Treasury funds that were currently being channelled through MI6 to opposition parties, bloggers and students in Iran who supported regime change.

He and Denton both knew, though, that it would take time to prove Leila's role in the wave of bomb attacks that had preceded Marchant's departure. An unknown cell in South India, with links to the Gulf, was thought to be behind the blasts. But the trail had invariably gone cold, the network analysis maps always had holes. The terrorists had been at least two steps ahead of MI5, prompting fears that they had inside help. MI6's role had been to explore the overseas links, and Leila, working for the Gulf Controllerate on the second floor of Legoland, had been a part of the team liaising with MI5. It was all so obvious now.

South India had been in the frame again for the attempted London Marathon attack, although the chatter and network analysis had increasingly pointed to a Gulf connection. That speculative link had since become a reality, thanks to Paul Myers, whose transcripts pointed to Iran's involvement, as well as Leila's.

'Should we have suspected her earlier?' Fielding asked. He was worried about Denton, who worked too hard and was always ill when he took leave, which was not often enough. (Fielding had to persuade him to use up his annual holiday allowance.) He had never seen him unshaven before, either.

'It depends on when we think she started to work for VEVAK,' Denton said.

'From the off, I fear. They must have made their

approach soon after her mother returned to Iran, and before Leila started at the Fort.'

'And the Americans? Did they know from the beginning?'

'No. It took them the best part of a year to notice her mother was back in Iran.'

'A year quicker than us.'

'Quite. Once Spiro had got wind of the mother's whereabouts, he used it to recruit Leila.'

'And Spiro had no idea she was already working for the Iranians?'

'None. Leila must have convinced him that she hadn't been compromised by her mother's move. The CIA was looking for someone close to the head of MI6. Who better than the lover of the Chief's son? Leila agreed to work for them. She could hardly believe her luck. It was her insurance policy against any future mole-hunt in Legoland.'

Fielding took a piece of flat bread and spread it with *labneh*. He gestured at Denton, inviting him to share his breakfast, but he declined. Denton preferred a sausage sandwich from the canteen.

'Leila's been very smart, Ian,' Fielding continued. 'If the West queries her actions, she knows they're consistent with her undercover role for the Americans. Why did she find herself near the American Ambassador, one runner in 35,000? Because she was working for the CIA, who were worried about an attack. Did she set up Marchant at the marathon, giving him his old phone? Maybe, but if she did, it was on behalf of the CIA, whose distrust of the Marchants was well known.'

Agreeing to spy for America, in other words, had provided Leila with the perfect operational cover for her real job: spying for Iran. A part of Fielding admired her technical prowess. The Service's instructors at the Fort spent weeks insisting on the need for good legends. Leila must have been listening.

But there was one thing that troubled him above all: why had she remained committed to working for VEVAK? If she was so concerned for her mother's safety, couldn't she have asked the Americans to protect her when they discovered that she was living in Iran? They agreed to pay for her mother's private hospital treatment, so why didn't she take them into her confidence, explain that VEVAK was threatening to kill her? Perhaps she was in too deep; but Fielding felt there was something else.

'We still don't know why she sabotaged the London attack,' Denton said, interrupting Fielding's line of thought.

'No.' Fielding picked up the transcript of the first conversation between Leila and her mother, on the evening after the marathon, and handed it to Denton. A section of the dialogue had been highlighted in green marker pen:

Mother (Farsi): '*You told me they wouldn't come. Others here have suffered, too.*'

Leila (Farsi): '*Never again, Mama. They won't come any more. (English) I promise.*'

Mother (Farsi): '*Why did they say my family are to blame? What have we ever done to them?*'

*   *   *

'You can see that the mother was clearly told that her family – Leila – was to blame,' Fielding said, watching Denton as he read the dialogue. 'When word reached Tehran that the bomber hadn't detonated his belt, VEVAK turned up and beat her mother's much-loved cook. If there was a deal between VEVAK and Leila, she had clearly broken it by preventing the attack.'

'And she didn't go through with it because of Marchant?' Denton asked, passing back the transcript. 'Because she didn't want her lover to die?'

Fielding hoped so. It would prove that Leila had a weakness – and spies lived for human flaws.

'Maybe her relationship with Marchant counted for something, I don't know. Perhaps she felt, for some reason, that a successful attack would have blown her cover. Either way, the Iranians stuck with Leila because she wasn't just working for MI6, she'd wormed her way into the CIA too. A priceless asset, in other words, who deserved a second chance. And she knows she can't afford to mess up again. We need to get to Delhi.'

But before Fielding had reached for his jacket, there was a commotion outside. He heard Otto swear – twenty-first-century expletives this time – and then the door swung open. Harriet Armstrong stood there, Sir David Chadwick by her side.

'We need to talk about Daniel Marchant,' Chadwick said.

37

Marchant stood in the shade of a stall selling strings of sweet-smelling jasmine, watching a group of bare-chested temple workers stride down the middle of the road. Their manner was urgent, almost sexual, with their shaven heads and toned bodies, wrapped in thin cotton *lunghis*. Further down the street, they turned into the main entrance of Mahabeleshwar Temple, the religious centre of Gokarna. A young Western couple passed by in the opposite direction. They were stripped to the waist too, except for her bright orange bikini top and his loose-fitting waistcoat. They both looked stoned.

Earlier, Marchant had walked around the temple's outer courtyard, where cows mingled freely with Hindu pilgrims. He had left his sandals beneath a sign saying 'Footwears Prohibited', and watched people going into the candlelit inner sanctum at the centre of the temple complex. The priests stopped Westerners from entering, unsure if they had bathed. Marchant caught a whiff of his own clothes, and conceded that they had a point.

According to Sujit, the man who had sat next to him on his bus journey to Gokarna, the town derived its name from the legend of Lord Shiva, who had once emerged here from the ear of a cow. Another story said it was the home of two brothers, Gokarna and Dhundhakari. Gokarna, born with cow's ears, wandered the world as an ascetic, while Dhundhakari became a notorious criminal. Marchant had enjoyed talking to Sujit, who worked as a journalist in Mumbai and had family in Gokarna, but he had resisted asking too many questions. Instead, he spent much of the time feigning sleep, thinking back to his earlier train journey.

He had stayed on the roof of the train until the next stop, where he had climbed down on the opposite side from the platform and stepped across the tracks to a deserted part of the station. He had told Kirsty and Holly that he was going as far as Vasai, further down the line. It might buy him some time, divert the police. He was still wary, though, and stayed on the platform for the rest of the night, like a stray dog hiding in the shadows, before heading for the bus depot at dawn.

The train search had worried him. Were they looking for someone in connection with the bomb at the Gymkhana Club? Or had the man on the platform at Nizamuddin station reported him? At least Gokarna would provide some cover. A steady flow of Westerners passed down the street in front of the flower stall, some with backpacks, others, like him, with no luggage.

Sujit had said that most budget travellers stayed at the Hotel Om, which was next to the government bus stop. They remained there for a day or two, recovering from their bus journeys, usually from Hampi, before leaving their luggage with reception and heading down to Gokarna's famous beaches in search of bongs and *bhang lassi*. Should he check in at the hotel, ask around about Om Beach? Uncle K had specifically mentioned the Namaste Café.

He decided against it. If the search for him should intensify, the police would focus on places popular with backpackers. Instead, he set off back down the street towards the temple, passing a large stable block, its studded wooden doors ajar. Through the darkness Marchant glimpsed a huge ceremonial juggernaut, standing at least twenty-five feet high.

He moved on, glancing at the local tribal women. They wore marigolds in their hair and nothing beneath their sari tops. Two Brahmins stopped to chat by a stall selling votive lamps and ghee, a solitary thread across their bare oiled shoulders. Marchant could feel the sap rising in Gokarna.

Earlier he had seen a Shivite *baba* sitting cross-legged in the doorway of the temple courtyard. He would drop some rupees into his lap and ask the way to Om Beach. Sujit had spoken of such people, said they were happy to discuss Eastern philosophies with naïve young Westerners – in exchange for a few rupees, of course.

'Do you know what "Om" means?' the *baba* said, his

limpid eyes looking up at Marchant through a blue haze of ganga smoke. Above him, a single strip of tube lighting dangled from the temple's painted doorway.

'The sound of the vibrating universe?' Marchant offered, thinking back to Monika's words at the airport in Poland. He was still wearing the pendant she had given him.

'The unstruck sound. Which place are you from?'

'Ireland. I need to meet someone at Om Beach.'

'It's not far from here. Ten minutes in a rickshaw. Ask any driver.' He paused, gathering his saffron robes around him. 'I went to England once, with my wife and son. Nottingham.'

Marchant was surprised to hear he had a family. 'Recently?'

The *baba* smiled. 'Before my wife passed away. *Om Namah Shiva.*'

'And your son?' The *baba* smiled again, but this time Marchant saw only sadness in his watery eyes. 'How long have you been here, in Gokarna?' Marchant continued, guilty that he might have disturbed the man's inner peace.

The *baba* lifted one hand, palm upwards, turning it from side to side as if he was weighing something. 'Twenty years, maybe longer. There are five beaches: Gokarna, Om, Kudle, Half-Moon and Paradise. Om is shaped like the Devanagari symbol. It is the most popular with Westerners. Paradise is the most remote. But there is a sixth that few ever reach. Shanti Beach. Ask the fishermen.' He paused, flicking the faintest glance at Marchant's pocket. 'The bond between father and son is never broken.'

Marchant gave him his rupees and left.

38

Fielding's office clock said 7.30 a.m.

'Apologies for the early start, but I'm afraid this couldn't wait,' Sir David Chadwick said, breezing past Otto, who stood in the doorway, a pained look of failure on his face.

Fielding never liked it when Chadwick set foot in Legoland, particularly when he had Harriet Armstrong in tow. They always had the air of estate agents measuring up a flat. It was no secret that the Chief's office was bigger than the Director General's in Thames House. The views were also better, much to Armstrong's annoyance.

This visit was different. It was unannounced, too early for Whitehall protocol, the bag-carriers and minute-takers. The envy was also not apparent. It reminded Fielding of the day they came for Stephen Marchant.

Fielding nodded reassurance at Otto as he ushered

Chadwick and Armstrong into the adjoining dining room. Denton followed.

'Take a seat,' Fielding said. The rising sun failed to raise the temperature of the room. Denton glanced at Fielding, but he was looking down at a handful of transcripts and files he had brought through with him.

'Harriet?' Chadwick said, sitting down next to Armstrong. 'Would you care to begin?'

They had chosen two seats at the end of the large oval table, as far away as possible from Denton and Fielding. For a moment Fielding felt as if he was present at a petty dispute in a provincial solicitors' office.

'We've just had the results back from new tests on the running belt,' Armstrong said. 'The lab sent them overnight. As you're aware, there was a TETRA-enabled detonation device attached to the charges. We knew it could only be operated on the TETRA network. What we didn't know was the number that a third party would have to call in on to detonate the charges, and who had that number.'

'We've always suspected it was Daniel Marchant,' Chadwick said, 'given that he had a TETRA handset with him on race day.'

'And despite the fact that he saved many lives,' Fielding said.

'But there was no proof,' Chadwick continued, like a politician ignoring a heckler.

'There is now,' Armstrong said. She hoped to fix Fielding with a thin grin, but the Chief had sat back, his long legs thrown to one side, his head turned towards

267

the window. Fielding knew what was coming. Leila had been too clever for them all. 'When we searched Marchant's flat, we retrieved his old TETRA handset, the one he had with him on the day of the marathon. He'd programmed in some speed-dial numbers – the office, Leila's phone, his father's home, and so on. But when we checked the office number, it wasn't the MI6 switchboard, it was the detonator on the running belt.'

Fielding continued to stare out of the window. Marchant, he was sure, had handed the phone back to Leila after the attempted attack, and she must have visited his flat after the race and planted it there. 'Just tell me one thing,' he said. 'Why didn't he blow the bomber sky high, taking the Ambassador and every fucking fun runner in London with him?'

Chadwick winced at the words. He had hoped Fielding would go quietly when he was presented with their evidence. 'Clearly he had a change of heart.'

'I'll say. He saved the Ambassador's life.'

'I gather from David that you were working on the assumption it was a set-up by the Americans,' Armstrong said, glancing at Chadwick.

'Not unreasonably, given that Leila's on their payroll.'

'Daniel was within the press of a button of murdering Turner Munroe. Do you really think the Americans would have risked that?'

Fielding said nothing. He almost felt sorry for Armstrong, with her misplaced admiration for Spiro, for America. It was the FBI's fault. On a recent visit to New York they had presented her with a jacket and a base-

268

ball cap, both emblazoned with the letters 'FBI'. She had even posed for photos in them. For a buttoned-up Whitehall mandarin, the culture shock had been exhilarating.

'Marcus, I'm afraid it doesn't look good for Daniel,' Chadwick said. 'I've already alerted the PM's office. We're going to need the cooperation of the Americans on this one. An MI6 officer nearly killing one of their most distinguished ambassadors isn't great for the special relationship.'

'Except that he didn't kill him.' It was almost an aside. Fielding had said it too often to care any more. He stood up and walked around the room, avoiding eye contact with Chadwick and Armstrong. His lower back was starting to ache. He had had enough of this game.

'We all know the Americans have made no secret of their concerns about MI6,' Chadwick said. 'But we can't pin this one on them, Marcus. They've been over it with Leila many times. She came off the course to alert MI5 as soon as she became aware of the bomber. She didn't know if Marchant was involved, but she couldn't take the risk, particularly in the light of her brief from the Americans.'

'We don't know why he had a change of heart out there,' Armstrong said, 'but perhaps it was Leila's presence by his side, in which case we should all be grateful that the Americans had the sense to keep such a close eye on him.'

'Are you suggesting that Leila talked him out of it?' Fielding asked. He was at the window now, his back to

Armstrong and Chadwick, wishing he was at Tate Britain across the river, before the crowds arrived. The night manager would often open up the gallery for him, let him walk the Pre-Raphaelite rooms on his own in the dawn light.

'Not directly, no,' Armstrong said. 'She had no idea what he was planning. But by being there, we think she had an effect on him, yes.'

'And she was running by his side because the Americans had turned her, not because of any genuine feelings she might have had for him, feelings that had been no secret to anyone at MI6 since their time together at the Fort?'

'You still have a very romantic view of Marchant, don't you?' Armstrong said, annoyed that she was addressing Fielding's back. 'Son of a distinguished Chief, best case officer of his generation, heroically saves the American Ambassador to London from a suicide bomber. How about son of a traitor, picked up where his father left off, gets within an inch of causing carnage in the capital.'

Fielding turned to face them, his tall figure silhouetted against the windows. 'My point is that we must be grateful they were lovers.' He paused. 'But I'm afraid we've all got it the wrong way round. It wasn't Daniel's love for Leila that stopped the bomb being detonated, it was Leila's love for Daniel. She was the one who had a change of heart.'

'We've been through this before, Marcus. It wasn't a set-up.'

'I know. Because Leila wasn't working for the

Americans.' He walked around to his seat, picked up the pile of transcripts and files and dropped them onto the table between Chadwick and Armstrong. 'She was working for the Iranians.'

39

Marchant listened to the rustle of the necklaces slung loosely around the cows' necks, made from seashells threaded with coarse coir twine. A small herd had gathered in front of the Namaste Café, meandering slowly towards a promontory of rocks that stretched out from the sand into the Arabian Sea. The café was in the middle of the beach, near the centre of the Om symbol. Marchant had seen the beach's auspicious shape from the top of the cliffs at the far end, where the rickshaw driver had dropped him.

Now he was watching the sun set, with a Kingfisher beer in one hand, a *chillum* in the other, thinking he could settle here for a year. His plastic chair was listing badly, its legs sinking slowly into the soft sand, forcing him to cock his head to level the distant horizon. Two human figures stood motionless on the far rocks, looking out to sea, their yogic poses silhouetted against the

272

vermilion-streaked sky. Further down the beach, a group of fishermen squatted around a wooden canoe, mending their nets. Monika would have enjoyed the scene, in real life as well as her cover one. Leila, he thought, would have told all the Westerners to go back home and find proper jobs.

He was beginning to accept now that Leila must have helped the Americans, unwittingly said something that made them think he was trying to kill Munroe at the marathon rather than save him. They had distrusted his father, and they suspected the son too. But had Leila really not known what she was doing? He hoped Salim Dhar would have the answer.

Other stoned travellers were sharing the view, chilled out in seats scattered around the café, chatting quietly. Marchant had two of them down as being from Sweden, two from Israel and one from South Africa. The Israeli couple, he guessed, had recently completed their national service (three years for men, twenty-one months for women). Behind the café was a small row of cubicles, each with a two-inch thick mattress on its sandy floor. Marchant had rented one of them for fifty rupees, and later paid an extra thirty for a mosquito net, when the biting started.

'It used to be more *shanti* here,' said Shankar, the bar owner, bringing Marchant another beer. He hadn't asked him yet about Salim. The Israeli couple were arousing his suspicion: the occasional look in his direction, the bulge of a mobile phone in the pocket of the man's shorts. 'Now there are too many Indian tourists.

They come to watch the hippies at weekends. Soon it will be like Goa.'

'The beer's good,' Marchant said, reading from the label, which hadn't changed since his backpacking days. '"Most thrilling chilled." Is it difficult getting a licence?'

'I give the policeman 4,000 rupees, they let me sell beer. Which place you from?'

'Ireland.'

'I tried it once. The Guinness beer.'

'And?'

Shankar shook his head from side to side in appreciation, but Marchant could see that he was distracted. He was looking down to the far end of the beach, at least three hundred yards away, where there was another, bigger café. Some sort of commotion had caught his eye. Marchant turned around to see.

'*Baksheesh* problem,' Shankar said. Marchant stared hard into the dying sun, shielding his eyes. He couldn't see anything unusual.

'He didn't pay up?'

'Maybe. They usually come at start of season.'

'Who? The police?'

Then Marchant saw them, a group of at least ten officers, led by a peak-capped man with a *lathi* in his hand.

'No problem, no problem. They are my friends.'

But Marchant could hear the tension in Shankar's voice. Without rushing, he stood up and walked around to his room at the rear of the café. There was nothing in it, because he had no luggage. Moving quickly, he

274

removed the plastic bag from the purse belt strapped to his leg, checking that his money and passport were inside. He then went out and walked over to the shade of some coconut trees, where hammocks had been strung between their trunks, and started to dig quickly in the sand. A few moments later he had buried his passport and money. He made a mental note of the nearest tree, and then looked over at the group of policemen. They had stopped at another small café, halfway between him and the end of the beach.

'I'm off for a swim,' he said to Shankar, who was busy stacking crates of empty beer bottles at the back of the shack. It was a futile gesture if he was hoping to conceal them. None of the other travellers seemed to have taken much notice of Marchant's movements.

'No problem,' Shankar said. 'The sea is strong.'

Marchant didn't want to leave his shirt and trousers lying around. Instead he ran down to the sea fully clothed, trying not to think of Stare Kiejkuty. He closed his eyes, took a deep breath and dived into the waves, telling himself that he wasn't about to drown.

'I'm afraid your allegations about Leila haven't played too well in Langley,' Carter said, glancing at the newspaper in his hand before putting it down on the park bench beside him.

'No one likes to hear that they've been betrayed by one of their own,' Fielding said.

'You know, I was sitting in on a Langley lecture the other day. The guy was telling all the rookies that money's no longer what traitors do it for. Divided loyalties, that's what they're about these days. Mother country calling louder than their adopted one.'

'So why don't you believe it about Leila?'

'She wasn't born in Iran.'

'She might as well have been. Close to her Iranian mother, fluent in Farsi. That's why we recruited her. She represented the future of the Service.'

They watched the stream of morning commuters cut through St James's Park up to Whitehall, a few runners weaving in and out of them. A cleaning van was making its way slowly along the path, its hazard lights flashing. To the left of their bench, a man was unchaining a stack of deck chairs. Spring had arrived, and the trees all around were blurred with blossom. In the distance, the London Eye rose above the Foreign and Commonwealth Office. It was where Fielding had first had his doubts about Leila, high above London in a capsule with Jago. Sometimes he longed for the innocent outlook of his godson, the untroubled optimism.

'They're disputing the Ali Mousavi mobile evidence, reckon the maltreatment of the mother was part of the bigger Bahá'í picture, nothing more. They don't buy that Leila was blown, Marcus. I'm sorry.'

No need to apologise, Fielding thought. She's working for you now, protecting your President. 'So I gather. Armstrong and Chadwick were the same. They think it's sour grapes on the Service's part. My revenge for Leila working for the Americans.'

'Are you safe? The job?'

'For the moment. Chadwick was brought in to steady the ship. He doesn't need two Chiefs taking early retirement. And you?' Fielding had heard rumours.

'I've been called off the Marchant case. Straker's brought back Spiro. He's flying into Delhi this morning.'

'Daniel Marchant wasn't trying to kill your Ambassador, you know that,' Fielding said.

'I wanted to believe it, Marcus, I really did. But we've been blindsided by Armstrong's TETRA evidence. The guy was within a speed-dial of blowing Munroe's head off.'

'Leila gave him the phone, trust me.'

'But it was Marchant's handset.'

'His old one. It was taken away from him when he was suspended. I've been through the records. Someone managed to check it out again, without signing for it.'

'It could have been Marchant, then.'

'He was suspended. Leila gave it to him during the race, and he handed it back to her afterwards. She must have planted it in his flat.'

They sat in silence, watching a squirrel approach them, looking for food. 'For a while, I thought our time had come,' Carter eventually said. 'Our chance to remind the world about the real meaning of intelligence. With Marchant's help, we could have found Dhar, played him back, started to whip AQ the old-fashioned way. Straker gave us our chance – twenty-four hours, he said. Now he's shuttered it. He wants Dhar dead, Marchant too. No nuances, no shade. The soldiers are running the show now.'

'Are those Spiro's orders?'

'I'm afraid so. And he only deals in dead-or-alive.'

'Does anyone know where Dhar is?'

'Somewhere on the Karnataka coast. The Indians are cooperating fully. They want the President's visit to go ahead as much as we do. A frigate from the Fifth Fleet is standing by.'

Marchant spotted the distinct outline on the horizon as he trod water, careful to keep his head above the surface of the sea. The ship was about two miles offshore, and looked like one of America's Littoral combat ships, the sleek, angular profile designed to reduce its radar signature. A large flight-deck was just visible, silhouetted against the orange horizon. Beneath the water, the new class of frigate had a trimaran hull for speed: forty-five knots.

Marchant's first thought was that it must be part of a wider security umbrella for the President's imminent visit, but he was only flying into and out of Delhi. Gokarna was hundreds of miles away, south of Goa. He looked again at the ship and tried to determine if it was on the move. After a couple of minutes, he decided that it was stationary. Its presence troubled him, and he turned back to face the beach, 400 yards away. He felt better looking at the land, more in control of the water around him.

The police had combed the beach's entire length, stopping at every café, and were now making their way back to the far end, where there was a way out onto the small road that led back to Gokarna. Marchant calculated that if he started his return now, they would have passed the Namaste Café and be almost off the beach by the time he reached the shore.

It was after two minutes of swimming that he noticed he was making no progress. While he had been treading water, watching the police, he had kept an eye on a small outcrop of cliffs, monitoring his position in case of currents. There had been little lateral movement, but he now realised that he had been drifting slowly out to sea. He should have gone easier on the *chillum*.

He kicked harder, and increased the frequency of his strokes. But when he stopped to look up, he knew that he had slipped further out to sea. He glanced behind him at the frigate, still out there on the horizon. For the first time, he felt a rising sense of panic. His arms felt heavier, the sea colder, deeper. He would be fine if he kept his head above water.

The sea was calm, but he faltered in his next stroke and swallowed a mouthful of water. As he choked, he remembered the cloth in the back of his throat, being worked in a circular motion, forcing itself deeper. He retched, seawater sluicing up his nose. The shore seemed to be slipping further away with each stroke, dropping beneath the gentle swell. The clingfilm would be next, a hose relayed into his mouth, deep down into his stomach.

But he never reached level three. Instead, he took a deep breath and dipped below the waves to a place where he could stretch his arms, kick for the shore. Here in the silence he could take control and confront the fear.

Sebastian was by his side now, no longer lying still at the bottom of the pool, but swimming up to the surface, smiling. He pushed on through the darkness, growing stronger with each stroke, until his lungs began to burst.

40

Paul Myers hadn't been hit so hard since he was bullied at school. He could have put up with the pain of a broken nose if it wasn't for his glasses, which had been knocked to the floor with the impact. They had been taken off him when he was blindfolded, and put back on over his hood, to the amusement of his attackers.

The sound of them being crunched under a heel hurt even more than the second punch, which split his top lip like a burst grape. Instinctively he curled up into the foetal position, but it was no good. There were at least three of them, and he was soon being kicked in the back. Their feet were accurate, targeting his kidneys. He had always been useless at fighting.

Myers had gone from one bar to another after Fielding had dropped him off in Trafalgar Square, hoping to drown his memories of Leila. He also had nowhere to stay (the friend's flat in North London had been a lie).

It was as he was wandering across St James's Park at about 9 a.m. that the van had slowly pulled up, hazard lights flashing. The usual park maintenance markings were visible on its sides, but the men who jumped out of the back doors weren't interested in sweeping leaves.

The journey lasted fifteen minutes. He had no idea where he was being taken, except that the sound of the van's engine echoed shortly before it stopped, suggesting that they had driven into a garage. Somehow he thought Leila was behind it, but he blamed her for everything in his life since he had discovered her betrayal.

As soon as the van's back doors were opened, the beating started. They dragged him out onto cold concrete, and the fall from the van should have hurt him, but he was so drunk that he didn't feel their kicks. He didn't even recognise the voice of Harriet Armstrong as she ordered his attackers to stop.

The three fishermen spotted the Westerner two hundred yards off the port bow of their wooden, fifteen-foot boat. The owner had told his son to alter course and pick him up. It wouldn't be the first tourist they had rescued, nor the last. They were usually drunk, high on skunk or acid. He had a cousin in Goa who said it was even worse over there. But Westerners had their uses. They liked having beach barbecues, and would buy tuna directly from his boat for prices three times as high as he could get at the market in Gokarna.

This one was far gone, he thought, as he and his son hauled the heavy body over the gunwhale. He had been swimming with all his clothes still on. Once the Westerner was curled up in the bottom of the boat, he nudged his stomach with his foot. The man groaned and vomited some seawater.

'He's probably one of Shankar's,' the boat owner said.

Marchant woke before it was fully light, and for a moment he thought he was in his childhood bedroom in Tarlton. The mattress was so thin it had taken him back, in the minutes before he was fully awake, to the time when he and Sebastian used to sleep on the floor in their indoor tent. But as his eyes adjusted to the orange light of dawn, he realised that the cotton above him was not a flysheet but a mosquito net.

He knew that he was lucky to be alive. The sea had drawn every ounce of energy from his body, and then worked on his mind. He had no recollection of being rescued, but he could remember being carried into his tiny room, the voice of Shankar, the café owner, enough to reassure him that he wasn't on board the American frigate.

He went outside, his legs shaky, and looked up and down the beach. It was empty except for the cows, which were standing in a group between the café and the sea, and a solitary squatting figure in the far distance. The sea was calm, lapping at the shore. And then he saw the angular outline of the frigate, still two miles off, slightly further down the coast. He knew he must find Salim Dhar today.

After retrieving his purse belt from the sand, Marchant came across Shankar at the front of the café, trimming a coconut husk with a knife before chopping its top off and inserting a straw. He placed it on a table next to a row of others, each with a straw sticking out. Overnight a turquoise fishing boat had been pulled up onto the beach, next to the chairs that were still littered across the sand. Its name, *Bharat*, had been painted in white lettering on the side, beneath the high-pointed bow. Something about the boat looked familiar.

'Who do I thank for rescuing me?' Marchant asked, sitting down next to Shankar. 'The owner of this?' He nodded at the boat.

'He says you shouldn't go swimming with clothes on.'

'I need to find someone. Brother Salim.'

Shankar stopped cutting at a new husk for a moment, and then continued.

'Can you help me find him?' Marchant asked, watching the knife. He knew he was speaking to the right person.

'So it was you the police were looking for?'

'Can you help?'

'The boat goes after breakfast.'

'Shanti Beach?'

Shankar stood up and walked away, dropping one of the coconuts into his hands. 'Breakfast. You ask too many questions.'

41

Fielding lifted the flute to his lips and began to play Telemann's sonata in F minor. He couldn't remember the last time he had been at his flat during the middle of a weekday. It reminded him of being confined to the sanatorium at school while everyone else was in their classrooms. Dolphin Square had been surprisingly busy when his driver had dropped him off at the side entrance. So life went on after the workers had left their homes for the office.

His driver had asked whether he should wait, and Fielding had hesitated. It wasn't a question of how long he would be, but of whether he would ever climb into the Chief of MI6's official Range Rover again. In the end he had told him to go back to the office. Now, as Fielding lost himself in Telemann's first movement, he hoped to find a reason to return to Legoland.

The most powerful person on the planet was about to

be under the protection of someone working for an enemy state. He wished he cared more. The future of the free world might soon be hanging in the balance. But it was up to Straker and Spiro and Armstrong and Chadwick now. They had conspired to turn Leila against him; they must live with the consequences.

He had provided the Americans with all the evidence in his possession, but it hadn't been enough. It was too circumstantial, the CIA said. More to the point, Leila was their prodigal signing, the agent who had saved an American ambassador's life. The CIA wasn't about to have her revealed as an Iranian spy by anyone, least of all by a compromised British spy chief whose ultimate loyalties the Agency also suspected.

Now they had taken Myers, an innocent man who had tried to do the right thing. MI5 were talking about a serious security breach, enough for a public prosecution. Leila would be called as a witness, to confirm that Myers had leaked confidential information on the night before the marathon. Fielding would be summoned too, asked to explain why Myers had taken transcripts off the Cheltenham site.

It took him a few moments to realise his phone was ringing. Very few people knew his home number. He walked over and picked up the receiver. It was Anne Norman.

'Marcus?' She had never called him that before.

'Anne?' He had never used her first name.

'There's someone who's very keen to speak to you. From India.'

'Who is it?'

'It's Daniel. Daniel Marchant.'

The boat left after breakfast, just as Shankar had promised. Marchant met its owner outside the café and walked with him down to the water's edge, where his son was stowing a tangle of blue fishing nets in the bow. The owner was jovial, with a proud potbelly, and was soon joking with Marchant about his misfortune the previous evening.

'You were floating in the water like a great big jellyfish!' he said, slapping him on the back.

Their laughter stopped, though, when Marchant nodded towards two local fishermen smoking *bidis*, who had stepped out from the shade of the coconut trees at the back of the beach and were walking across the sand towards them. He knew at once from their detached manner that they had come to take him to Dhar. They looked on silently as the owner and his son struggled to launch the boat, helped by Marchant. Once it was afloat, the two men waded out into the shallow water and climbed aboard, ignoring the son's offers of assistance. The owner threw Marchant a nervous glance, started up the engine and steered the boat out towards the headland.

To his relief, Marchant couldn't see the frigate on the horizon any more. He looked inland at the rocky coastline and the hills beyond, one of which was topped with a communications mast covered in satellite dishes and aerials. In the past, he would have been depressed by its presence in such a rugged, timeless setting, but he knew they were everywhere in modern India, and today the sight of its distinctive red and white stripes reassured him.

After twenty minutes, Marchant spotted a small beach where some huts, made of laterite bricks cut from the local Konkan soil, had been built into the hillside. He thought he could make out one or two Westerners on the beach, but the owner kept going down the coast. If it wasn't for the two silent men sitting behind him on the boat, Marchant would have enjoyed the spray and the sunshine of the open sea, but their stony presence was a constant reminder of what lay ahead.

An hour later, the owner finally nudged the tiller away from him and steered the boat towards the shore. The son jumped out first, and dragged the boat ashore. Marchant stepped down into the shallow blue water and walked up onto the beach, followed by the two fishermen. It was in a small cove, barely fifty yards across, and sheltered on both sides by steep cliffs. At the top of the beach was a tatty shack made from wood and woven palm leaves, and a few hammocks hung in the dappled shade of some coconut trees. A sign said 'Shanti Beach Café', painted in the colours of the Indian flag. There were no Westerners around, no sign that anyone was staying here. As Marchant took in the view, the two men pushed him forward, signalling for him to walk on.

He followed them to the shack, and they led him in through an open doorway. Inside was a small table, and a man standing with his back to them, talking on a mobile phone. He turned briefly to look at Marchant, a cigarette in his hand, and continued to chat quietly in what sounded like Kannada, the local language. He was better dressed than the fishermen, new jeans, printed shirt, sunglasses perched on the top of his head. For a moment his boyish good looks reminded Marchant of Shah Rukh Khan. Marchant glanced at the faded postcards that had been stuck to the central wooden post holding up the roof: London, Sydney, Cape Town.

It was a reasonable effort at cover, Marchant thought.

'Welcome to the Shanti Beach Café,' the man said, putting away his phone. He looked Marchant up and down. 'Just our sort of guest.'

'I've come to see brother Salim,' Marchant said, tensing his stomach muscles. A part of him expected to be punched, bound and hooded at any moment.

'He's been waiting for you. It's a long walk from here. I don't know who you are, where you've come from, but these two will kill you if you try anything. Salim's orders.'

Four hours later, Marchant reached the crest of the hill and looked back down over the tops of the dense vegetation towards Shanti Beach. It had been a hot, hard climb, and he was out of breath, dripping with sweat. The two fishermen pushed him on. '*Chalo*,' the taller one urged. Neither had said anything else to him for the whole journey, ignoring his attempts to speak Hindi.

Marchant walked on from the crest, enjoying the first stretch of downhill since they had set off from the beach. He wondered whether he would ever leave this beautiful place alive. A pair of Brahmani kites soared high above him, enjoying the thermals. Why had Dhar agreed to see him? And would he have any answers about his father? The Namaste Café must have been used by Uncle K as a contact point when he was trying to run Dhar. Word would have reached him that a white man had asked for 'brother Salim'.

The sound of a gunshot made Marchant drop to the ground and look around desperately for cover. For the first time since they had left the Namasté Café, the taller fisherman, who had kept walking as if he had heard nothing, smiled at Marchant, lying in the red dust. It was an awful smile, teeth stained with blood-coloured betelnut juice. Another shot rang out. Marchant listened carefully to it this time, calculating that it was from a high-powered rifle, fired from as close as twenty yards away. He had excelled in his fire-arms training at the Fort. Looking along the path ahead, he saw a figure approaching, a .315 sporting rifle slung over one shoulder. He knew at once that it was Salim Dhar.

42

Leila listened as Monk Johnson finished running through the itinerary of his new president's forty-eight-hour visit to Delhi. There were more than two hundred people in the hall, about as many as it could hold. They were almost all Secret Service personnel, who had been in India for the past month as part of the Presidential Advance Team, trying in vain to impose their fixed manual of security demands on a very fluid country. There were a few CIA officers present, too, including Spiro, who was sitting on the stage next to Johnson, sweating in the heat. The US Embassy air conditioning was struggling to keep a lid on the temperature.

Johnson, head of the Advance Team, stood in front of a detailed satellite image of New Delhi, with key landmarks highlighted in red: the Red Fort, Raj Path, the Lotus Temple, the US Embassy and the Maurya Hotel, where the President would be staying. To the right of this there was a larger, more detailed aerial image of the Lotus Temple complex to the south of the city, with a red route highlighted down a tree-lined avenue leading up to the temple. At various points along the route, times had been written, also in red: 5.28 p.m.; 5.30 p.m.; 5.35 p.m.

Spiro wiped his forehead with a handkerchief, preparing his notes before he spoke. Leila had come to know him well in London – too well. He never missed an opportunity to flirt, didn't bother to disguise the glances at her 'cute ass'. But she had no option but to put up with his attention. He was her American handler, the one who had debriefed her after the marathon. He was also her biggest ally, rejecting Fielding's allegations about an Iranian connection when William Straker, the DCIA, had put them to Spiro, and defending her again when David Baldwin, head of the CIA's Delhi station, had raised his own objections about her prominent role in the presidential visit.

So she had joined in the cheering when Spiro had walked into the embassy that morning, straight from the airport. His recall to Langley hadn't gone down well with the footsoldiers, who were reassured by his straight-talking manner. Johnson had been pleased to see him, too. Spiro seemed to have taken most of the credit for saving the US Ambassador's life at the London Marathon.

'Any more questions about the threat matrix?' Johnson asked.

'Might POTUS try to work the people outside the

Lotus Temple?' asked Baldwin. 'In my experience, crowds in India are either too polite or rioting.'

Baldwin shared Spiro's muscular style, but he was one of the few who hadn't welcomed his arrival. Baldwin, a South Asia specialist, felt that Spiro was on his patch. He wasn't in love with India, but he understood its people, and almost felt protective of them. And unlike Spiro, he wasn't trying to get into Leila's panties.

'No chance,' Johnson said, walking over to the projected aerial image of the temple's gardens. 'We have to keep him moving to these times.' He pointed to the numbers written in red, dotted along the main avenue leading up to the temple. 'He's got a seven-minute walk through the fancy gardens, down the main four-hundred-yard avenue. They wouldn't let us bring the cars any closer. I can't emphasise it enough: this is the most vulnerable point in his entire forty-eight-hour stopover, so all units need to be in tight on him. At 5.35 p.m. he'll pause to be greeted at the foot of the steps leading up to the temple by a delegation of senior Bahá'ís. They've all been vetted. One of them will present a garland, placing it over the President's head, and we'll all back off. A couple of seconds, nothing more. It's the money shot, and the photos need to go around the world. They won't appreciate any ugly Security Service agents ruining the frame.'

'Can't we land him in any closer, bypass the long walk?' a young, shaven-headed man asked.

'Look, I'd land Marine One on top of the goddamn building and winch the President down through a hole in the roof if I could, but the White House needs the avenue, temple in the background, symbol of world peace. This trip is all about hearts and minds, remember. New president, new beginning. Once he's on those steps, we're fine.' Johnson pointed to the aerial image again. 'There are high walls on either side, here and here.' Five cascades of steps led up through a narrow, high-sided approach to the main temple entrance, beneath one of the twenty-seven 'petals' that formed the building's distinctive roof.

'He'll attend a short ceremony inside, along with a couple of hundred Bahá'ís, then leave by Marine One from the south side and go straight back to Palam airbase. They wanted the temple full, but the Indians couldn't guarantee full security screening.'

'Have they guaranteed anything on this trip?' Spiro asked. The room laughed politely.

'This temple's for Bahá'ís, right?' another Security Service officer asked.

'That's correct,' Johnson said.

'And if the Bahá'ís come from Iran, are they, like, Muslims?'

'Kind of,' Johnson replied, looking across at Spiro.

'Not exactly,' Baldwin interrupted, standing up from his front-row seat. 'They have their origins in Shia Islam, but that was over 150 years ago. Today's Shia clergy regard them as heretics, infidels, a threat to Islam. The Republican Guard in Iran are all over them right now. They're the country's largest religious minority, and the most persecuted. Leaders executed for apostasy, schools closed down, denied passports, barred from government jobs, civil rights withdrawn.'

'Which is why POTUS is paying them a call,' Spiro said, reasserting his authority over the gathering as Baldwin sat down again. 'Symbolic support for regime change. Leila, would you care to enlighten these ignorant people further?'

Spiro threw Baldwin a glance as Leila walked from her third-row seat to join him and Johnson on the stage. For a moment she was standing in the light of the projector, an image of the Lotus Temple playing across her face. She moved to one side, putting a hand up to shield her eyes.

'There are more than five million Bahá'ís in the world,' she began, emotion rising in her voice. 'My mother happens to be one of them. The biggest population is in India, the second largest is in Iran, where it all started.' She paused, composing herself, glancing at Baldwin. 'They believe that Moses, Buddha, Krishna, Jesus, Mohamed and Baha'u'llah, the religion's founder, were all messengers of the same universal God. Baha'u'llah was born in nineteenth-century Persia, so it's a relatively new religion. He believed in spiritual unity, world peace, compulsory education for all. He was also against any form of prejudice.' Leila stopped again. 'I'm sorry,' she said. 'It's the heat.'

But everyone knew it was more than that.

'You can begin to understand why POTUS is so keen to visit the temple,' Spiro said, stepping forward to stand beside her. 'You want to take a break, babe?' He had one arm around her now, squeezing a shoulder.

'I'm fine, really,' Leila said, pouring herself a glass

of water from a plastic bottle on the table beside her. 'The Bahá'í House of Worship, better known as the Lotus Temple, was designed by an Iranian architect. Its distinctive shape is based on a partially open lotus flower.'

'It kind of reminds me of the Sydney Opera House,' Spiro said.

'They say it's the most visited building in the world,' Leila continued. 'Everyone's welcome: Hindus, Jews, Christians, Parsees, Muslims, you name it. The President will enjoy his visit. It's a very special place.'

Leila went back to her seat, but she was desperate to get out of the stuffy room, out of Delhi, away from India. She wanted to be with her mother.

'Thanks, Leila,' Spiro said. 'We appreciate it.' The room applauded, several of the Secret Service officers turning in their seats to look at her. Spiro glanced at Baldwin as he continued. 'Given her specialist knowledge, Leila has been asked to join the POTUS party for this leg of the trip, representing the Company.'

'With the greatest respect to Leila here, isn't that a little unorthodox?' Baldwin asked. 'We all appreciate what she did in London, but . . .'

'No, David, it's not unorthodox,' Spiro interrupted. 'Not at all. It's a great honour for the Company, that's what it is.'

'The honour's all ours,' Johnson said, sensing the tension. 'The President wants to thank Leila personally for her good work in London, as all of us in the Service do.' Another round of applause spread across the hall.

'It's no secret that we owe Langley. And it's no secret that we don't like to admit it. Needless to say, we're not expecting to have to rely on Leila's heroics this time.'

43

There was something about the network of cave-like huts on the hillside that reminded Marchant of Tora Bora. He'd never been to Afghanistan, but he had seen the satellite images, the route Osama Bin Laden had taken when he had given the Americans the slip. Each of the wooden shacks had been built deep into the red Konkan hillside. The one he was now sitting in went back twenty feet, although from the outside it looked like a small, single-room shack. There was no one else inside it apart from Salim Dhar, who had a restless energy about him as he brewed up a saucepan of milky cardamom *chai* on a small gas stove. Outside the door, a man sat on a plastic chair with an AK47 across his knees, smoking a cigarette.

'We have so much in common, you and I,' Dhar said in perfect English.

'Except that I put the milk in afterwards, and you boil it all together, along with a couple of kilos of sugar.'

'And who has the better teeth?' Dhar said, turning to hand Marchant a stainless steel beaker of tea, holding it by the rim. His smile was perfect white.

Marchant was struggling to understand the warmth of Dhar's welcome. From his Africa days he was used to the hospitality of enemies, that polite respite from hostilities while warring factions broke bread together before the slaughter. But there was something different going on here, and he didn't know what it was.

From the moment Dhar had greeted him at the bottom of the hill with a wide smile and a warm embrace, Marchant's mind had raced with possibilities. The taller of his two escorts had been dispatched up the hill, where Marchant noticed a number of men dotted around the rocky ridge. The second fisherman had accompanied Marchant and Dhar down through a deep valley of coconut groves and dense jungle, at the other side of which was the collection of huts. At least ten men were sitting around, some smoking, all with guns.

Marchant clocked a mix of nationalities: North African Arabs, Middle Eastern. No one seemed too bothered by his arrival. He wondered whether Dhar had concocted a cover story to reassure them about his presence. But did Dhar really know who he was? Was he aware that, until a month ago, his visitor spent his days and much of his nights working for an organisation dedicated to eliminating people and places like this? But Dhar had appeared relaxed, asking about his journey, the Westerners on the beaches, how he found the climate – the small-talk of casual acquaintances.

Now, though, as Dhar sat down at the flimsy table opposite him, his head beading with sweat, Marchant sensed that the conversation was about to change. Possibly his life, too. He thought of his father visiting Dhar in jail, and felt the pit of his stomach tighten. Had he been welcomed equally warmly? Were the Americans right to question his father's loyalty to the West? Marchant reminded himself that Dhar had attacked two US embassies in cold blood, killed many US Marines.

'You look a bit like him, you know,' Dhar said in English. 'A family likeness is there – the good looks.' Marchant sipped his tea, grateful for its spiced sweetness. Dhar was wearing a T-shirt cut off at the shoulders, revealing muscles that could only have been toned in a gym. He was tall, his face long and angular, with a skin colour much lighter than that of the local Karnatakans. The nose was prominent, the eye-sockets deep, but none of it seemed out of proportion or surprising. Perhaps it was habit, but Marchant kept glancing at Dhar's low, distinctive earlobes. They were the hardest parts of a face to disguise.

'It's good of you to see me,' Marchant said.

'My fight is not so much with the British, although your government's support for the infidel is craven.' At a flick of a switch, Dhar's voice had hardened into the familiar tones of the *jihadi*. 'I received a message that you might be coming.'

'Who from?'

'An old family friend.'

300

Marchant assumed it must have been Uncle K. 'I need to know why my father visited you in Kerala.'

Dhar smiled at Marchant again, in a way that disarmed him. He was holding all the cards.

'He wanted a name. Someone in London.'

At last, Marchant thought. He had come a long way to hear this. 'Why did he think you would tell him?'

Dhar paused, glancing out of the door at the guard. His voice became quieter.

'Because I had once – foolishly – agreed to assist our family friend.'

'And did you give my father a name?'

'No. I couldn't help him.'

'Couldn't?'

'I didn't know it. He said someone in London was destroying all that he had worked for. From the inside. I couldn't help him.'

'Do you know the name now?'

'No. These things are kept separate.'

Marchant was suddenly very tired, even more tired than he had felt in the marathon. The hike had been bearable in the heat, knowing that ahead lay a chance, however slim, to restore his father's reputation. But now he was finally here, sitting opposite Salim Dhar, one of the world's most wanted, and it had all been a waste of time. Dhar didn't know a damn thing.

'My father lost his job shortly afterwards,' Marchant said, angry now. 'Then he died, of shame.'

'Some say it was the infidel Americans. Doing our job for us. Someone in MI6, close to the Chief.'

Marchant looked up at him. 'But you don't have a name.' He paused. 'Why did you agree to see me?'

'Why?'

'You had no choice with my father. You were in prison when he visited. But with me, you could have had me killed.'

'Because there's something you need to know. Something Stephen told me.' Marchant flinched at the use of his father's first name, his mouth turning dry. Dhar's liquorice eyes had begun to glisten. 'He was my father too.'

44

Fielding put down the phone and looked around the room, his mind working fast. There was no question Daniel was telling the truth. It all made sense now: the payments each month, authorised by Stephen Marchant, to Dhar's father. His predecessor hadn't been trying to bring on a potential asset; it was a personal allowance, prompted by guilt, paid for by the Service.

The dates fitted, too. Stephen Marchant had overlapped with Dhar's father at the British High Commission for six months at the beginning of 1980, the year Dhar was born. It was then that he must have met Dhar's mother, in the months before returning to Britain for the birth of Daniel and Sebastian, when he was without his wife in Delhi.

He picked up the phone again and rang Anne Norman, asking to be put through to Ian Denton, who listened quietly to what Marchant had told Fielding on the phone.

'Where was he calling from?' Denton asked.

'He wouldn't say.'

'But he was with Salim Dhar.'

'No, he'd just left.' There was a pause, too long even for the taciturn Denton. 'Ian?'

'We might not have much time.'

'Can you contact Carter? Straker won't take my calls any more.'

'The phone, Marcus. If Daniel was talking on a targeted mobile, Fort Meade will have picked it up and passed it on already.'

'That's why we need to speak to Carter.'

'Isn't he out of the loop now?'

'Not yet. He'll understand what this means.'

'And you think it's going to help our case with Langley?'

In the few minutes since taking Daniel's call, Fielding had felt only relief, finally knowing why Stephen Marchant had travelled to India on an unauthorised visit, a trip that had always troubled Fielding because it had been so out of character. There had been no mention of any name, no mole uncovered, but at least Fielding now knew that the journey had been made for private reasons, not national ones. It might lower Stephen's reputation in some people's eyes, but for Fielding it meant professional exoneration for his predecessor. Denton was right, though. He always was. In the American mind – Spiro's, Straker's – it would be interpreted quite differently: as further proof that the former Chief of MI6's loyalties were questionable.

'Carter will understand,' Fielding repeated. 'It explains Stephen's visit, why he travelled to Kerala. That's what was bothering them all so much, wasn't it? He was a philanderer with a conscience, Ian, not a traitor. Doesn't this prove it?'

'It will prove only one thing to them: that they were right to go after him.'

Fielding didn't care any more what the Americans thought. It had always been Stephen Marchant's dream to recruit someone like Dhar. In recent days, Fielding realised it had become one of his own, too. Wasn't that why he had let Daniel try to find him? Now they knew who Dhar really was, a high-level penetration of AQ had finally become a possibility. He wasn't about to let the Americans pass up the chance. There would never be another opportunity like it. And who better to recruit Dhar, he thought, than Daniel Marchant, his half-brother?

'He never really got over the death of Sebbie,' Marchant said, sipping at his second cup of cardamom *chai*. He wished there was something stronger to drink. 'None of us did.'

'Was he like you?' Dhar asked.

'Sebbie? More serious than I was. Troubled at times. Used to wake me with his nightmares. Shit hot at maths, though. Drove me mad. Always ahead of me at school.'

Dhar smiled. 'Stephen said that one day you would come.'

Marchant tried to picture the two of them together. 'Do you think he wanted you to let me know?'

'I was angry when he first told me, cross that it had taken him so long.'

'My mother would have died if he had ever gone public about it. She was very vulnerable.'

'My mother too. That's why I forgave him. He told me there wasn't a day in his life when he hadn't thought about me, wondered how I was getting on. But my mother had made him swear that he would never visit me, never try to make contact, never tell anyone. My father still doesn't know. He thought the money was from her family. He used to complain that they hadn't paid him enough dowry. Stephen agreed to her wishes, but said that it had always been his plan to come and find me when I was eighteen.'

'What delayed him?'

'Do you know where I celebrated my eighteenth birthday? In a training camp with my Kashmiri brothers.'

'He might have ruined your reputation.'

'I might have ruined his. He always sent money, though.'

'For how long?'

'Until I was twenty-one. I guess it was him. We weren't rich. My parents worked in the embassies. My father filed infidel invoices, my mother was paid a pittance for looking after expat children when their parents went out to drink. Both of them were treated like pigs. But we were never short of money. My mother said it was tips. She kept a roll of 500-rupee notes hidden behind the *puja* cupboard.'

'Your mother was a Hindu?'

306

'Both of them were. I converted to Islam when I left school. Did everything I could to distance myself from my father, his *kafir* world.'

'You weren't close then.'

Dhar laughed. 'When I found out he had nothing to do with me, it all made sense. The rows, the lack of any bond like those I saw between other fathers and sons. It was such a relief.'

'Maybe he did know?'

'No. He always wanted me to be more like him. To my shame, his favourite job was at the US Embassy. He loved everything American, even wore a cowboy hat and boots to the office fancy-dress party. But he didn't see it. How they treated him, laughing behind his back. I saw it, and I knew he was so, so wrong. He sent me to the American School in Delhi – the worst years of my life.'

Dhar stood up, slinging a small rucksack on his back. 'I have to go. You must stay here for a few days, then they will take you back to Om Beach.'

'Will I see you again?'

'Never try to contact me, for your own safety. I'm your only brother around here.'

'And you can't give me a name?'

'No.' He paused. 'I'll ask.'

'Where are you going?'

Dhar turned back at the doorway, smiling. 'Family business. *Inshallah*.'

45

'Sons turn out in the strangest ways,' Carter said. 'My youngest is in a goddamn thrash band.' Carter was sitting in the back of a black people carrier, Fielding and Denton opposite him at a small foldaway table. They were heading west on the M4, planes landing at Heathrow in a steady procession to their left. He had never seen the Vicar so quiet. 'Besides, Marchant was sending his family money long before he became a *jihadi* warrior.'

'Straker won't buy it, though, will he?' Denton said.

'No, he won't. Which is why we have to get ourselves out to Delhi. I'm not going to sit here quietly while our new President's life is on the line. Hell, I voted for him. You're still the Chief, Marcus. I'm still head of Clandestine. Let's pull some rank here while we're both in play.'

'I shouldn't have taken the call,' Fielding said, looking through the tinted glass as another plane came in to land.

It was a sight that still made him nervous, after what had nearly happened at Heathrow a few years earlier. 'If Daniel had just called the switchboard, he could have been dismissed as a renegade trying to come in from the cold. But he asked to speak to me, and I took the call.'

'So we're heading for Fairford,' Carter said. 'In my untracked vehicle, not yours.'

Denton's phone started to ring. He answered it, listened, then hung up. 'That was Anne. They've come for you in the office, Marcus.'

Marchant had been lying on the *charpoy* for over an hour, waiting for his moment. The guard stood up from his chair, glanced in his direction, and walked down the hill towards another man who had called him. They were both laughing at something.

Marchant had spotted the old Nokia handset while he had been talking to Dhar, but assumed that he would take it with him. It was partially hidden under a copy of *The Week*, an Indian news magazine, in a pile on the dusty floor. Had Dhar left it there on purpose, knowing he would find it? To create a diversion, buy Dhar some time? He swung off the bed, one eye on the doorway, and picked up the phone. He pressed the power button and rolled it up in his shirt, hoping to muffle any start-up tone. It vibrated briefly.

He knew that there was a high risk that it was a targeted unit, but he had to get news about Dhar and his father to Fielding. He may not have the name of a mole in MI6, but at least he had an explanation for the unorthodox trip to Kerala that had so concerned the Americans. He pressed at the familiar digits with shaking fingers, praying that the phone had international access. Then he heard the ringing tone of a London number, and breathed in deeply, a sound that was heard two thousand miles away, in the headphones of a young operator at the National Security Agency in Fort Meade, Maryland.

Denton clipped the safety belt across his lap, and looked around the small cabin of the Gulfstream V: six seats, all buttermilk leather and chrome, a single divan and a mahogany-panelled buffet unit. Fielding fastened his belt opposite him, and caught Denton's wry smile. The irony of senior intelligence officers fleeing Britain in a plane used for rendition flights was not lost on either of them. Carter was up with the pilot, briefing him on the route. He lifted a headphone from one ear and turned back to talk to them.

'The pilot's just filing some dummy flight plans,' he said, louder than he needed to. 'We're operating under special status, but he says UK traffic control's gotten a little stricter in recent months.'

'Like hell it has,' Denton whispered to Fielding, as Carter put his headphone back on and faced the front again. 'Did you see where they put them?'

'I didn't want to look.'

'Behind the buffet. Enough to put you off lunch.' Denton had glanced through the door that separated the back of the plane from the main cabin. The contrast with the plush interior couldn't have been greater. All the fittings had been stripped, leaving the bare-ribbed shell of the plane. Fixed to the matt metal floor were two small steel rings, three feet apart. There was a dark mark between them, where Denton assumed the human cargo had sat, feet and hands restrained. It might have been blood, or something worse, but the traces of pain remained. Had Daniel Marchant been shackled there on his flight to Poland? And, before him, Khalid Sheikh Mohammed?

'Welcome to Air CIA,' Carter said, sitting down next to Denton. 'Twelve hours till touchdown in New Delhi.'

Denton hadn't heard him. He was watching the blue flashing lights on the road beyond Fairford's perimeter fence. At the same moment, the pilot called for Carter to return to the cockpit. Denton caught Fielding's eye, and nodded out of the window.

'There's still time for you to go, Ian,' Fielding said. 'You don't have to be here.'

Denton ignored his Chief. He knew they were right about Leila. Earlier, the three of them had entered the airbase with little difficulty. As far as the RAF was concerned, Fairford was now a standby facility. The USAF ran the place, keen to ensure the safety and secrecy of its B-2 Spirit Stealth bombers, as well as the occasional rendition flight. The guards on the main gate knew Carter well and had waved him through, but Denton feared that the phones would be ringing in Whitehall and Washington. It all depended on how much authority Carter still wielded, whether Straker had done the maths, and concluded that he was working with Fielding.

The twin turbojet engines whined as the pilot nursed the plane across the tarmac towards the end of the three-kilometre-long runway. Denton unclipped his seatbelt and went forward to Carter. For a moment, Fielding thought he was taking up his offer to get off the plane.

'Everything OK?' Denton asked.

'We're just clarifying with Langley that I'm on official Company business,' Carter said.

'You mean a rendition flight.'

Carter laughed. 'Routine Clandestine work.'

'Have you seen the police activity on the perimeter?'

'Relax, it's nothing. Just a bunch of plane-spotters, happens all the time. Guess the Spirit's flying today. We always ask your police to clear them away. Nobody knows the Vicar's on board, Ian. We don't do passport control on these planes.'

46

William Straker sat back in the DCIA's office in Langley, Virginia, and looked at the photos of his two boys on his desk. He had been an only child, and envied the camaraderie that his sons already enjoyed. He hadn't checked, but he guessed Harriet Armstrong in London was a single child, too. She shared his natural distrust of others.

'It's a final green, Harriet, we're going in now,' he said on speaker-phone. 'Fort Meade picked up the call earlier. The strike point's been relayed to the USS *Independence*.'

'The Prime Minister has requested that Daniel Marchant is taken alive,' Armstrong replied.

'I was afraid you'd say that. The DNI wants all threats in the region eliminated. And Dhar's currently top of the lone-wolf list.'

'Marchant might be useful,' Armstrong said.

'You're not going soft on me, Harriet, are you?'

Armstrong said nothing. 'India won't allow Predator use in their airspace, so we're sending in Seals, supported by some token Black Cats to keep Delhi onside. I'm sure your Prime Minister appreciates we can't take risks with a presidential visit. There are too many already on this trip. Monk Johnson's a wreck.'

'We understand the threat, of course we do, but Marchant is a British citizen, and the PM is adamant he is not killed. We currently have an SAS unit on standby in Delhi, ready to help.'

'You know, I think we can manage this on our own, but thanks for the offer. Here's what I'll do. Once we've pulled Marchant out of the jungle, he's your prisoner. You might get a bit more out of him than we did in Poland. How does that sound?'

Not great, Armstrong thought. Body bags didn't make great interviewees. 'I'll inform Cobra of the offer. It's convening now.'

'Your cooperation is appreciated, Harriet. You and I think the same. You saw the TX details of the call?'

'Earlier, yes.'

'Jesus, we were right about Stephen Marchant. Like father, like son. But what about Marcus? Daniel's put through to his home, then the Chief chooses not to report the conversation to anyone. And now he's gone AWOL. I thought this guy was on our side.'

'It also bothers the PM.'

'Glad to hear it,' Straker said, failing to detect much sincerity in Armstrong's reply. 'Does the PM know about Chadwick, too?'

'David?'

'Sir David, knight of the realm.'

'What about him?' Armstrong tightened her grip on the phone. She had always liked Chadwick, even fancied him in her earlier Whitehall days. She wouldn't hear a bad word said against him.

'Seems like he's been signing up to some illegal websites over here. The FBI passed over the credit card trail this morning, thought we should know.'

Armstrong, her resentment rising, wanted the conversation to end. She didn't believe a word. The Americans were still on the warpath after removing Stephen Marchant, but this was new territory. They would go after the PM next.

'How illegal?'

'I hope he hasn't got children.'

Marchant slipped the mobile phone back under the magazine and lay on his *charpoy* again, watching the guard walk back up the hill towards him. He looked in briefly on Marchant then sat down, picking at his teeth. It had been good to hear the Legoland receptionist's voice. The best ones worked on the emergency number. Her warm, reassuring tones had contrasted sharply with Anne Norman's brusque manner.

Fielding had said very little. They both knew that the less time they spoke, the less chance there was of the call being traced. But it had been hard to convey everything quickly and cryptically. The most important thing had been to provide Fielding with the real reason for his father's trip. He had also wanted him to know that Dhar might be turned. Dhar would never work for America, but the notion of him spying for Britain was suddenly not so implausible.

The implications of his father's revelation had not yet fully sunk in, he knew that: the opposite lives his sons had led, each one's existence on a separate continent, unknown to the other, despite being born within months of each other. Marchant knew that by ringing Fielding, immersing himself in his old professional world, he was avoiding the personal consequences. His father, who had spent a lifetime uncovering other people's secrets, had been carrying around the biggest one of all. Did he think worse of him for it? He feared the Americans might.

A commotion outside broke in on his thoughts. A man was coming up the hill with a large sheet of cardboard, cut out in the shape of a human figure. He was talking excitedly, a small group of men following him, looking at the effigy. Marchant couldn't understand what he was saying, but he heard Salim's name mentioned, and recognised the figure. It was of the previous US President, wearing a cowboy hat and boots.

One of the men barked an order at another, who pulled out a cigarette lighter and held it to the image, dropping it to the ground when the flames caught. But before the curling fire had reached the President's head, Marchant saw quite clearly that there was a small hole between the eyes, made by a single bullet.

Spiro leant in towards Leila and touched her hand. 'You

don't have to do this, you know,' he said, maintaining the contact longer than she would have liked. 'The threat level is high. There are others who can take your place.'

'Like Baldwin? He doesn't seem very pleased to see me here.'

'The guy's a loser,' he said, looking around the restaurant. 'All hat and no cattle.'

Spiro had been drinking all evening – their last chance for the next forty-eight hours, he said – and was starting to worry her.

'It's important I'm there. My mother will be proud that her daughter's showing the US President around the biggest Bahá'í temple in the world. It's important for me, too. I need to draw a line under all that's been said, reassure the doubters.'

'Who cares what Baldwin or the Brits think?' Spiro said, topping up her glass with wine. She shouldn't have agreed to dinner, but she was indebted to Spiro, and needed his ongoing support. She glanced around the restaurant. It was on the roof of their hotel, the lights of New Delhi spread out beneath them as two musicians from Rajasthan worked the candlelit room. With a different man the scene might have been romantic, she thought, trying not to picture herself and Marchant together.

'They're pulling the Vicar in, too,' Spiro said. He was pumped up, unrelaxed, his leg bouncing beneath the table. 'Never liked the guy.'

Leila knew all about the allegations Fielding had made, that she was working for Iran, but she hadn't heard of his apparent suspension.

'Why?'

'Daniel, your former squeeze. Seems he made a call to London. Spoke to Fielding on a phone used once by Salim Dhar. Thank God Fort Meade had their pants up and their headphones on for a change.'

Leila was relieved to hear that Marchant was still alive. She had feared the worst after the Gymkhana explosion. What remained of the book at the club's reception had confirmed that a 'David Marlowe' had been signed in as a visitor, but his body was never found. She hoped one day to talk to him, explain it all, but time was running out.

'Where was he calling from?' she asked, struggling to conceal her interest.

'Somewhere south of here. We were right to man-mark him in London, Leila. You did a fine job. It turns out the whole lot of them were at it: Marchant, his father, Fielding.'

'Was Daniel with Dhar when he called?' Her voice was more anxious.

'We sure as hell hope so. But you don't need to trouble yourself about him. What do you say to a drink back in my room?' He forced his leg between hers under the table.

'I must do a bit more reading up on the Bahá'ís,' she said, pushing back her chair. 'I'd hate the President to think I'd just screwed my way to the top.'

'I'm not sure you heard me,' Spiro said, holding her forearm. She looked around the restaurant for support, but no one had noticed. Spiro's breath was sour, his lips oily from the earlier *biryani*. 'I've been asked a lot of questions in recent days, told a lot of folk to trust you. Men like Baldwin. I think that deserves a little payback, don't you?'

47

Marchant heard the mobile phone begin to ring moments before the Sikorsky Seahawk came in low over the tree-tops. He rushed to pick it up just as the guard outside fell to the ground, a single sniper shot to his chest.

'Get out of there now,' a familiar female voice urged. As he tried to place it, a loud explosion ripped the roof off the hut, knocking him to the ground. He started to crawl, but his eyes were filling with warm blood from a cut to his forehead. Wiping his face, he rolled across the dusty ground to the back of the hut, where he slid out through a hole that had been torn in the palm-woven panelling. The air was thick with the sound of gunfire, urgent shouts – American, Indian, Middle Eastern – and the cry of crows.

Marchant kept thinking of the crows, what they were doing in the middle of a firefight, as a group of Black Cats moved down the hillside towards him. They must have walked, taken the long route, he thought. If it hadn't been for them, he would have escaped. Two of them lifted him up and dragged him semi-conscious towards the winch rope of the Seahawk, now hovering above the clearing.

'No Dhar,' Marchant heard one of the Black Cats say into his helmet mike, as he rose above the coconut canopy into a cerulean sky.

Leila looked up to the very top of the temple ceiling, where a lotus-flower pattern blossomed at its apex. Early-morning sunlight was streaming in through the windows, bathing the interior in an ethereal glow. Pews had been arranged in neat rows across the large open space, and Leila sat down at the end of one of them. The temple was almost deserted, except for a few cleaners polishing the floors and a group of Indian police officers who stood at the main door. The temple complex had been swept four times in the last twenty-four hours by the Secret Service, and would be checked twice more before the President's visit in the evening.

Leila glanced around, then pulled out a piece of paper and began to read from it quietly, tears filling her eyes. '*O thou forgiver of sins, open thou the way for this awakened soul to enter thy kingdom, and enable this bird, trained by thy hand, to soar in the eternal rose garden. She is afire with longing to draw nigh unto thee: enable her to attain thy presence.*'

She had heard the news about her mother two hours earlier. Something had made her want to ring Tehran from the moment she had woken. Already her mind was playing tricks, rearranging the sequence of events so that she somehow knew her mother was dead before the woman on the phone had confirmed it. The woman, a neighbour, had been sitting with her mother all night, comforting her as she slipped away. She shouldn't have told Leila, but clearly she needed to speak to someone.

'*She is afire with longing to draw nigh unto thee,*' Leila continued, the words blurring in front of her. '*Enable her to attain thy presence. She is distraught and distressed in separation from thee. Cause her to be admitted into thy Heavenly mansion.*'

The past twelve hours had been the worst of her life. She had stayed up late reading about Fariborz Sahba, the Iranian architect behind the temple. Her mother had spoken often of him and his wonderful house of worship, which she had visited soon after its completion in the 1980s. Sahba had chosen the metaphor of a blossoming lotus flower in the hope that a new era of peace and religious tolerance would emerge out of the 'murky waters' of mankind's history of ignorance and violence.

Spiro was ignorant of many things, but last night was the first time he had been violent towards her. She had tried to resist, to talk him out of it, but he had threatened to tell Monk Johnson that she was behaving erratically. Nothing could jeopardise the presidential pageant, or the leading part she had been asked to play in it, so she had followed him out of the restaurant and back to his hotel room.

Afterwards, in her own room, she had taken a shower,

sobbing as she scrubbed herself with sandalwood soap. Then the tears had cleared and she had set to work, researching the Bahá'í faith online with the zeal of a dying patient desperate for a cure: the simple process of religious conversion that required a 'declaration card' to be filled out; how the rural masses had been targeted by Bahá'í missionaries in post-Gandhi India, many of them signing up to its appealing message of a united mankind with a single thumbprint. And the British weapons inspector David Kelly, who had converted to Bahá'ísm four years before his mysterious death.

By the time dawn broke, her research had better prepared her for the news of her mother's death, which only seemed to confirm in her tired mind the belief that she had known about it already. She felt closer to her mother, understood her life better, and knew how to pray for her in death. Her understanding of the Bahá'í faith was still nothing compared to her mother's, but it had grown in recent months, preparing her for this day.

Now she was here, in the Lotus Temple, waiting for her Security Service colleagues to arrive, and she must try to put her grieving on hold. As an intelligence officer she was used to protecting her emotions, partitioning off her inner life in order to play a part, but she knew that the next few hours would test her skills to the limit.

'With tearful eyes she fixed her gaze on the Kingdom of Mysteries. Many a night she spent in deep communion with thee, and many a day she lived in intimate remembrance of thee.'

She dabbed at her eyes with a tissue and looked around

the temple, drawing strength from its beauty. Monk Johnson would want to walk through the President's journey one more time, down the avenue, up the five flights of steps and into the protection of Sahba's petals. Leila felt protected too, with her own declaration card in one hand, a page of prayers in the other, about to convert to the religion of her mother and hoping to be forgiven for the choices she had made and the actions she was about to take.

48

Marchant lifted his head towards the cell door and listened to the bolts being pulled back. Both of his eyes were heavily swollen, and he could hear better than he could see. As far as he could tell, he was in the basement of the American Embassy in Delhi. He had been hooded on the Seahawk flight, his wrists shackled, and then beaten by two men he took for Seals.

There was an avenging energy about their assault that made Marchant wonder if they were the same two who had waterboarded him in Poland. But they didn't speak, either to him, or to each other, so it was hard to tell. Perhaps they were just venting their frustration that they hadn't found Dhar, knowing that their own butts would be whipped for having returned empty-handed on the eve of a presidential visit.

Marchant went with the blows as much as he could, but it was a cowardly assault, and his anger stopped him from slipping into unconsciousness as quickly as he would have liked. Instead, he rolled around the cold floor of the helicopter, trying to protect himself by tucking up his knees, and spitting out as much blood as he could to stop it congealing later in his throat.

He was lying on the floor again now as the cell door swung open, letting in a cool draft from the air-conditioned corridor outside. He steeled himself for another beating, but the blows never came.

'Daniel?' It was the same voice he had heard on Dhar's mobile: Harriet Armstrong's.

He heard her walk towards him as the heavy cell door was closed and bolted behind her. She came over to where Marchant was lying.

'I was going to ask if you're OK. Can I get you some water?'

Marchant didn't know what to say or think. This was the woman who had helped to drive his father from office, and had led the calls for his own suspension. What was she doing here? And why had she phoned him in the jungle?

'I wasn't expecting your call,' he managed to say. Armstrong passed him a plastic bottle. He held it up to his lips with both hands. They were bound together in front of him now, rather than behind his back. He dropped the bottle after a few sips, and Armstrong picked it up, holding it to his lips again. Then she put it on the ground and helped him sit up against the back wall of the cell.

'Thanks,' he said. Armstrong said nothing. He heard

her walk away from him and knock on the cell door. After a few moments the two bolts were pulled back. Another rush of cool air.

'Get me some warm soapy water, a cloth and a doctor,' her voice echoed down the corridor. 'And if anyone questions you, tell them to call William Straker in Langley.'

'Sir, I've got Carter on the line,' the junior officer said, standing like a bellboy at the door of the Maurya Hotel's Presidential Suite.

'Carter?' Spiro asked, walking across the main room, his mind on other things – Leila's ass, when he could be with her again. 'Is he back at Langley, or still showboating in London?'

He glanced around at the desk, the deep leather armchairs, the plasma screen on one wall and the large glass bowl on the low Rajasthani coffee table. A single lotus flower was floating on the water. Monk Johnson had asked him to take one final look at the suite. Everything seemed to be in order.

'He's here, sir, in Delhi.'

Spiro spun round to face the junior officer. 'Here? What the hell's he doing here?'

'He's at the airport, sir. Flew in on a Gulfstream this morning. The Indians are awaiting our authorisation before allowing him to disembark.'

The last thing Spiro needed was to have Alan Carter in Delhi. He would call Straker, find out what was going on. Carter had been pulled off the Marchant case when he went soft on the British renegade. This was Spiro's shout now, an opportunity to rehabilitate himself after Poland. The DCIA had charged him with coordinating the Agency's role in the presidential visit – his last chance, Straker had said. He wasn't about to let Carter embarrass him again.

'That's the first sensible thing they've done in days. Let Carter fry. Tell the Indians there's a problem with the paperwork. I'm sure they'll understand.'

Salim Dhar pushed his way through the crowded alleyways of Old Delhi, thinking about his contact. Would he be a *farangi*, or dark-skinned, like his target? All Dhar knew was that he worked at the infidel's embassy in Delhi. He turned into Kinari Bazaar, sidestepping a woman with a wicker basket of baby aubergines balanced on her head. On either side of him as the lane became narrower, sparkling wedding gear lit up the shop windows: grooms' turbans, brides' bangles, embroidered jackets glistening with thick silver thread, garlands made from rupee notes, lace tinsel, giant rosettes.

He felt at home here, reassured by the warren of lanes and Mughal doorways, the call of a nearby *muezzin*, the teeming company of Muslim brothers. He turned into Dariba Kalan, the street of pearls and precious stones in Shah Jahan's day, now famous for its gold and silver jewellers. To his left a *jalebi wallah* scooped out bright orange strands of syrup-soaked batter from a pan of oil and shook sugar over them. On a normal day, Dhar would have stopped to buy some, but today wasn't normal. He glanced at his watch and moved on towards the Jama Masjid, looking out for a cycle rickshaw.

The arrangement had been designed to mirror the chaos of Chandni Chowk. His contact would pass by the mosque's main entrance at around midday. More important than the exact time was the person in the back seat of the rickshaw, who would be wearing a black baseball cap. The rickshaw would stop outside the mosque, where its passenger would step out and pay off the driver. Dhar would then climb in and ask to be taken to Gadodia Market, just off Khari Baoli. Before the rickshaw set off, however, his contact would approach and ask if he was going anywhere near the town hall. Dhar would confirm that he was, and they would set off together in the rickshaw through the back streets of Chandni Chowk while he was briefed on the evening's itinerary.

Dhar liked the plan, because the noisy crowds offered good cover and the congestion would make it impossible for anyone to follow them without being noticed. But he was becoming anxious when, at 12.15 p.m., no cycle rickshaws had stopped outside the mosque. He looked at the people around him, one of whom must be his contact. To avoid attention he had agreed to have his shoes shined, the 'semi-deluxe' service.

Then he noticed a rickshaw appear in the distance, in the midst of a sea of people flowing up Dariba Kalan. The scene reminded him of the television images he had seen of the London Marathon, heads bobbing up and down, everyone focused on the road ahead. As the rickshaw drew near, zigzagging through the crowd, he could see someone wearing a baseball cap in the back. He paid off the shoe boy and glanced around. Still there was no one he could identify.

The rickshaw driver was now outside the mosque gates. Dhar stepped in closer, keeping an eye out for similar movement around him. The passenger climbed down from the rickshaw, not looking up. Dhar nodded at the driver, letting him know that he was his next fare, then asked for Gadodia Market. The driver gestured for him to get in. Not a flicker of recognition from anyone. Dhar settled back on the thin plastic cushion.

'*Chalo*,' he said to the driver, already admiring the coolness of his unseen contact. And then a figure appeared from nowhere at the side of the rickshaw.

'Are you going near the town hall?' The question was asked in perfect Urdu.

Dhar smiled. 'Get in,' he said, making room next to him. He hadn't been expecting a woman.

49

'The Prime Minister was adamant that you shouldn't be killed,' Armstrong said, wiping the last traces of blood from Marchant's bruised face. She put the sponge back in the bowl, red strands swirling in the soapy water. 'The Americans weren't so concerned. Their minds were on other things. We compromised.'

'You mean they sent for you. Very reassuring.'

But Marchant was pleased Armstrong had come. He could see out of both eyes now, the cuts in his forehead neatly stitched, and he was wearing a clean, if ill-fitting, set of clothes: jeans and a collarless cotton shirt. Two wooden chairs had been brought into the cell when the doctor had checked him over. The woman sitting in front of him was very different from the frumpy figure he remembered from London, less stiff, more feminine. Perhaps it was the cream *salwar khameez*, simply embroidered at the front. He had only ever seen her in dark trouser suits.

'Daniel, there's something we need to talk about. It's Leila.' Marchant had to suppress an involuntary start. It was strange to hear her name again. 'Marcus Fielding has made some very strong allegations about her since you've been away.'

'She was working for them, wasn't she?'

'For who?'

'Langley. She set me up at the marathon. It's the only explanation. She could have explained everything, cleared my name, but she didn't.'

Armstrong paused. 'Did Leila ever talk to you about her mother?'

'Not often.'

'Did you ever meet her?'

Marchant was struggling to work out where Armstrong was going with her questions. 'She never encouraged it. Why?'

'But you knew where her mother was?'

'In a home. Hertfordshire, I think. Leila was embarrassed about her.'

'Her mother went back to Iran soon after her father died. She never set foot in a British nursing home.'

Marchant said nothing. He thought back to Leila's tears, the phone calls, the reluctance to talk, her worry that her mother was being mistreated.

'The Americans knew,' Armstrong continued. She could have chosen to be triumphant, but she appeared to take no satisfaction in what she was revealing. 'They used it to recruit Leila. Her vetting officer thought the mother was still in the UK. Leila never informed him that she'd gone back to Iran. The officer's been suspended.'

'Did the Americans tell you she was working for them?'

'Eventually. Chadwick put on a brave face, said we already knew. But they never told us how they turned her. She knew her career would have been over if MI6 had found out her mother wasn't still in Hertfordshire. The Americans threatened to inform her vetting officer. It kept her loyal to Langley.'

'Why are you telling me this?'

'Because Fielding said something else.' She paused. Her tone was almost maternal now. 'He thought Leila was ultimately working for Iran.'

'Iran?' Marchant said quietly. He knew as he repeated the word that Fielding was right. It was the final leap he had never been able to make, but the Vicar had, his judgement unswayed by love.

Fielding knew that time was running out. It was almost fifty degrees on the tarmac where the plane was parked, in a quiet corner of Indira Gandhi airport. The aircon unit was on the blink, and the plane didn't have enough fuel for another flight, even if the control tower gave them clearance, which was unlikely.

Fielding held Carter's mobile, waiting for MI6's station head in Delhi to call him back. An alert would have gone out to all the Service's staff to report immediately if there was any word of Fielding's whereabouts. But the local station head owed his promotion to the Chief, who had nothing to lose.

The phone rang in Fielding's moist hand. He looked

at Denton and Carter as he listened, both of them stripped down to their shirts, buttons undone, dripping with sweat. Denton was the worse of the two. He had never been good in the heat, always preferring the cooler climes of Eastern Europe. After a few moments Fielding passed the phone back to Carter.

'They're sending out a refuelling truck in ten minutes,' he said quietly.

'Thank God for that,' the pilot whispered, his voice drained of all its earlier confidence.

'They'll load enough fuel to reach the Gulf. You can make your own way home from there.'

'What about you?' Carter asked, wiping his brow.

'One of our local agents is on board the fuel truck,' Fielding said. 'I'm going back with him to the depot, and on from there to find Leila.'

'Fielding never believed that your presence at the marathon was anything other than chance,' Armstrong continued. 'It made him look elsewhere for answers. Leila's mother is a Bahá'í – a persecuted religion in Iran. The Iranian Ministry of Intelligence and Security saw an opportunity to blackmail Leila in London as soon as her mother touched down in Tehran. If Leila didn't agree to work for them, they would kill her mother. No one would notice – Bahá'ís are being killed and imprisoned all the time.'

'What made her go back to that?' Marchant asked, but he already knew the answer.

'Her mother country. It tends to call loudest when it's in trouble.'

Leila had spoken about it once, how her mother longed one day to return to her place of birth. She must have finally decided that time was running out. Her husband was dead, and Iran, despite its problems, held more for her in old age than Britain ever would. It had only been her daughter who kept her there, and she was embarking on a life of foreign postings.

'And the rest of you believed I was trying to take out the US Ambassador at the marathon?'

'The TETRA phone evidence seemed incontrovertible.'

'It was Leila who gave me the phone.'

Armstrong paused again. 'We managed to establish that it was linked to the explosives on Pradeep's running belt. There was a pre-programmed speed-dial number, listed as the main switchboard at MI6. If you'd rung it, Pradeep, you and many others would have died.'

Marchant had been so close to calling Leila on that number. She had even urged him to dial it. He felt sick. *If you don't hear from me in fifteen minutes, try calling the office. Speed-dial 1.'* He remembered the exchange vividly, like much of what was said that day.

'You know it wasn't my mobile,' he said, swallowing hard, still thinking of the look in Leila's eyes when she had handed him the TETRA unit. 'My old one maybe, but it was Leila who brought it with her.'

'That's what Fielding said, what you told us in your debrief. But I'm afraid we all believed Leila, who debriefed very differently. MI5 was finally allowed into Legoland yesterday. We found the person who signs out the handsets, sweated the truth out of him.'

Marchant knew what that meant, but he felt no sympathy. All he could think of was that Leila had been prepared to kill him.

'It seems she used her charms to check out your old phone without actually signing for it. She told him it was for sentimental reasons.'

For the first time, Armstrong's tone was condemnatory, as if she could stomach the treachery, but not the promiscuity. Marchant's response was entirely personal, too. The implications for his country would have to wait. Leila had betrayed him.

He had come to accept that her failure to exonerate him after the race could not be easily explained. Some sort of collusion with America had been the most likely reason, but now he knew it was worse than that. Far worse. He tried to hang on to the fact that she had chosen not to separate him and Pradeep into a thousand body parts. '*Did you try ringing me? Don't, OK? Please. Just don't.*' Her voice had been insistent, but it wasn't much consolation. Leila was the mole. His heart was hardening instinctively, to protect him from the blast, but he knew it was too late.

He remembered that night at the Fort when she had come into his room at dawn, how he had told her he wanted to keep their relationship separate from the deceit of their chosen profession. But he had slowly relented, won over by her laughter and love. Now it appeared that there had been no distinction for her. It had all been work: one big, dirty, duplicitous job.

Was that the Leila he had known? He *had* to believe

that a part of what they had meant something to her. The Iranians must have presented her with such a hideous alternative that she was forced to go along with their plan.

'So are you and Fielding best friends again?' he asked.

Armstrong ignored the sarcasm. 'He's disappeared. We think he's here in India, trying to find Leila.'

'Is she here too?' Marchant couldn't conceal his interest.

'She asked for a transfer to the CIA station in Delhi, before Fielding found out.'

'Why Delhi?'

'She wanted to protect the President.'

They looked at each other for a moment. An image of Leila and Dhar together flashed through his mind. He had to get out of there.

'Have you come to release me? We need to find her.'

'That's not in my gift, I'm afraid. We failed to convince Langley that Leila has betrayed them as well as us. I'm not sure we ever will. At least Straker's allowed me to debrief you about Salim Dhar. He remembered your stubbornness in Poland. You're meant to be my prisoner.'

She looked at the bowl of bloody water.

'You can tell him that Dhar headed north, two hours before the Seals arrived.'

'Thank you.'

'And that he likes shooting US presidents for target practice.'

50

Dhar watched the rickshaw driver's legs seesaw through the Chandni Chowk traffic. 'You will only have one chance,' the woman next to him said. 'At 5.35 p.m. the President will pause at the foot of the five flights of steps leading up to the Lotus Temple entrance. He will be greeted by a delegation of senior Bahá'ís. One will present him with a garland of flowers. At this point, and this point only, his security detail will withdraw a few steps. Your line of sight should be clear.'

'I won't miss,' Dhar said. '*Inshallah*.'

They sat in silence, watching the sea of faces flow past them on either side. She had already been through all the practical arrangements for the evening and there was a sense that their meeting should now come to an end.

'It must have been difficult, so much time-passing with the *kafir*,' Dhar said. Across the street, two Western tourists, money belts slung below their thick waists, were

338

taking photos of a man with no legs, perched on a board with wheels, pushing himself along with raw knuckles.

'Those who work with animals get used to the smell.'

They were still wary of each other, both retreating to the muscled vernacular of the *jihadi*. There was no reason for either of them to trust each other beyond this short encounter. But there was something about the woman that intrigued Dhar. Her head was wrapped in a black scarf, concealing most of her face except for her big Meenakshi eyes. She spoke perfect Urdu, but with a slight accent that Dhar couldn't quite place.

'Some people are saying that the Americans were behind the *jihad* in Britain, the petty squabbles of the enemy doing our work for us.'

'Is that what they say?' she asked.

'The talk is of nothing else. The American infidel recruited someone to destroy its allies from the inside.'

Dhar had a question for his passenger before he dropped her off at the town hall: the name of the insider in London. His father, whom he had met only once, was dead, but he still needed to know, for himself, for his brother.

'The enemy within has succeeded,' she said. 'The Britishers are facing turmoil.'

'*Inshallah*.' The rickshaw speeded up, free of traffic now. 'Your work is at the infidel's embassy. You must know who this person is in Britain.'

'Why do you ask?'

Because his *jihadi* world, so recently turned upside down, would begin to make sense again if he could be certain that it was an American who had betrayed his father. But he said nothing.

'The infidels believe it was one of their own,' she continued, 'but the credit lies elsewhere. Not with Britain or America, but with someone, a woman, who tricked them both.'

'Another woman?' Dhar shifted in his seat. 'It would be an honour to meet her,' he said quietly, without conviction.

'An honour?' she asked. 'What's honour got to do with it?'

'It can't have been easy. Like you, she was living amongst the infidel, but acting in the name of Allah.'

'Was she?'

But even Dhar wasn't sure any more.

51

Straker took the call in one of the small private booths in the White House's refurbished Situation Room complex. Moments before, he had stepped out of the Telecommunications Room next door, where the Vice President, the Director of National Intelligence, the White House Chief of Staff and a raft of other security advisers who wanted his job had been waiting for him to assess the threat matrix in India. It was a meeting he had been postponing ever since word had reached him that Salim Dhar had not been captured in Karnataka.

'Harriet, I hope you have some decent CX for me. Otherwise I'm going to have to dunk our friend Marchant's head in the Arabian Sea. Tell me he knows where Dhar is.'

'Marchant was meant to be my prisoner.'

'He was alive, wasn't he? That's all your PM wanted.'

'Barely. Dhar left two hours before you reached the hideout, heading north.'

'Great. Marchant told you nothing else?'

'Dhar was shooting at Texans before Daniel reached him.'

'Texans?'

'A target in the shape of your previous President.'

'Jesus, we need to take this guy down.'

'Leila too. She might be working with Dhar.'

It was at moments like this, when he needed to punch someone, that Straker wished he brought a basketball into the office, as other DCIAs had been known to do, but it wasn't his style to bounce balls down the corridors of power.

'I'm touched by your interest in an Agency employee, Harriet,' he said, failing to conceal his anger. 'Really, I am. But we've run the rule over Leila many times. Monk Johnson is the most paranoid man I know, and he's happy to have her meet his President. She saved the Secret Service's butt in London, remember? Spiro's looked into her case. Every goddamn analyst in Langley has taken a look. It doesn't stack up. She's clean, she did us a favour, she saved one of our ambassador's lives. She's a fucking hero, for God's sake.'

'Daniel Marchant thinks she was working for the Iranians.'

'Marchant? We've just airlifted the kid out of a terrorist's hideout in the Indian jungle. Give me a break here, Harriet. He tried to kill Munroe. He's an enemy combatant, like his father, another one of Dhar's British buddies.'

342

Armstrong looked around the room she had been given in the American Embassy. It had started with Straker's crass attempt to destroy Chadwick's reputation, but now her disillusionment with America had grown into something more general, a weariness with its ways that she had once so revered.

'Give me a little longer with him,' she said.

'Do what you have to, Harriet. We need to neutralise Dhar. I've told the embassy that Marchant's yours, but we don't have much time.'

Armstrong hung up and dialled through to the guard-room in the basement, where Marchant was being kept. Then she made an encrypted call on her mobile to the MI6 station chief in Delhi, one of Fielding's old friends. If the Chief was in town, he would know.

52

Marchant couldn't decide if it was a good or bad development that his guards were taking him out of his cell. The hood and cuffs should have made him fear the worst, but there was something about their manner that gave him hope. Their body language was routine rather than rough.

'Where are we going?' he asked, not expecting an answer. The brightness of a Delhi day was forcing its way through the hood as they walked slowly up some stairs.

'For a little drive,' one of the guards said. 'With your new best buddy.'

The next moment, Marchant felt the full heat of an Indian summer hitting his face like a hair-drier. One of the guards ducked his head and helped him step inside an air-conditioned vehicle of some sort. It felt spacious rather than cramped as he sat down in a back seat. The sound of a sliding door told him it was a people carrier.

He sat in silence as it drove off, aware of a number

of other people inside. Nobody talked except for the driver, an Indian, who muttered as he waited to pull out into the traffic. Daniel could smell jasmine incense.

'So, how old were you when he died?' a voice from the seat next to him asked. It was Armstrong's.

'Who?' Marchant was troubled by her tone. He guessed that there were five of them in the car altogether: the driver, Armstrong, his two US Marine guards and himself. Armstrong seemed to be addressing the gallery, her maternal manner a distant memory.

'Oh, come on, Daniel. Sebastian, your brother. The one you've blamed for so much in your life. The death you could have prevented, the reason for the survivor's guilt that drove you to drink.'

Marchant tried to work out what was going on, why she was so obviously talking for the benefit of others. Her approach was unnatural, her tone forced.

'He was eight. We both were.'

'Twins. Of course. Tell us what happened.'

'Where are you taking me?' Marchant asked, but he already knew. He just wasn't sure why.

'To where it all went wrong for Daniel Marchant,' she said. 'I thought it might be useful if we returned to the beginning. It might help us work out how it all could end.'

She touched his hand, then spoke more quietly, as if just to him. 'Here, put your seatbelt on. You'll need it.'

'I have a question for you,' the woman said as she stepped down from the rickshaw. 'Why did Stephen Marchant, the infidel spy chief, visit you in prison?'

Dhar instinctively looked around, then composed himself. 'Is it common knowledge?'

'It was one of the reasons he was removed from his office in London.'

'The *kafir* was desperate, tried to recruit me. Why does it matter?'

'Some of our brothers were concerned. They couldn't understand what he wanted with you.'

'He would have been slaughtered if it hadn't been for my chains.'

'And the son, they say he came for you too.'

Dhar was worried now, troubled by how much this woman knew. Did others also know?

'Why should the son wish to find me?'

'He was a spy for the infidels, like his father. He also lost his job.'

'Our female comrade in London did well to bring down the house of Marchant,' Dhar said, managing a thin smile. It wasn't returned.

'Some brothers tried to kill the son, at the Gymkhana Club. They were worried about you.' She paused. 'But he is on the run, still alive.'

For a moment Dhar thought he detected emotion in her voice, disguised like his own.

'Not if he finds me.'

They looked at each other, eye to eye, and then she was gone.

'We were driving back from Chanakyapuri,' Marchant began. 'My mother, Sebbie, me.' His hood tasted of stale clothes. 'Usually we drove around in our Ambassador, but it was being fixed by a garage so my father had arranged for us to borrow a vehicle from the High Commission. It was used by the traffic police, a *desi* version of the American Jeep.'

'Nice wheels,' one of the guards said from the front. 'Got one in the garage back home.'

'Not these.' Marchant paused. 'Death traps. No safety belts in those days. Our driver, Raman, was normally so careful, but he was angry that day. The petrol pump attendant had ripped him off, served us up short. Raman disliked that more than anything. My mother was anxious, too. We had an *ayah* coming for a job interview, and we were late. She hated being late. So we were rushing, heading down towards Saket on a main road.'

Marchant was aware of the car slowing down. When it stopped, his hood was removed by one of the guards. He blinked in the bright sunshine.

'Was this the place?' Armstrong asked.

Marchant looked at the traffic all around him. They pulled over on the side of a busy road, on the edge of a big junction. Then he glanced at Armstrong in the seat next to him, and tried to work out what was going on. He had been right about the number of people in the car. The two Marines were sitting up front with the driver, who was tapping the steering wheel nervously. It was a dangerous place to have parked. Armstrong must have asked them to leave her and Marchant on their own in the back.

'I can't be sure,' Marchant said. 'It was more than twenty years ago.'

347

'Try to remember,' Armstrong said quietly. 'Because we're not going anywhere until you do.'

Fielding climbed into the back of the cotton-white Ambassador and turned to look at the airport behind him. The Gulfstream was still sitting on the Tarmac, shimmering in the hazy heat. At least it had fuel now, and Denton and Carter would soon be clear of Delhi's intolerable summer. They had been reluctant to let him go on his own, for their different reasons, but they knew it would have been impossible to smuggle three men out on the fuel truck, even though security at the airport was lax. 'Don't let her even get near the President, if only for me,' Carter had said.

As the car drove off, with Prasannan, the local agent, sitting in the front, Fielding wondered what he would do if he found Leila. He knew he must stop her. It wasn't enough to know that he had been right and the Americans were wrong. But he was a marked man himself now, on the run like Daniel Marchant. He assumed it was Armstrong who had entered his office in London. She would have loved marching into Legoland with a warrant, tearing the place up, questioning everyone.

'The traffic is very vigorous today,' Prasannan said, turning to Fielding. 'It's the President's visit.' The driver nodded in agreement. He was sitting almost sideways-on to the steering wheel, his back pressed against the door, one leg jigging up and down. Fielding thought he looked unduly anxious, even for someone about to drive through Delhi.

'Do we have an itinerary yet?' he asked.

'I have a copy here, sir, acquired from the city police.' Prasannan waved a sheet of paper in the air. Fielding thought he looked nervous too.

'Where's the President going today?'

'He started at the Gandhi memorial, then visited the Lokh Sabha, the lower house of parliament. Lunch at the American Embassy was followed by Lodhi Gardens and then the Red Fort.' Prasannan looked at his watch, then back at the sheet of paper. 'He should be on his way now to the Lotus Temple, before a state banquet tonight hosted by the Indian President at the Rashtrapati Bhavan.' He paused. 'Sir, there is . . .'

'What's the Lotus Temple?' Fielding interrupted, remembering something he had once read.

'The Bahá'í house of worship. Built like a giant lotus flower. You will have seen photos of it. Very nice place,' Prasannan added, rocking his head proudly.

'Bahá'í? Why's he going there?' But Fielding already knew the answer.

'To show solidarity with the Bahá'ís of Iran. Sir . . .'

'We need to be at the temple now.'

'Sorry, sir, there is one thing else. I have an urgent message from Harriet Armstrong. First we must go to Saket.'

Prasannan fastened his safety belt.

'The police said later that the traffic lights were faulty,' Marchant said, speaking slowly. The air conditioning was on, but struggling. 'I remember seeing a traffic policeman

349

– the thick white gloves – so perhaps the lights were out and he was in charge. Raman thought it was clear to go. We were at the front of the queue, but ten yards back from the junction for the shade. It was hot in the jeep, no A/C, of course. We accelerated forward, in case anyone tried to move in front of us, and then I just remember this awful noise of twisting metal and the policeman's whistle, a desperate shrill sound that went on and on, as if he was trying to undo what had happened. The bus, a government one, had been coming from the left, and didn't stop at the junction. Maybe it was going too fast, or the driver just ignored the policeman. It pushed our jeep thirty yards down the road.'

'And you were unhurt?'

'I was thrown across the back seat, so was my mother. But Sebbie . . .' he paused, thinking back. 'It was Sebbie's turn to ride in the front with Raman. He loved Sebbie, loved us both. Sebbie was sitting on the left, by the door. He took the main brunt of the impact.'

Marchant looked up just as the British High Commission Ambassador hit them, pushing its proud Morris bonnet deep into the front passenger side of the people carrier in a shower of glass. Armstrong must have seen it moments before the impact, because she had reached a protective arm across him. The two Marines and the driver had no warning. In the slow, panicked seconds that followed, after their car had been shunted sideways across the junction, Armstrong slid open the side door and nodded for Marchant to get out. One of the guards was conscious, hanging forward in his seatbelt, but the other one appeared to be dead. The driver was slumped over the wheel, his chest jammed against the horn.

'Bloody hell, I can't do much more,' Armstrong said. 'Find her, and stop whatever she's started.'

Marchant realised that Armstrong couldn't move. Her left leg was bent forward at the knee.

'I can't leave you like this,' Marchant said, unscathed for the second time in his life.

'It's better I'm found with them. Now go. Get on with it. The Chief's waiting.'

'Daniel, over here!' a voice called from across the road. Marchant turned to see Marcus Fielding in the back of a rickshaw. The three-wheeler swung out into the road, where the traffic had come to a sudden halt, picked Marchant up and drove off in the direction of the Lotus Temple, a policeman's shrill whistle fading behind them.

53

Salim Dhar brought the US President into focus with the telescopic sights of his semi-automatic Russian rifle. He seemed smaller than on election night, when Dhar had watched him on TV milking the adoring American public. A large group of suited Security Service personnel were bunched around him as he walked down the tree-lined avenue towards the Lotus Temple. They were scanning the crowd with the worried urgency of parents in search of a lost child. A clean shot was impossible, the President's head partially obscured all the time. For a moment Dhar began to doubt the plan.

He and the woman had synchronised their watches in Old Delhi, close to Chandni Chowk's clock market, the biggest in Asia. Most of them were fakes, unlike his own, a Rolex Milgauss, given to him by Stephen Marchant as he left the jail. Made in 1958, it had been designed to withstand strong magnetic fields, Marchant had explained. Dhar hadn't worn it when he met Daniel, unsure how their meeting would go, but it was on his wrist now. He needed to keep perfect time with the West.

It was 5.33 p.m. The President was moving at a steady pace, waving at the crowds, but equally concerned that the TV cameras were getting a clear view of him. Dhar had similar worries. He was one thousand yards to the north, lying on the flat roof of a two-storey building that formed part of a small housing estate near a large school. The owner, a brother who worked for India's Forest and Wildlife Department, was away on leave, but he had hidden the Dragunov sniper rifle before he went, just as the woman had said he would. The gun had been used against tiger poachers, and Dhar recognised it as an SVD59, a model favoured by the Indian army. Two brothers had recently been killed in Kashmir by a Dragunov's steel and lead bullets.

The whitewashed roof was hot, but at least Dhar was out of direct sunlight. He was also out of view of the three helicopters, two American, one Indian, that were circling low above the temple complex. They had been in the air all day. According to the woman, Delhi police officers, accompanied by members of the Security Service, had also searched every house within a two-kilometre radius of the temple.

All the houses on this particular estate had water tanks on their roofs, but the brother's had been raised eighteen inches off the ground, resting on breeze blocks. It was also the only one with a false bottom, where the gun had been hidden. From the air, the tank looked identical to all the others. It was impossible to see Dhar, who was lying in the gap between the roof and the bottom of the tank, his gun resting on a tripod. The only risk was from the infrared cameras that Dhar assumed were strapped to the undersides of the helicopters. But the water above him had been in the sun all day, and he hoped that its heat profile would mask the warmth of his body.

The President was well within range of the Dragunov, a weapon Dhar had used with accuracy at fifteen hundred yards, but he was still nervous as he panned the sights away from his target. For a moment he was distracted by some movement in the VIP enclosure, behind the avenue. A tall white man was trying to push his way through the crowd. Dhar moved on, panning across the remainder of the avenue, then settled on the first step, waiting for the President to enter the frame. He rested his finger on the trigger. It was 5.34 p.m.

Fielding was still a hundred yards away when the President approached the foot of the first flight of steps leading up to the Lotus Temple. The rickshaw had dropped him and Marchant off on the western perimeter of the temple complex, and they had pushed their way through some of the thousands of people who had gathered in the gardens to see the new leader of the Western world.

An armed Indian policeman blocked their way at a checkpoint. He was not letting anyone beyond it, even when Fielding showed his British security pass. Fielding felt a wave of relief as he leaned against the hot metal barrier, suddenly exhausted by the heat. It was up to Marchant now. He was the only one who could stop Leila.

'You go on alone,' Fielding said, shaking Marchant's hand. 'Good luck.'

The formal gesture surprised Marchant, until he felt the roll of rupee notes pressed into his moist palm. He slipped them into his pocket and moved quickly to his right, following the crowd barriers for thirty yards until there was a gap, manned by another policeman, younger than the first one. Marchant looked around and spotted a vendor selling souvenirs: wooden snakes painted in American colours; toy rickshaws with the President's name stencilled on their plastic windscreens. He was also selling disposable cameras. Marchant went up to him, and bought a camera for too much. It wasn't the time to haggle.

Beyond the barrier a group of well-dressed Indians, all saris and *sherwanis*, were mingling in the VIP enclosure with military brass, their uniforms blooming with medal ribbons. Marchant looked around quickly, thinking fast. The enclosure was on the south side of the main avenue, where it met the steps going up to the Temple.

'I need a good photo,' Marchant said to the policeman, showing him the camera. A bunch of 500-rupee notes was clearly visible in his hand. 'Please.'

The policeman glanced up and down the line of the barriers, then looked back at Marchant. His bruised face worried him, but not enough. He took the money with the deftness of a pickpocket, frisked Marchant thoroughly and let him through. There were barely twenty yards now between Marchant and the temple steps. He spotted Leila in amongst a detail of nervous Security Service agents. She was talking to the President, who was just visible in the middle of the group.

The President seemed to be listening intently, his head cocked towards Leila on his right. For a brief moment, Marchant felt proud of her. A group of Bahá'í officials was waiting patiently for the party to reach them at the foot of the steps. As they drew near, the security detail, including Leila, momentarily withdrew, allowing TV crews and photographers to capture the President and the Bahá'ís seemingly on their own, against the dramatic backdrop of the Lotus Temple, framed by the tree-lined avenue. Marchant glanced at his watch: 5.35 p.m.

He needed to get closer to Leila, but it was impossible. Security Service officers were everywhere now, their backs to the President, shouting at people to stop pressing against the metal barriers that separated them from the presidential entourage. The VIPs had grown boisterous, excited that the President had stopped in front of them. Marchant pushed through the crowd, upsetting people as he went.

He thought about calling across to Leila, but she wouldn't hear him above the noise. Whatever was about to happen, he knew her life was in danger, whether the threat to the President came from elsewhere or from her. Marchant scanned the crowd, searching for something, anything, that might buy him a few seconds.

Leila had now moved back up alongside the President.

What was she doing? What had she done? In the same moment, she turned northwards, staring out beyond the gardens and scrubland. Marchant followed her gaze, towards a housing estate in the middle distance, and froze.

'Leila!' he screamed.

The atmosphere around the table in the White House Situation Room was tense, the low ceiling adding to the pressure. Dhar had still not been found, and Straker knew his job was on the line. The Director of the Secret Service, sitting to his right, was also feeling the heat. An occasional frozen frame on the screen didn't help to ease the tension, the images suffering on their way from a military satellite orbiting at 7,000 mph high above the dust of Delhi.

'Just keep him moving,' Straker said to no one in particular, loosening his collar. The President had paused for a moment too long at the end of the avenue for the TV crews.

'We need these images for the morning shows,' said the Chief of Staff, who was sitting to Straker's left. 'Is he looking a bit shiny in the heat?'

'You'd look shiny in ninety-five degrees,' Straker said, as the President stopped at the foot of the first flight of steps. Come on, he thought, get your butt inside the safety of the temple.

Straker was to repeat many times what he thought happened next, to colleagues, to Congress, to his conscience. As the President's protective detail withdrew

357

for the money shot, Leila scanned the crowds and spotted something that alarmed her. She couldn't be sure, but her training suggested that it was the glint of a telescopic lens caught in the low sun, at a distance of one thousand yards to the north. Without any regard for her own safety, she stepped forward to shield the unprotected President, an American hero to the end.

Dhar's line of sight was suddenly perfect. He found the President's choice of a cotton Nehru suit even more offensive than his predecessor's cowboy boots, but he didn't need any further incentive. *Inshallah*, his job was almost done. The President was alone, his figure filling the lens as Dhar traced the crosshairs over his chest and neck, and up to his forehead, which was beaded with sweat.

But as he squeezed the trigger, distilling in that moment a thousand thoughts of anger, from his first day at the American School to the death of his father, a woman stepped forward and stared back at him through the lens. Dhar recognised the big eyes as the high-velocity bullet impacted between them, knocking her backwards and removing part of her skull.

In that shard of time, where there was no place for shock or regret, Dhar knew that he had killed the person who had betrayed his father: her job at the American Embassy, the English-accented Urdu, her seeming affection for Daniel Marchant. They all surfaced at once to shout out her guilt, which should have made missing the President more bearable.

A second shot was out of the question. The President

had been thrown to the ground and smothered by a blanket of Security Service officers, as if he was on fire. There would be another opportunity in the future, Dhar told himself, but he knew it was unlikely. It no longer seemed to matter, either. He left the rifle where it was, hidden under the water tank, slid through a hatch in the roof, and made his way down to a rickshaw parked in the street below.

Marchant saw Leila pirouette to the ground, her spilt blood darkening the President's white suit. He tried to push through the boiling crowd, but his world was slowing down, falling silent. The women all around him were mouthing muted screams, the men running everywhere and nowhere. A tide of people was carrying him away from Leila, out to the dark depths of the Arabian Sea, to level three. Sebbie was there, lying on the floor of the pool. Then he heard the sound of a police whistle and saw him on the road, twisted and bloodied, alone, eyes open with fear and confusion.

He saw Leila, too, ignored at the foot of the temple steps as the President was bundled away towards Marine One, its blades starting to stir the hot evening air. How could they leave her on her own like that? He was by her side now, lifting her wet head in his hands, shielding her from the downdraft.

'Leila, it's me, Dan,' he said through his tears. 'It's me.'

But he knew it was too late. He bent over her, shoulders shaking, and kissed her still warm lips goodbye.

54

'As far as we're concerned, she took the bullet that was meant for our President,' William Straker said on the secure video link. Daniel Marchant turned away from the screen to the window. A Dutch barge was making its way up the river below Fielding's office. 'That's pretty special in our book, a loyal Agency employee who made the ultimate sacrifice,' Straker continued. 'The President wants a full state funeral.'

'And we'll be there, of course,' Fielding said. 'Leila was an extraordinary woman.'

Marchant caught Sir David Chadwick raising his eyebrows at Bruce Lockhart, the Prime Minister's foreign policy adviser, who was sitting across from the Chief.

'We appreciate it, Marcus, really,' Straker went on. 'It's at times like this that Britain and America need to stand as one. No one here forgets the night after 9/11, when the Chief of MI6 somehow got a plane into Virginia to be with us. That's how it should be. Madam, sirs, thank you.'

The screen went blank, and the six of them sat quite still, listening to the sound of an aircraft flying over London towards Heathrow. Harriet Armstrong, crutches propped against her chair, glanced at Chadwick, who looked away. It was Marchant who finally spoke.

'Have they seen all the evidence?'

'Everything,' Armstrong said.

'And they still believe she was working for them?'

'No. But they need to believe she was,' Fielding said. 'The alternative is unthinkable. And why not? She saved their President. You heard Straker. She "took the bullet". In the West's war against terror, she's a hero. And at the moment, America needs heroes. It doesn't need traitors.'

'So why did they agree to release me?' Marchant asked. Two Secret Service officers had started asking questions when they took Leila's body away in an ambulance and Marchant had insisted on accompanying them. An hour later he was in the cell in the basement of the American Embassy again. He had finally arrived back in Britain earlier that morning, landing at Fairford, the airbase he had flown out of two weeks earlier with a hood over his head.

'In return for Britain publicly believing in Leila too.'

'And that's enough for them to free me? They thought I was involved in a plot to kill their Ambassador to London, that I was a traitor.'

Fielding shuffled his papers and looked around the room. The hesitation made Marchant feel uncomfortable, excluded. 'There's something more. What? Tell me.'

361

'Leila sent me an email on the morning of the day she died,' Fielding said, looking straight at Marchant. 'In it, she provided the time and place of what would have been the next arranged dead drop with her Iranian handler. It was here in London, Hyde Park. We put the spot under surveillance, even though the world knew Leila had been killed. Someone from the Iranian Embassy duly turned up, in case she'd left something before she went to India. This man was unknown to us, not on the diplomatic list. Harriet pulled him in.'

'He was senior officer in VEVAK, and he told us everything, in return for letting him leave the country,' Armstrong said. 'When Leila started to work for the Iranians, how they had given her no choice because of her mother, how the Americans recruited her. But it seems Leila struck a better deal than we thought. In some ways a very brave, selfless deal. In return for her spying for Iran, VEVAK would not only keep her mother safe, they would also suspend all police activity against the Bahá'í community in Iran.'

The room fell silent. 'The latest human rights data appears to bear this out,' Denton said quietly. 'The number of Bahá'ís persecuted in the last six months is the lowest since the '79 Revolution.'

'We sent a transcript to Langley,' Fielding said.

'And? What did they say?' Marchant asked.

'Nothing,' Fielding said. 'We didn't expect them to. Two days later, they agreed to a complete rehabilitation of your father. Lord Bancroft will be filing his report shortly. It will conclude that there is no evidence to doubt

362

his loyalty to his country. There will be a full memorial service in Westminster Abbey, attended by the Prime Minister and the US Ambassador to London.'

'All references to Salim Dhar and his family have been deleted from your father's records, both here and at Langley,' Armstrong added. 'Privately, they still maintain that we're honouring a traitor. Privately, we think they're doing the same. But the world will never know.'

'One day the truth will come out about Leila, though, we've insisted on that,' Chadwick said. 'Fifty years from now, historians will discover how she sabotaged our investigations into a terror campaign in Britain. Not only that, but it appears she was the main UK point of contact for the terrorists. It was a South Indian cell, your father was right about that.' Chadwick looked Marchant in the eyes for the first time. 'What Stephen didn't know, what none of us knew, was that it was being run out of Tehran.'

'Stephen visited Dhar, a rising star in the *jihadi* firmament, because he had hoped Dhar might know something about the cell,' Fielding said.

'He also wanted to meet his son for the first time,' Marchant interrupted. Chadwick winced.

'Stephen was convinced that this cell had help from inside the Service,' Fielding continued, as if he hadn't heard Marchant. 'He was right about that, too. But the Iranians had kept Dhar out of the loop. He couldn't tell Stephen who was behind the attacks in Britain, or who the mole was, because he didn't know.'

'Will the Iranians use him in the future?' Lockhart

asked. 'He managed to eliminate Leila, one of their most priceless assets, someone who had infiltrated two Western intelligence agencies.'

'Their interests might overlap again,' Fielding said. 'But it was an unusual alliance. Maybe that's why no one saw it. We think Dhar's future lies with AQ. The *jihadi* chatrooms are jubilant, praising him for getting so close.'

'But is he ours?' Lockhart asked. Marchant knew he was the only one who could answer the question. It had been on everyone's lips from the moment the meeting had started.

'Dhar is his own man,' Marchant replied.

'His war is with others, though, not with the British.'

'So far his targets have all been American.'

'Will he ever try to make contact?' Lockhart asked.

Marchant remained silent. He knew that a part of him hoped so.

'We have to leave this to Daniel,' Fielding said. 'We think Dhar's only motivation will be personal. Family business,' he added, looking at Marchant.

'But if he does?' Lockhart persisted.

'Then this whole operation is deniable. Dhar is currently the most wanted man in the Western world. If contact was ever established between him and Her Majesty's Government, it's clearly not something we would boast about.'

'In the unlikely event of him becoming a British asset, the PM must be ring-fenced, is that clear?' Lockhart said, looking around the table. 'He cannot be told, under any circumstances. Only the six people in this room will ever know.'

55

Marchant stood outside Legoland, on the Thames path, looking across the water to the Morpeth Arms. It was where he and Leila had sometimes gone after work in the early days, after they had graduated from the Fort. He had had time to think about her betrayal, about when the deception must have started, whether he had missed any obvious clues. It was easier to assume that her treachery had begun as something small, pieces of information here and there in return for her mother's safety in Tehran, but that slowly it had gained an unstoppable momentum of its own, ending with the Americans recruiting her too, providing perfect protection against the hunt for a mole in MI6.

Leila was certainly right to have feared VEVAK's threats to her mother. The day before the President's visit to the Lotus Temple, a mob in a poor suburb of Tehran had dragged an old Bahá'í woman outside and stoned her. She had died in the night. Had VEVAK begun to suspect that Leila was losing her nerve?

Marchant turned away from the river and looked behind him, distracted by a noise. A yellow London Duck was coming down the slipway. The amphibious vehicle rumbled to a stop beside Marchant, who spotted Fielding sitting in the bow.

'Hop on,' he called down to Marchant.

Two minutes later, Marchant was sitting at the front of the Duck as it made its way towards Westminster, too low in the water for his liking. But he had his own particular reasons to fear water, and tried to take comfort from the other passengers, sitting towards the stern, who seemed untroubled.

'I've always wanted to go on this bloody thing,' Fielding said. 'Hear what they tell the punters about Legoland.'

'And?'

'The usual Bond nonsense, M's office. Although he did point up to the right windows. I must have a word afterwards. Are you all right? That was quite a meeting to fly into today.'

'The Americans are sticking to their story, then?'

'It's the most convenient lie for everyone. And it's bought us some leverage on the subject of your father.'

'Sometimes I wonder if Dhar did know Leila was the mole.'

'And that's why he shot her? I doubt it.'

'There was a real bond between Dhar and my father. Dhar spoke very fondly of him, even though they only met the once. That attack on the US Embassy in Delhi

– I checked the dates again. It was just after my father died. Dhar was an angry man that day.'

'Shooting the President of the United States would have been a far greater act of revenge than killing Leila.'

Marchant wasn't so sure, but he knew that his own emotions were still too raw and confused for him to make a clear judgement of what had happened and why. Leila had betrayed a father; now she was dead, killed by a son. Greater forces seemed to have been at work.

'I had a call this afternoon from Paul Myers, down at Cheltenham. He wanted to tell you himself, but he was wary of bypassing official channels.'

The Duck was passing the London Eye, sinking even lower into the water as it turned around and started to head upriver again.

'How is he? He used to have quite a thing about Leila.'

'Bruised. Armstrong's people were a little heavy-handed with him. He's come across an email account, thinks it's Leila's.'

'Anything in it?' For a moment Marchant hoped she had written him a message explaining everything, but he knew there was no simple answer.

'Empty inbox, nothing sent. But he found this in the drafts folder, attached to a blank email addressed to you.'

Fielding reached into his jacket breast pocket and handed Marchant a pixellated A4 printout of a photo. It was of a small Indian boy, staring at the camera, holding a woman's hand. Both figures were a little stiff, unsmiling.

'The image is dated,' Fielding said. 'In the bottom

corner. The Jpeg was called "Pradeep's son, safe and well".'

Marchant looked at it for a moment, grateful that the marathon bomber's son had survived. VEVAK had clearly decided that Pradeep had done enough, dying so publicly on Tower Bridge. He was grateful to Leila, too, for letting him know. She must have tracked the family down when she was in Delhi, using her VEVAK contacts.

'There's something else you should know,' Fielding said. 'Armstrong got quite a lot out of the Iranian we brought in. Personal stuff we didn't want to air in the meeting. We've all wondered why Leila didn't tell us, or the Americans, as soon as she was compromised. It would have saved a lot of trouble, but not, it seems, her mother. They had someone outside her house twenty-four hours a day, ready to kill her the moment Leila told anyone she was working for them.'

'She had no choice, you mean.'

'She was close to her mother, as you know.'

'When did the Iranians first make contact?'

'Even before she turned up at the Fort, I'm afraid. That's what I wanted to talk to you about. Harriet asked the Iranian a lot of questions, for your sake. She must have warmed to you in Delhi.'

'Like a mother.' Marchant managed a smile.

'Initially, when she was working at the Gulf Controllerate in London, the Iranians just asked Leila for general information. It was only at the end that they asked her to target you personally, once they realised how close the two of you had become.'

'Very comforting. Except that the "general information" she provided led to my father's departure. It's hard to forgive her for that.'

'She couldn't go through with the marathon attack, you know that. It was her one weakness as a traitor, her strength in other ways. We think she was meant to kill you, frame you at the very least. It was when they increased their demands that she insisted they stopped all attacks against Bahá'ís, not just against her mother. A courageous call.'

'And they agreed?'

'Until they began to doubt her commitment in Delhi. The Americans found a Bahá'í declaration card in her room. She converted on the day she died. The Indian press have picked up on it. The plight of the Bahá'ís in Iran is getting a big play around the world: "Brave Bahá'í woman saves US President from an evil, Iranian-backed assassin."'

But Marchant wasn't listening any more. His staff phone, a new TETRA unit, not his old one, had buzzed in his pocket. No one had his number yet. He assumed that it must be a routine test message from Legoland, but it wasn't.

'Are you all right?' Fielding asked, as Marchant read a text.

'Fine,' Marchant said. 'It's good to be in London again.' They were near the Houses of Parliament, coming alongside the Embankment. 'A chance to catch up with old friends.'

'The captain's letting me off here,' Fielding said. 'I

have a meeting at the Travellers with the new head of Clandestine Europe.'

'Who's that?'

'James Spiro, God help us. Sadly, his predecessor, Carter, resigned. Took a job in the private sector. Look, why not stay on board, enjoy the trip. You're not expected back at your desk today.'

'I will. Thanks.'

Fielding stood up, putting his hands to the small of his back, then steadied himself on the railing as the Duck bumped against the pontoon. 'It's good to have you back, Daniel. You should never have been suspended.'

'And Armstrong's pleased, too?'

'Harriet? She's a pussycat these days, ever since she realised we were right about Leila. Five and Six have become allies. Almost.' He paused. 'When do you think Dhar will try to make contact? Six months? A year? You know there's no hurry.'

Marchant glanced again at his mobile and slipped it back into his jacket pocket. The two men looked at each other for a moment, an unspoken knowledge passing between them. Then Fielding was gone, lost in the crowds of tourists, as Marchant headed out to the middle of the river, the low yellow bow pushing against a racing tide.

ACKNOWLEDGEMENTS

There are some people I can't openly thank, but MF, DM and HA know who they are. Ditto DB in America and AM in Iran. In India, C. Sujit Chandrakumar offered his usual wise counsel and, along with Kinjal Dagli, oiled my rusty Hindi. Mammen and Philip Matthew welcomed me to Kerala almost fifteen years ago and have been incredibly supportive ever since. The Dominic family, too, have been generous hosts over the years. Thanks also to Ramachandran Nair and Chandar Bahadur, wherever they are now, and to Vivek Kumar, who emerged out of the blogosphere to help with Stephen Marchant's detention.

In Britain, Nick Wilkinson, a fellow Wiltshire man, took time off from writing his history of the D Notice Committee to shed warm light on the darker recesses of Whitehall. Mark Mangham, David Robson, Justin Morshead and Judith Stevenson all read early drafts, offering invaluable advice and suggestions. Thanks too to Doug and Jane, Neil Taylor, Peter Foster, Chris Yates, Tor and Ed, and to Giles Whittell for the bet – won by him but on me. *The Big Breach*, Richard Tomlinson's classic account of life as an MI6 officer, remains a unique and recommended read. And David Cornwell reassured me on a Cornish clifftop that times might change, but spying will always remain the same.

The *Daily Telegraph* kindly sent me to India a few years ago and subsequently gave me the security of a great day job in London, allowing me to pursue the far riskier business of writing fiction. The Weekend team (Casilda Grigg, Stuart Penney, Jenny Martinez and Jodie Jones) have been particularly supportive.

At HarperCollins, my editor, Robert Lacey, spared many blushes with his razor-sharp eye, priceless notes and high intelligence standards. Any mistakes that remain are mine. Thanks, too, to Ilsa Yardley. I have been lucky enough to know Patrick Janson-Smith since long before he agreed to publish me. His early interest in *Dead Spy Running*, first as an agent and then as a publisher, kept me going on the FGW train to London, where most of this book was written. Six years earlier I had signed a copy of my second novel: 'For Patrick, one of these days . . .' and now it has happened. I couldn't think of a better home than one with a Blue Door.

Janklow & Nesbit, my agents, have been the epitome of friendly professionalism. Thanks to Kate Weinberg for the introduction and to Rebecca Folland, Kirsty Gordon, Tim Glister, Lucie Whitehouse and particularly to Claire Paterson, unquestionably the best agent in town (and, sadly, a quicker marathon runner than me). I'm grateful for her editorial insights, cool head and chutzpah. I'd also like to thank Sylvie Rabineau in Los Angeles, Jeanne Allgood and McG at Wonderland Sound and Vision, and Ollie Madden at Warner Brothers in London.

It's my family, though, who deserve the biggest thanks of all: my late, loyal father, Peter Stock, for showing the way; Andrea Stock for her encouragement; Stewart and Dinah McLennan for the London eyrie; Andrew Stock for marathon tips (he's quicker, too); Felix, for his unbridled enthusiasm for this story in its early days; Maya for watching the sun rise with me; Jago for his sheer joyfulness; and most of all, my wife, Hilary, who has made it all possible with her patience, understanding, humour and love. This book is dedicated to Hilary because without her, it simply wouldn't have happened. Thank you.